The author, Dougie Macfarlane, was born in rural Western Australia in 1954 and grew up in the bush. He attended the University of Western Australia from 1972 to 1976. He graduated BSc math in 1975 and DipEd in 1976. He has been a teacher in primary and secondary schools in two countries, a bartender, a private math tutor, a wine sales manager and a bagpipe maker. For thirty years, he lived in Scotland, but now he lives as a writer in the Netherlands.

For my wife, Bernadette. It would not have been possible without you.

Dougie Macfarlane

MARTINUP

Growing Up in the
Australian Bush

AUSTIN MACAULEY PUBLISHERS™
LONDON • CAMBRIDGE • NEW YORK • SHARJAH

A CIP catalogue record for this title is available from the British Library.

ISBN 9781528983020 (Paperback)
ISBN 9781528983037 (ePub e-book)

www.austinmacauley.com

First Published (2020)
Austin Macauley Publishers Ltd
25 Canada Square
Canary Wharf
London
E14 5LQ

My dad, Laurie, for teaching me to be honest and my mum, Kathie, who always had faith in me and her gift to me of "The Children Encyclopedia".

Table of Contents

Synopsis	11
The Vengeance of the Mallee Root	12
The Wonders of Science	27
The Incarcerated Priest	46
The Glasgow Kiss	60
The Unfortunate Demise of Giovanni	75
Where's My Farm?	90
Drug Addicts and Communists	105
An Outbreak of Conjunctivitis	118
A New Day Dawns	132
The Divine Miss Henderson	146
It's a Pig's Life Down on the Farm	160
Lord of the Manor	174
Testing Times	189
An Unlikely Hero	202
Epilogue	217

Synopsis

The year is 1967 and Martinup, (pop. 5,000) situated in rural Western Australia, is much unaffected by the sixties revolution that is sweeping the rest of the world.

Brian MacArthur and his best friend Trevor are finding it hard to adjust to the strange new world of high school. As there is nothing to offer in the way of entertainment at home, they amuse themselves in the bush, but their apparently harmless activities have unforeseen and unfortunate consequences.

Paul, the boys' teacher, coming to the town straight from the city on his first teaching post, struggles to cope with a demanding profession, separation from his girlfriend and life in a small country town. He has nothing in common with his housemate Jacko, a teacher from the primary school, and conflict is inevitable.

Father O'Neill, the parish priest, hides a dark secret and longs to leave the town. An incompetent altar boy, a recalcitrant confessional door, an incomprehensible housekeeper and an inquisitive Jesuit sent to investigate financial irregularities in the parish accounts add to his woes.

The Vietnam War is increasingly messy and Australian's involvement beginning to be questioned. Roger, Brian's longhaired, dope-smoking older brother knows he must pass his first-year university examinations or face possible conscription. Lured into an ill-timed anti-war demonstration by his extremist girlfriend Suzie, a riot ensues. Local aborigines ask him a question he cannot possibly answer.

Trevor and his mother see a massive change in their lives and Brian, with a foolish experiment involving a rusty bolt, inadvertently causes the deaths of countless people. Well, nearly.

The Vengeance of
the Mallee Root

'Whatcha doin' this arvo?' Trevor asked.

Brian had been daydreaming. The afternoon February sun glared down ferociously despite the fact that it was well after three thirty. The two boys were cycling home after what seemed an endless school day that they had with a double period of science in the morning and finished with a torrid double period of maths in the afternoon.

They were rapidly finding out that Thursdays at high school were a drag.

'Dunno.'

Brian's mind was still in Mr MacDuff's maths class. It was so unbelievably awful. He had quite enjoyed maths at the Convent school but this was something else. Mr MacDuff was definitely a weirdo. He was a little old man with a peculiar high-pitched voice. When he scribbled on the board, his bald patch gave him the appearance of a faceless person with a chin beard. When he addressed the class, Brian's attention would be drawn to his eyes. Framed by big black-rimmed glasses, the lenses had the same dimensions as beer bottle bottoms which made his eyes appear to be a series of concentric circular lights. But what was most disconcerting of all was his habit of apparently scratching himself inside his loose-fitting corduroy trousers.

Whatever he had been saying that afternoon about algebra, had been lost amidst Brian's simultaneous fascination and revulsion. The nuns had never been like this!

And his oral hygiene was truly astonishing. A sharp intake of breath was necessary for survival whenever he ventured close, which fortunately wasn't very often. Brian had quickly learnt not to invite him over to explain himself personally. The lad was quite pale and faint after Mr MacDuff finally left him on the first occasion the teacher had been called over.

Mr MacDuff was the only teacher to be awarded not one but two nicknames, "pocket billiards" and "fart breath".

He put his reverie into words,

'Why don't we set fire to Mr MacDuff?'

'He'd most likely do that himself if he had a box of matches in 'is pocket,' was his mate's retort prompting Brian's: 'an' then his breath exploded and blow 'is head off.'

This sent them both into hysterics and nearly dislodged Brian from his bike as the wheel caught a stone by the roadside. Side by side they swapped the endless inane babble of boyhood hilarity as they made their way homeward through the dust and heat.

The two boys were getting used to the new daily routine which was to be with them for the next five years. At the last siren, it was the mad rush to the metal lockers outside Room Ten for books and files and plastic lunchboxes which had that curious smell found nowhere else in nature. Then they would be swept across the Quadrangle with the hordes of other kids converging on the same exit. Different groups moved at different speeds. The faster ones were invariably "bus kids" from out of town who were totally reliant on the various privately owned buses outside the school to convey them to and from their farms. They were therefore always paranoid about being late. The sequence ended with a violent crush of bodies and bags and books in the main doorway, a scene relished by the school bullies and detested by the sole teacher on duty whose onerous task it was to prevent it.

Then to the bike racks and FREEDOM!

The trip home would take about twenty-five minutes as the boys lived on the other side of the railway line which effectively divided the town.

The journey would take them down the hill past the opulent homes of the retired farmers who had made a lot of money when wool sold for a pound per pound and then wisely decided to get off the land. They were the "*nouveau riches*" of Martinup, which is not quite accurate as all the riches were relatively "*nouveau*" in Australia anyway, having only arrived in the virgin bush a mere hundred years previously. They rapidly dispersed the incumbent residents who had been there a good bit longer and who certainly weren't interested in *"riches, nouveaux"* or otherwise.

Farmers were known colloquially as "cockies", a term of endearment if you were one of them or a term of contempt if you weren't. The houses they chose for their retirement reflected their taste and style. Big. Preferably on two levels as most Australian homes were bungalows. Swimming pool because water was expensive. Spanish-style arches as some had been to Europe for the first time. Exotic palm trees and of course a two-car garage even if the missus couldn't drive. And to top it off, the newest luxury in 1967, a TV aerial which needed to be about fifty feet high as the nearest transmitter was on the coast about a hundred miles due east. Channel choice was limited: you had a choice of the ABC. Unfortunately, the picture quality was invariably poor. It was a bit like having the radio turned up loud between stations while watching a snowstorm.

The two boys rounded the corner at the bottom of the hill and cycled past the seemingly endless rows of pastel-coloured-galvanised-iron-roofed-asbestos-bungalows-on-stilts (the wooden stilts being for air circulation, a precursor of air conditioning) which were the temporary homes of teachers and other government officials who had been posted to the country either as an initiation or a demotion. Lifeless, soulless places, they provided little more than a roof over the heads of their tenants during the week. At the weekends, they lay even more silent as their occupants had invariably fled back to the city on the Friday night.

They crossed a wasteland called imaginatively "The Park", then over the bridge of the Creek which had last seen water in the floods of 1963 but was now a tangled mass of kikuyu and old car tyres, then around the primary school (which was Trevor's old school) and bumped and rattled their way across the railway lines.

All the while the afternoon sun beat down.

Sweaty and exhausted, the conversation between the two boys had tailed off. Home was in sight.

Trevor's house was first.

'See ya t'morra!' he shouted as he free-wheeled his bike to the gate.

Then, 'Wait a minute! I've got something to show ya. Just chuck yer bike over there.'

Brian leaned his bike against the fence and followed his mate around the side of the house as it was the custom in the country to enter by the back door rather than the more obvious front door.

He waited on the back step.

Trevor's mum emerged from the gloom of the doorway opening onto the back verandah, the glow of her cigarette clearly discernible in the darkness.

'C'mon in son. It's bloody hot out there.'

Brian liked Trevor's mum. She was the only adult he knew who swore and smoked. In fact, she smoked so much that she had a nicotine-stained face which gave her the appearance of a permanent tan even though she was rarely seen outside the house. Her dress sense was somewhat eccentric. She favoured old-fashioned floral cotton dresses which stopped mid-calf and set off the ensemble with work boots normally seen on men. And no socks. Brian mused that it was probably just as well that she didn't go out much. He knew she liked a drink too because of the ever-present pile of empty Penfolds sherry flagons at the back door. Brian followed her through the fly-wire door and into the darkness of the kitchen.

It took his eyes a minute to adjust to the feeble light that struggled through the fly-stained net curtains on the only window. Newspapers and teacups littered the table. Dishes and other assorted crockery fought for space on the sink. Here and there ashtrays overflowed. Mrs Stewart may not have had the cleanest kitchen in the world, but for all that there was an atmosphere of comfort and tranquillity about the place and Brian always felt quite at home there.

'Ya wanna cuppa tea, Brian?'

'Yes please, Mrs Stewart, Milk and sugar.'

Trevor's mum busied herself with the kettle on the cast iron range. The fire was always on but curiously never seemed to give out any warmth. It was always cool and dark at Trevor's place despite the searing heat outside.

Trevor emerged from the greater gloom which was the interior of the house holding an open book.

Brian recognised it immediately. It was a volume of "The Children's Encyclopaedia". His Aunty Betty in Perth had a set but he hadn't been impressed with his initial cursory glance at one of the volumes. It was very old fashioned, mostly about the might of the British Empire and how brave soldiers from around the world were set to crush the evil Hun on the Western Front. That and silly poetry and boring black and white photos of armless Greek statues.

Trevor cleared a space on the table with his elbow and set down the book.

The title caught Brian's eye, *"HOW TO MAKE A HOT AIR BALLOON"*.

He was immediately less cynical of the dusty tome and his eye quickly scanned down the page: tear-shaped pieces of tissue paper glued together at the edges would form the body of the balloon. A circular piece of tissue at the top sealed the structure. A wire ring at the bottom held the mouth open. The hot air was supplied by a burning wad of cotton wool, soaked in methylated spirits and held in the centre of the opening by another piece of wire running across the diameter. Simplicity itself! Brilliant!

'I'll definitely be into that, Trevor.'

'What's that?' asked Trevor's mum advancing on him with the cup of tea.

'School science project Mum,' Trevor interjected. Margaret Stewart, despite her inclusive attitude towards young folk, like all adults had reason to fear the combination of adolescents and things flammable. The summer had been long and hot. All it took was a stray spark to start a bushfire which could consume everything in its path. White Australians feared these savage infernos more than anything else although they had in fact always been a feature of the landscape. Indeed, the bush *needed* fire for regeneration.

'Yeah. Science project,' Brian concurred absent-mindedly as he sipped the tea, his eyes still glued to the page.

A hot air balloon out of tissue paper? Could it really be that simple to make?

Mrs Stewart casually remarked to her son that the firewood supply was getting low.

Brian suddenly remembered his own obligations. There were mallee roots waiting for him at home that needed his attention.

'Sorry Mrs Stewart. I've gotta go. Me mum wants some wood chopped and it's after four o'clock already. I'll see ya later mate.'

Trevor followed him to the front gate.

'I reckon I'll have a shot at this balloon thing. I know we've got some tissue paper kickin' about somewhere.

I'll drop round to your place later on, prob'ly after tea.'

'Rightio,' said Brian easing his front wheel through the gate. 'Oh, and tell your mum she makes a great cup of tea. Sorry I didn't have time to finish it.' With that, he pushed his bike homeward. He'd just lied through his back teeth. The tea tasted awful but Brian was beginning to learn the subtle art of diplomacy.

His mind turned to the hot air balloon that would soon lift gently from the silent, and dusty town of Martinup and soar ever upward and far, far away. Wouldn't it be amazing to be aboard a balloon? He wondered what his home town would look like from the air. He wondered how far it would go. To the sea?

But that was over a hundred miles away. Over the sea? His imagination was running away with him.

He parked the bike at the side of the house. Brian's home was bigger than Trevor's. It was a rambling whitewashed brick bungalow with the regulation twin features of verandah and patch of kikuyu that served as a lawn. This ubiquitous African grass thrives in suburban Australia It remains green in the summer (provided the sprinkler is kept on regularly) but you could not have a picnic on it as its leaves are sharp enough to cut flesh. The front lawn served as a totally subconscious reminder to the descendants of white settlers from cooler climates of "home". It was unthinkable not to have a front lawn (and a back lawn if the property was big enough as Brian's was) despite the fact that the grass consumed precious water, needed constant mowing and couldn't be sat on.

To the front of the house was the bush, a precious but fragile remnant of what the place used to be like. Tall gum trees towered over a tangled mass of smaller jam trees, white gum and thick grass, the vegetation so thick that the eye could not penetrate more than fifty yards of it. The White Man has a special fear and distrust of the bush and its indigenous inhabitants which was perhaps why it was cleared so quickly and ruthlessly soon after

17

their arrival. Brian grew up knowing that it was not safe to walk through long grass or even to walk along the few paths through it without adequate footwear. The dugite, the local venomous snake, was particularly feared and although he had not personally encountered one, he had seen discarded skins and plenty of dead specimens on the road.

Brian walked around the side of the house under the shade of the trees (almond + plum trees) and ducked under the grape vine heavy with fruit that guarded the back door. His mother, as always called to him as he crossed the creaking lino-covered floorboards of the back room.

'Is that you, dear?' the voice came from the pantry just off the kitchen.

'Yeah, Mum.'

Brian dropped his schoolbag by the bed and started to change out of his school clothes.

'Change out of those hot school clothes and have a cup of tea.'

Brian cheekily mouthed her words in the wardrobe mirror as he struggled with the knot of his school tie.

She had said the same thing to him every day after school since Grade One.

Brian had recently acquired the room. He was the youngest of a family of four boys. John, the eldest, was an accountant in Perth. He earned a lot of money and didn't come home often. Then there was Richard, a weedy-looking chap with terminal acne and chronic short sight who was studying to be a priest at a seminary in Melbourne who was seen even less, which was a relief for Brian because they couldn't stand each other. Roger, the previous occupant of Brian's room was the most exotic. He was Brian's favourite brother. An undergraduate at the University of Western Australia, Roger was also a hippy with long hair and outrageous clothes. He was a vociferous opponent of the Vietnam War in which Australia was becoming increasingly involved. His views would often bring him into heated conflict with his parents. Roger would be home at Easter and Brian was looking forward to it even though it meant giving up his room for a week.

Brian joined his mother in the kitchen.

'Have nice day at school, dear?'

Brian thought for a moment, '*Did she really want to know the truth? Did she really want to know about Peter Haddow's intentional or unintentional flatulence in science this morning? Or Kevin Shearer's lunchtime joke about the new male sex drive pill which had to be swallowed quick or else you would get a stiff neck? Or worse still about Mr MacDuff?*' So he erred as always on the side of caution leaving Mrs MacArthur like so many mothers wondering about their offspring's reticence to talk about school.

'Yeah, it was alright.'

His mother had retreated into the pantry where she was preparing plums for jam.

'There's some mallee roots that need to be chopped up the back.'

'Yeah, I know. I'm just on my way.'

'Have you got homework?'

'Yeah, a bit of science.' The evacuation of the science lab that morning due to Peter Haddow's intentional or unintentional flatulence flashed through Brian's mind but again he kept his mouth shut.

'I'll do it tonight.'

He squatted on the back step and hauled on the heavy boots obligatory for wood cutting. His brother Roger had taught him the trade early, probably as an excuse for getting out of doing it himself, but it was a necessary chore and Brian generally enjoyed it. It was certainly better than picking up rotten fruit from under the trees in order to prevent blowfly infestation. That was not a nice job. But then, chopping mallee roots was a different matter altogether.

The wood heap was at the back of the house beside a corrugated iron woodshed. His father had built it with the intention of storing chopped wood, but as its open side faced south, where the rain usually came from, it proved rather useless as a storage area. So he built a bin by the back door instead. A lane ran behind the heap and a post and wire fence bordered the property. A well-worn stump stood embedded in what must have been millions of chips, the accumulation of years of his father's and older brothers' intimate encounters with the local varieties of timber.

From an axeman's point of view, some of these varieties were better than others. Jarrah blocks split beautifully, cleaving under just a tap of the blade. Karri was good too but a little more effort was required. Red gum and white gum were harder still, especially so if the wood was still green. The grain was wavy and Brian knew from bitter experience that a hard blow would often result in the axe buried in the wood.

He spent many unhappy hours, attempting to part *"chopper"* from *"choppee"*.

But the hardest of the lot was the mallee root.

The mallee root gets its name (perhaps not surprisingly) from being the root of the mallee, a rather nondescript shrub-like tree indigenous to the area. The cockies hated the mallee along with the rest of the bush and ripped it out with gusto to make way for fields of wheat and oats and barley that could only be sustained by liberal applications of the fertiliser superphosphate. The useless mallee roots were piled in rows as tall as a man and hundreds of yards long over the newly cleared landscape and, when the wind was in the right direction of course, torched.

But townsfolk, like Brian's old man, recognised the potential of this natural resource, for the mallee root burned hotter and cleaner and longer than any other wood known to man. Well, that was what he told Brian but John MacArthur was known to exaggerate from time to time, especially to his youngest son. A load of mallee roots had been dropped off the previous day by a mate of his father's in exchange for a dozen eggs and a cardboard box full of fruit. John MacArthur was always in a good bargaining position on the black market at this time of year with laying poultry and numerous fruit trees coming into season.

With the axe on his shoulder, Brian surveyed the heap. He hated mallee roots. He knew what they were like. They were complete *"bastards"*.

Apart from their colour, a dirty grey, no two mallee roots were remotely similar. They ranged in size from that of a man's fist to twenty, or even thirty-pound monsters. They were all shapes, knots, hollows, with bits sticking out that must once have been the roots and stems of their previous existence. Now they were gnarled and knobbly dead things locked together in a pile.

He wrestled one from the stack and balanced it on the block, not an easy task in itself due to the complexity of its shape.

Next, he inspected it for weak spots or cracks in its convoluted grain, for he knew that a random blow with the axe could result in several things, all of them unpleasant. First, the axe head could rebound with wrist-juddering violence from the target, leaving nothing more than a faint scar on the surface. Second, the axe head could shear off the face of the root and bury itself in the axeman's boot (as had apparently happened to his father when he was Brian's age, and although economical with the truth at times, he had the scar to prove it). Thirdly, and more likely, the axe head could dislodge a shrapnel-sharp piece of the root, sending it at high speed in any direction.

'This is a bit like diamond cutting,' he mused to himself as he studied his first victim, having read in the National Geographic about the cutters in Amsterdam who would take weeks examining the flaws of a gem before committing themselves to a final tap.

He stood back eyeing off the weak spot he'd identified and raised the axe behind his head.

Thunk!

'Bingo! You beauty!'

The first mallee root had succumbed meekly into three roughly equal sized pieces which Brian cheerfully tossed into the waiting wheelbarrow.

'Right,' he said, 'that's one down and...ah...um...lots to go.'

He selected the next one from the heap and went through the same routine of positioning and analysing and finally raising the axe for the fatal strike eye fixed on the likely weak spot...

'HEY, SHIT HEAD!'

The axe head now flew with a volition of its own, temporarily without the guiding eye of its owner, the latter having swung towards the direction of the noise. The metal blade collided with the slanting side of the root and sheared off, burying itself in the chips beside the block. In the process, it dislodged three razor sharp chunks which were now flying in three different directions. One was on a course which would take it inches past Brian's right ear. The second was travelling straight for Trevor's head for it was Brian's best mate who had just arrived on his bicycle in the lane with the ill-timed exuberant greeting. The third was on its way to the galvanised iron walls of the woodshed.

'FAAAACKING HELLL!' intoned the boys simultaneously but their cries were drowned out by the clattering roar of mallee root chunk number three colliding with the shed wall. Brian heard a wasping sound by his right ear and ducked a good half-second too late anyway, dropping the axe in the process.

Trevor's fate looked more ominous but as he was a little further away from it all, he had a slight advantage. He ducked what was apparently an ever-increasing piece of dark matter on a collision course with his forehead. The piece of mallee root did little more than graze his hair on the way through before disappearing in the long grass across the lane. It did, however, have the indirect effect of knocking Trevor off his bike leaving him in a tangle of wheels and spokes in the dust.

'G'day!' said Trevor from inside his bike. 'Shit, that was a bit close!'

Brian was still too stunned to speak.

His mother's voice rang out from the back door.

'You all right, Brian?'

'Yeah, Mum. A bit of mallee root hit the shed.'

'That's all! That's all! Moaned Trevor still recumbent, confined by a tangled mass of metal. 'I'm lucky I've still got me bloody head!'

'Well, it's your own stupid fault, you silly bastard, sneakin' up on a bloke like that,' said Brian, straddling the wire fence to help his friend. 'What are you doin' here anyway? I thought you were comin' over after tea?'

'I thought I'd show you what I'd done so far, but I think it might be knackered now.' Trevor was at last free of the bike and was scrabbling around in the schoolbag that was lashed to the carrier behind his seat.

'Yeah, think it's buggered alright,' he said ruefully as he gently retrieved what looked to be a pile of coloured tissue paper.

'What is it?'

'It's the balloon. Well, it was 'till I fell off me bike. I had a shot at it after you left, but I dunno if it's any good.'

The boys inspected Trevor's effort on the ground behind the woodshed.

Spread out, it measured about eighteen inches by twelve and looked not too bad until Brian picked it up for closer inspection. The metal ring which was to hold the mouth open and contain the cotton wool bud fell off immediately. Brian picked it up and turned it over in his hand.

'What did you make this out of?'

'Piece of coat hanger.'

'Reckon that's a bit heavy mate.'

'Yeah, s'pose so.'

'And the sticky tape makes it heavier still.'

'Yeah.'

Brian turned it over. In doing so, the seams parted.

'Well the glue's still wet of course!' said Trevor pre-emptively and somewhat peevishly as he felt his pioneering aeronautical efforts were being unjustly criticised.

He changed the subject.

'Have you got any metho?'

A thought flashed through Brian's mind, '*I know why there's none around your place, 'cos if there was, your mum would prob'ly DRINK IT! HA! HA.*'

Wisely, he kept his mouth firmly shut. That wasn't funny. Maybe he was becoming more diplomatic. Or maybe it was just called growing up. Maybe he was finally learning that you don't say the first thing that comes into your head if you want to keep your friends. So instead he offered cheerfully,

'Yeah. I'm sure me mum's got some in the pantry cupboard,' then added,

'Look, I've still got these bloody mallee roots to chop, it'll be tea-time soon and there's that stuff for science, so why don't we leave this till tomorrow and the two of us work on it round at your place?'

Trevor mumbled in agreement and started to pack the balloon away.

'Hey Trevor! Did you know you've got a big hole in your strides?'

A triangular piece of material of the regulation grey school trousers was hanging from the seam, exposing his underwear.

'Oh, shit!' Trevor exclaimed as he vainly tried to peer over his shoulder and simultaneously feel his bum with both hands.

'Bloody hell! I musta' done that when I fell off me bike. Oh well. I'll sort it out when I get home. See ya later!'

With that, he threw his leg over the bike and disappeared down the lane.

Brian retrieved the axe and glared at the pile of mallee roots as if they were his mortal enemies and this was a fight to the death.

'Right,' he muttered murderously. 'I'll have you!' He wrestled a big one from the top of the pile and dragged it to the block. He drew a deep breath and raised the axe.

A piece of mallee root the size of a brick, launched itself at high speed from the main body the instant the steel blade of the axe made contact. It would travel just a few feet, completing its journey in a very, very short time. Its destination was Brian's left kneecap.

On the other side of town, a car pulled up beside one of the pastel-coloured asbestos houses reserved for teachers. As the dust settled, the driver, a cleanshaven young man in his early twenties removed his sun glasses and leaned over to put them in the glovebox. He gathered the pile of paperwork scattered over the passenger seat and eased himself out from behind the steering wheel.

He looked tired and even though he was back from work, there was still much that needed to be done before the following day. He was a teacher at the high school. The subject he taught was science. His name was Paul Newton. Effectively, he was the teacher of one hundred and forty children, ranging from first year to fourth year. The red class register which he now carried under his arm along with all the other books and papers contained the names of all his students. Two of the names in one of his first-year classes were those of Brian MacArthur and Trevor Stewart.

He mounted the wooden steps slowly and propping the fly-wire screen door open, unlocked the front door.

Ignoring the pile of unwashed dishes at the sink and the empty beer bottles on the floor which had been steadily accumulating from the beginning of the week, he settled at the Laminex-covered kitchen table and set about sorting the paperwork. There was a lot of work to be done. Tomorrow he knew the first years were carrying on with air pressure: it was chemistry in the afternoon with the fourth years, they were writing up the first experiment, but what did he have period two?

His concentration was interrupted by the roar of a high-powered car coming up the street. The tyres screeched as the vehicle lurched to a halt outside the house.

'Oh no! It's him back already,' Paul groaned. 'I'll never get any work done around here. Bastard!'

The axe clattered into the wheelbarrow as Brian, clutching his left knee with both hands performed a silent one-legged hopping dance around the wood heap for maybe thirty seconds, or it could even have been longer. After however long it took for the pain to subside from "excruciating" to "intense", all he could manage to growl through gritted teeth was "Bastard"! When it had fallen to "dull roar", he had made his mind up. Plan B. He would scour the heap for little mallee roots. Anything. "*Anything that didn't need to be hit by an axe!*"

He limped back to the heap and like a madman tugged away at the tangled mass of wood flinging anything that roughly matched the dimensions required for his mother's stove. Surprisingly, he found quite a few, but he knew that at the end of the day, Plan B was necessarily self-defeating. There would come a time when once again he would have to face big roots with an axe, those monsters he was currently treating with contempt. They would come back to haunt him. There was no escape.

By the time his father's car pulled up the drive. Brian was heading across the back lawn with a pile of mallee roots teetering in the wheelbarrow.

'Well, done son,' his father said cheerfully, making his way to the back door.

'Still plenty of mallee roots up the back?'

'Plenty,' said Brian manoeuvring the wheelbarrow past the grapevine trellis and up against the wood bin.

After his father had disappeared, through clenched teeth, he muttered, 'Yeah, plenty of 'em… Bastards.'

When the washing-up was done, Brian retired to his room to listen to the radio and to do his homework. It was not long before his mind had switched to his latest craze. After an hour, he'd made a cardboard template for the tissue panels and constructed the circular wire mouthpiece from some fine fuse wire he'd found in the shed. He was getting tired now. His mother called to him from the kitchen that there was plenty of hot water for a bath if he wanted, which in fact was just what he needed.

He eased himself over the tub as his left kneecap shot him a reminder of the afternoon and squatted in the twelve inches of water which was the total capacity of the wood-fired hot water system.

He thought back over his first week of high school which was rapidly coming to an end. He had met most of his teachers by now and apart from Fart Breath, they seemed ok. He still had trouble finding the right room. There were so many of them. But all in all, it hadn't been too bad.

'No, not too bad,' he mused out loud to himself absent-mindedly as he lay back in the tub.

Brian thought of his best friend and what life would be like without a father. Peter Stewart was never the same man after the prison camps in Burma. He died when Trevor was just three.

It was great having a mate like Trevor. someone to do things with, even though they were not even supposed to be friends. Kids who went to the "state school" regularly hurled abuse at those from the "convent school" and of course vice-versa, but since the two boys lived so close and had known each other since they were toddlers, the Great Religious Divide never troubled them, nor to be fair was it actually taken seriously by anybody. Martinup, along with the rest of Australia, was an exotic mixture of nationalities and faiths. There were Poles, Italians, Greeks, Yugoslavs, Presbyterians, Methodists and even the occasional Jew. They all got along pretty well in this new country full of opportunities to work hard and make lots of money.

In fact, the only people who didn't fit in were the ones who had been there before anyone else. The Aboriginals. But Brian didn't know too much about them. He was only thirteen years old and had a lot to learn. Now he was tired and the bath water was getting cold.

The light of a full moon filtered through the almond tree and illuminated half of the bedroom.

It looked like an enormous balloon.

On the floor, a first-year science text book lay undisturbed in a school bag.

The Wonders of Science

Australia has been invaded by aliens from Outer Space! Brian has seen the lights of their flying saucers streaming high overhead in straight lines, heading south. He has heard the news on the radio that Perth was captured and that Albany was to be next! People have been told to stay inside and not to answer a strange knock at the door! But that was just what was happening! They were here in Martinup! He could see them through the net curtains of the back window! There was at least a dozen of them, all of them dirty grey in colour, all different shapes, blots, hollows, with bits sticking out of them and eyes on stalks, like...sort of...mallee roots! They were stomping around the garden! But he had to go to the toilet! He was bustin'! The dunny was down the back! He had no choice! He burst through the back door and ran up the garden path! The biggest alien spotted him! He raised a stick-like limb and an electric-blue ray struck Brian on the left kneecap! He went down in agony! There was no escape!

AAAAAAAAAAAAAAAAAAAAAAAAAAAAAAGH!

The morning light was streaming in through the window when Brian shot bolt upright in bed, his left kneecap having just sent him another gentle reminder of the wood heap. He threw off the blankets and gingerly inspected it from inside the drawstring top of his pyjamas. It was quite red and swollen, 'Mallee roots!' he growled under his breath inadvertently inventing another obscenity for his collection.

'Brian!' called his mother from the kitchen. 'What's all the noise about?'

'Sorry, Mum. Me knee's a bit sore. I got hit by a piece of mallee root yesterday, but it's ok now.'

He lied, fearing an application from his mother of some horrendously painful antiseptic that she kept especially for such events in the bathroom cabinet.

'Maybe we should put some flavine on it?' his mother shouted.

'No, it's alright, Mum, honest!'

Brian was by now carefully easing his injured leg into his school trousers, making a face as he did so.

'There's Iodine there too.'

Brian raised his eyeballs skyward and sighed.

'It's ok, mum!'

Mary MacArthur detected the hint of annoyance in her youngest son and refrained from suggesting "Dettol" and got on with making his lunch, pausing to shout, 'Come and have your breakfast or you'll be late for school!'

'Just coming Mum!'

Brian adjusted his school tie in the mirror grateful that she hadn't suggested that bloody "Dettol".

He grabbed his schoolbag from under the bed and limped through to join his mother in the kitchen. The radio on the sideboard was on as usual with the seven o'clock news: "*...in Da Yang yesterday, Australian troops came under heavy enemy fire...*"

'Porridge?'

"*...three Viet Cong were killed in the attack and early reports suggest there were no Australian casualties...*"

'Uh, yeah thanks Mum.'

"*...speaking from Canberra, the prime minister, Mr Harold Holt said...*"

'Toast?'

...represented a firm commitment by the Australian people to the war which would prevent the spread of....

'Uh, yeah thanks.'

"*...domino effect spreading to neighbouring countries...*"

'I'll just turn that thing off,' said his mother easing herself behind his chair. She was not keen to hear about Vietnam. Although her two eldest boys were safely beyond the government's age requirements for Conscription, Roger was liable for call-up. She was immensely relieved at the news that he had decided to go to university and was therefore ineligible for military service as full-time students were exempt. But that situation could change if things didn't get better. At least her youngest boy was safe for the time being.

Brian suddenly realised that his father was absent.

'Where's Dad?'

'He had to leave very early for a meeting with a client in Esperance.'

Brian's father was an accountant and often had to travel far and wide for business. In this case, he faced a five-hour journey on less than adequate roads and he quite wisely elected to travel in the early hours before the heat set in.

His mother returned to the pantry. She had been up since her husband had left preparing pears for bottling. It was a long and complicated process perfected by the Vacola Fruit Preservation Company and heralded by the authors of "The Golden Waffle Cookery Book" (the Australian housewife's bible) as "revolutionary" despite the fact that fruit had successfully been preserved in cans since the early part of the century.

Essentially, the fruit was cut up and packed into heavy glass jars. Sugar syrup was added, a rubber ring put on the top followed by a metal cap and finally a spring steel clip. The jars were then loaded into a metal container, water added and the whole thing loaded on the stove to be boiled for a couple of hours. All the while the temperature had to be monitored constantly.

In theory, the jars were by then hermetically sealed and thus preserved. In practice, the caps rusted producing tiny, almost undetectable holes and the rubber rings perished; either one or both defects resulted in a failed jar, and of course over time, the number of viable caps and rings steadily diminished. An abundance of fruit and an Irish inheritance of frugality effectively sentenced Mary MacArthur to a lifetime of fruit bottling, sadly much of it unsuccessful.

'Right, I'm off Mum.'

'Alright dear. Your lunchbox is in the fridge.'

Brian collected his lunchbox and shoved it in his bag and headed out the back door.

It was not until he crossed the creek that he suddenly remembered. Science first period and he'd forgotten to do his homework. To a lot of boys of his age this would be a matter of monumental unimportance but to Brian, it was most definitely not. Perhaps it was due to the example of the rest of his family. All his brothers had excelled at school. Or maybe it was because of his early schooling. He had been well primed the previous year that homework would be expected of him at the high school. 'Lots and lots of it,' he'd been told in no uncertain terms. But above all, maybe it was because he had been brought up a Catholic, for Catholics, amongst other things to be sure, believe in guilt. Indeed, was it not St Thomas Aquinas who once proclaimed: 'Give me the boy and I'll soon make him feel guilty?'

'Right,' he said to himself grimly. I'll do it first thing when I get to school. What time is it?'

His watch showed twenty to eight. That was ok. He could make it if he kept the speed up.

John MacArthur glanced at his watch.

'Good,' he said to himself. 'I should get there just after nine. That gives me plenty of time to get this business sorted out. It shouldn't take too long and then I can head straight back again.'

He did not enjoy the annual trip to Esperance. It was a long, straight drive through featureless scrub and the road was not particularly good. To avoid the heat, he'd set off early from Martinup but it was warm already with the sun just clear of the horizon, its rays reflecting off the dusty windscreen and partially obscuring his vision. He'd managed to keep to a respectable sixty-sixty-five miles per hour for most of the journey despite the need to watch out for pot-holes in the road.

He reached across for his cigarettes which were perched on the dashboard, momentarily taking his eyes off the road. At that instant, he became aware of something big coming in from the left at an angle. Collision was inevitable. He knew immediately what it was and instinctively swung the car to the right. The wheels hit the gravel of the roadside and a barrage of stones struck the underside of the vehicle as it started to broadside out of control in a cloud of dust and scorching rubber.

Brian leaned his bike into the corner for the run up the hill to the school, the last leg of his frantic journey. He stood on the pedals to overcome the resistance of the slope, hauling up on the handlebars to maintain his balance, every so often getting a stabbing pain in his injured kneecap for his efforts.

'C'mon!' he urged himself. Another glance of the watch revealed eight o'clock. By now he was through the school gate and freewheeling towards the bike-rack.

'C'mon! he muttered as he rammed the bike home, grabbed his bag and hobbled his way through the main door.

He was early enough, alright. The Quadrangle was almost deserted. He hurried as fast as his damaged limb would allow to his locker outside Room Ten, threw himself down on the wooden slatted seats that ran along the wall and grabbed his science book and file that he kept his work in from the bag.

'Page 42 questions one to five,' he mumbled to himself, flicking through the pages of the text.

'Got it. Right One. '*Explain how a suction cup works*,'

Blank. He didn't have a clue. Suction? Something to do with air pressure? It must be something to do with air pressure because that was what the topic was called, he reasonably concluded. It had been explained the previous day but then the Haddow incident interrupted proceedings.

He had to write something so he began:

HOMEWORK

P-42 (1)

Air pressure causes

'G'DAY BRIAN!'

The voice roaring a greeting into his left ear had the predictable result of jolting his entire body off the bench sending the book and file flying along with pens pencils, the whole lot clattering and scattering on the concrete floor. And of course, triggering a surge of pain from his dodgy knee.

'TREVOR! Will you bloody well stop doing that!'

'Sorry mate, but see what you did to me yesterday!'

Trevor turned his backside to Brian. The seat of his pants was held together by an irregular line of thick, bright red stitching running the perimeter of the damaged area. 'I thought I'd stitch it myself. Me mum was feelin' a bit tired last night.'

'*Oh yeah?*' thought Brian.

His mate continued, 'Hey, you know what, I was thinkin' about this balloon right? Well…'

The conversation between the two continued oblivious as they were to the steady increase in the school population that was happening around them. It was cut short by the blast of the siren.

31

'Oh shit!' said Brian realising that it was too late now and he might as well face the music. Maybe Mr Newton would forget that they'd been given homework? Maybe it didn't really matter anyway? But deep, deep, deep in the inner being of his psyche, Brian knew there was no rational argument that could compete with GUILT. So, with head bowed he grabbed his stuff and limped after the others up the steps to the science lab and stood along with them in a line, like the proverbial lamb to the slaughter.

'SETTLE DOWN QUICKLY PLEASE! We've got a lot of work to get through today. Homework from last night. Page forty-two, questions one to five I believe.'

Brian groaned and arranged his work on the desk in front of him.

Paul Newton was new to teaching. In fact, he wasn't sure he wanted to be a teacher in the first place but nothing else appealed and further studies were out of the question, so here he was in Martinup of all places in front of thirty adolescents. He missed his girlfriend. He missed the beach. He had never really been out of the city in his life and now he was sharing an awful asbestos house, miles from anywhere with a frightful yobbo who drank beer all night and told filthy jokes by way of conversation. And this clown *actually taught at the primary school!'* It was unbelievable. *'But tonight,'* he thought, *'I'm out of here, straight back to the city.'* Meanwhile, there was the last day of his first week in Martinup High School to be endured.

He scanned his hand-written register of the still barely-familiar names.

'...CHAPPEL...Kenneth...CLELIAND...Brian...HADDOW S, Peter...Oh, yeah that's the little shit who farted yesterday. I'll not give him a chance to perform again. Let's see...' he mused.

'Brian MacArthur. Where are you?'

Brian was, in fact, not surprised to hear his name called, for he believed in a vengeful God. With a sigh, he rose to his feet.

'Brian,' said Mr Newton, mentally repeating the name to himself, 'how do suction cups work?'

Brian stared at the page before him. There was nothing else for it but to read the three words he'd written. But as he did so, something incredible happened. He began to remember the explanation from the previous day. He started cautiously:

'Air pressure causes…' and pretended to struggle to read his own invisible writing as the words came one by one into his head…'the…cup to stay…in place…when the air is pushed out…a low pressure area is formed…inside…the rubber…prevents the pressure…from being equalised.' He paused, somewhat stunned. He knew what he had just said was right. Maybe God was not so Vengeful after all. He could not believe his luck.

'Very good Brian!' said Mr Newton enthusiastically and turned his attention away. 'Now question two.'

'How…?'

Brian slowly seated himself on the laboratory stool. He was still coming to terms with his unexpected salvation when a poke in his ribs from Trevor brought him back to the real world. 'Lucky bastard! Brilliant piece of bullshit!' he whispered. Brian shrugged his shoulders. Who was he to explain Divine Providence?

Mary looked at the clock on the mantelpiece. Ten past nine. He would call soon as he always did. She turned back to the pantry where the first half dozen jars of pears were cooling. As she watched, the clip of one jar popped up. She sighed, emptied the contents of the jar into a dish and transferred it to the fridge.

'I mentioned briefly yesterday about the mercury barometer…' Mr Newton was scanning the list of names on his register again… 'Trevor Stewart, Trevor could you tell us about how a mercury barometer measures air pressure?'

Trevor rose confidently to his feet because he knew about this. It was in a book he'd just got out from the library and science was a bit of a hobby for him. But he wasn't prepared for was the roar of laughter that went up from those behind him. He had forgotten his efforts in embroidery.

From that day on, Trevor had a new nickname: Redback. It was a reference to a small venomous native spider which inspires particular fear amongst White Australians, all of whom once had outside toilets. For the Redback loves cool, dark places, its favourite haunt being just under the seat.

The class was quiet. The instruction had been to read up to page fifty and to copy out the diagrams but Brian's mind was away in the world of hot air balloons. He was idly sketching in the margins of the paper the ways in which the tissue panels would fit together and how many of them would be needed, a bit tricky because it was now a three dimensional problem. He started to draw another configuration, oblivious to his teacher standing behind him.

'So, this is the diagram of an aneroid barometer is it Brian?'

'Ah…no sir,' said Brian weakly attempting to surreptitiously cover the page with his elbow.

'No, indeed it is not. Could you see me after class please?'

With that Mr Newton swept on with his inspection tour of the class while Brian emitted a low groan and slumped his shoulders.

'You're in trouble now mate,' said Trevor helpfully.

At nine forty the phone rang. Mary MacArthur ran from the kitchen to the hall. She was beside herself with worry. She knew something was wrong.

After what seemed an eternity, the siren sounded to signal the end of the first period. Amidst the confusion of departing boys and girls, Mr Newton called out that there was no homework, which raised a cheer from the mob, wished everyone a happy weekend and then immediately motioned Brian to come to the front bench. Trevor waited outside the door for the fireworks.

'…but you must remember to keep the weight down. That's absolutely essential. Let me know how you get on…'

'Thanks a lot Mr Newton.' Brian had a huge grin on his face as he made his way to the door.

'What's wrong with your leg?' the teacher called after him.

'Hit by a mallee root,' said Brian, the injury being so common in those parts that he didn't think further elaboration was necessary, inadvertently leaving his teacher completely in the dark.

'Oh, of course…yes, oh and Brian, one last thing…' Brian paused in the doorway and turned.

'…Do your homework next time won't you?'

Brian smiled, nodded and hobbled out the door to inform his best friend that the Children's Encyclopaedia had been around a long time and that the new teacher was a good bloke.

A scuffle at the door heralded the arrival of Mr Newton's next class. He groaned inwardly. It was 3B4, a small group but big trouble. He went to meet them.

As Trevor and Brian made their way past them deep in conversation, a leg was thrust out by the tall dark-skinned boy at the back of the line. The trip was perfectly timed and both boys clattered to the ground.

Laughter erupted from all sides.

'BRIAN!'

From his prone position, Brian looked back at Mr Newton. But it was not at him that the teacher was glaring. His fury was directed at the grinning aboriginal boy who had just created the disturbance.

His name was Brian Grady. His life was very different from that of Brian MacArthur. There were lots of Grady's in the area and the family had been in Martinup a lot, lot longer than the MacArthurs, who had only arrived in 1950. The first white man came in 1834.

Sergeant Anderson wiped the sweat from his brow with the dirty handkerchief and stuffed the sodden cloth back into his breast pocket. The heavy scarlet woollen uniform sapped his strength. The sturdy cloth was not designed for this climate. He longed to rip the whole lot off and dive into a pool of clear water. But that was out the question for a man of his station and they had seen no water for three days. The heat and the dust and the flies made things difficult enough but finding a path through bush like this on horseback was very nearly impossible at times.

He was still shocked by the climate and wondered at his sanity for volunteering to come on this expedition south from the fledgling Swan River Colony which itself was barely five years old. The whole country was still virtually unexplored and it was just seventy years since Captain Cook had established a penal colony at Botany Bay on the other side of this island continent. Fears of French Imperial claims to the western half of the continent (they had already explored the south western coast naming Point d'Entrecasteaux and Esperance and had the cheek to set up a whaling operation in the Southern Ocean) inspired London to instruct Major Lockyer to claim that vast, largely unknown territory for the British Crown without delay.

Sergeant Anderson had been ordered to find water, an obvious requirement for any future settlement inland. Having found it, a base, effectively a police station, was to be established and word sent back to the Swan River Colony and on to the coastal port of Fredericktown so that a permanent settlement could be made to accommodate the ever-growing number of immigrants from England eager to farm their own land.

Word had it that there was water in abundance in an area about one hundred miles SW of the Swan River and about the same distance north of Fredericktown.

They had been in the saddle for nearly a week.

Sergeant Anderson brushed the flies from his face and adjusted the chin-strap of his helmet, now sticky with sweat and mentally assessed their progress:

The blackfellow appears to be reliable, for the time being at least. Without him and those like him that could be trusted, the damn country would never be civilised. *'One bit of bush looks exactly like another to me. Quite amazing how they do it, even without one of these,'* he mused to himself as he eased a brass pocket compass from his breeches and confirmed their course was indeed correct, SW.

He ducked the bough of a tree as it loomed up.

'SLOW DOWN A BIT JACKIE!' he shouted at the aboriginal tracker ahead, on foot, clad only in a pair of rough cotton trousers barely visible in the thicket of trees and long grass ahead of the two mounted policemen.

The sergeant changed his position in the saddle, then turned and addressed his subordinate:

'How are you, Constable? Still managing I trust despite these trying conditions?'

The tall young police constable that brought up the rear of the small expeditionary party bit his tongue before answering. He hated this upper-class English bastard. He hated the sound of his accent. He hated this godforsaken country. But it was still better than the filth and poverty of Limerick where all he could look forward to was an early grave. He was here to advance himself. This was a new land of opportunity.

He could even put up with this toff in the new police station if it meant he could get on in life.

'Thank you for asking, sir. As well as can be expected,' came the obsequious reply.

But his superior was not listening.

'What's that you say? Well done Jackie! I'll ensure you are well rewarded for this!' The sergeant was leaning over in his saddle listening to the tracker who had hurried back through the bush with urgent news.

'Constable! He says he's found it! Water! Lots of it, just ahead!'

The horses had already sensed salvation and without encouragement surged forward until they crashed out onto the sandy banks of a broad pool, dragging behind them the reluctant mules, their backs loaded with provisions.

On the opposite bank, a young aboriginal woman watched the intruders through the undergrowth. Her people were called Gnoongah which can only be translated as 'People' since that's all there was in the south west of Western Australia since time began. But these intruders were known about. Word had spread through the bush from north and south. The strangers already had a name amongst the Gnoongah. They were called Wadgellah and this was the first time she had seen them. Now they had come to her land, this special place where the water was always constant and food was plentiful. They had come to The Water where her ancestors had drunk and swam and fished; where countless members of her race had lived their dramas of betrothal and betrayal, of love and hate, of peace and war; where the sacred songs of initiation were sung and spirit dances danced to ensure the abundance of the kangaroo, the possum and the goanna. They left no sign that they had ever been there, no building nor monument, not even (in that area) a rock or cave painting or artefact of any kind to record their passing. No sign, that is, except to her and her people.

The Gnoongah thrived in that area simply because of the water. The abundance of game it attracted could then support a reasonable population of small kinship groups. Other people lived in the harsh desert further inland. They were much fewer in number in keeping with the availability of their resources. They spoke a completely different language and had customs that were very different to the Gnoongah. This girl belonged in this place. She could live nowhere else. She and her kin owned the land in as much as the land owned them and always had done; indeed, the notion of "owning" someone else's land was to her an oxymoron. Although there were at times arguments and fights, it was always to do with matters of a cultural nature, of inappropriate behaviour or totem violations. No war was ever fought over land. The bush and the Gnoongah were as one, unchanged for ten thousand?…Twenty thousand?…A million years?

Her people and her own life were unique in the world and probably the oldest in continuous existence.

And now the Wadjallah had come to The Water. They had come to Maadenup, her place. And she could not understand why they would even want to do that. They did not belong here. This was not their place.

Having watered the horse, the constable remounted to get a better view of his new home. As he cast his eyes around edge of the lake, he caught a glimpse of naked female flesh in the bush on the other side. It rapidly disappeared from view.

'Oh, yes!' he whispered. 'I think I shall like it here very much!' and grinned broadly.

Then his mind turned to other matters. With luck, he might be soon promoted and be in charge of this area. '*Sergeant,*' he mused, '*Sergeant Patrick O'Grady.*' His name would live on in that area for generations.

'Have you got the stuff?'

'Sure have,' said Trevor as he struggled through the door with a large cardboard box.

Having survived their first week of high school and with no homework to do or mallee roots to chop, the boys had gone straight after school to the shed at the back of Trevor's place.

Don't you reckon, you should let your mum know you're here?'

'Naah, it'll be alright. She'll know where I am and this won't take too long anyway,' replied Brian with an air of nonchalance.

The shed had once served as Peter Stewart's workshop. His tools were all still pretty much where he had left them. Jars of nails and screws, pots of paint and other things cluttered the shelves that lined the walls. From the ceiling, a ladder and a chainsaw were suspended. A cobweb-covered window with a cracked pane overlooking the bush shed some light on the workbench, upon which along with other things were the parts of a model aeroplane under construction. The whole shed was a treasure trove for a young boy. Trevor had effectively inherited it along with the role of man about the house. Brian never brought up the subject of Trevor's dad. Even though Brian was the older of the two by just a month, it was Trevor who seemed to be the more mature one.

'Nice place this,' said Brian gazing around as if he had never been there before. 'I wish I had somewhere like this at home.'

Trevor smiled ruefully to himself and wondered if the loss of a father could be compensated by the gain of a work shed but he kept his thoughts to himself.

'Yeah, it is nice, isn't it? Let's see what we've got here.' He poured the contents of the cardboard box on the floor. Out tumbled a pile of junk; brown wrapping paper, Christmas wrapping paper, aluminium foil, cellophane and at last, tissue paper…loads of it.

With Brian's cardboard template they set to work with scissors to cut out the panels. Their enthusiasm and concentration for the task was such that neither noticed the passing of time nor the approach of Mrs Stewart across the back lawn. She put her head around the door just as the balloon was almost complete.

'You in there, Brian?'

'Yes, Mrs Stewart.'

'I've just had a phone call from your mum. She wants you to go home straight away.'

'Is anything wrong?' asked Brian suddenly a little concerned.

'She didn't say but she sounded a bit upset, so I reckon you better scoot off.'

'Fair enough, Mrs Stewart, I'm just on my way,' said Brian rising to his feet.

'This glue will have to dry and the best time to try a launch is sunset when it's usually dead calm,' said Trevor and continued, How about tomorrow about six o'clock up by the race track?'

'I'll see ya there,' said Brian heading for the door.

'And, don't forget the metho!' his mate called after him.

Even though it was not a great distance home, the journey seemed to be much longer than usual. Pedalling furiously, his mind was working overtime. Why was his mother upset? Or was she upset? Mrs Stewart got things wrong from time to time. Was it dad? Had something happened? Has he had an accident or something? Was he dead?

When he saw his father's car parked outside the front of the house, he knew something was wrong alright, something terribly wrong. His father never left the car at the front. It was always parked either in the drive or in the garage. He slowed his bike down on approach. The car was covered in dust. As he got off his bike, he saw the left-hand side of the vehicle and gasped. The fender and the front passenger door were battered in and there was blood everywhere. Not only was his father dead, it looked like he had killed someone in the process!

Thoughts racing and heart thumping, he hauled his bike through the front gate and dumped it at the side of the wall. What had happened? Was he really dead?

As he came through the back door, he could see his mother at the kitchen table with her head in her hands.

She looked up at him with tears in her eyes and said the words he'd been dreading,

'Your father had an accident.'

Suddenly it all made sense. All that thinking about what it would be like to be fatherless, just like Trevor…

'What happened?'

'He hit a kangaroo just before he got to Esperance.'

Before he could ask anything else his father who been attending to the lawn sprinkler outside, came through the back door.

'Hello, Son! How was your day at school? Mine wasn't very good!'

It took Brian a split second to respond to this new reality having already come to terms with his father's demise. It was like seeing a ghost. An instant later and he was across the room with his arms around his father's neck.

'Ouch,' groaned John MacArthur and smiled as he gingerly lifted off his son's embrace.

'Are you alright, Dad?'

'Yeah, just a couple of cuts and bruises, like this one,' He pointed to a small cut above his left eye.

'I'll put some flavine on that.'

'No, it's alright, Mary, honestly,' said John and winked at Brian.

Mary smiled at him and wiped away a tear. She had been worried sick all day since he'd called her and even though she knew he was alright, the thought of what might have been had driven her to distraction. And there was still all that distance to come back. She still wasn't sure herself of all the details and her husband had arrived barely minutes after she had telephoned Margaret Stewart to send Brian home. But she'd had quite enough for one day and busied herself in the pantry getting tea ready

'So, what happened Dad?' The boy was keen to know all the gory details.

The big man eased himself into a chair and at length told how, after hitting the animal, he managed to bring the car under control and safely to rest just off the road. The kangaroo had been killed in the impact. Amazingly enough, the car was still driveable and as he was just ten miles out of Esperance, he was able to limp into town, phone his wife and even get his work done. The local garage owner was once a customer of his and offered to bring the car back. A tow truck was due to make a trip to Perth and as Martinup was on the way, John MacArthur had his car towed home while he sat in the cab and chatted to the driver.

John MacArthur had indeed been fortunate, not just in the chain of circumstances following the accident, but by the fact that he had survived an impact with a full-grown male grey kangaroo relatively unscathed. Found all over the continent, they had adapted well to the clearing of the bush, unlike countless other smaller mammals which became extinct. The Greys flourished in the new open country unconstrained by fences, having the ability in full flight to jump a barrier twice the size of a man. Often encountered in the early hours of the morning or at sunset on country roads, this variety of kangaroo represented a real driving hazard. The one that hit John MacArthur's car a glancing blow was the size of a cow. It was not unknown in the case of a head-on collision for a beast to come straight through the windscreen and end up on the back seat, literally alive and kicking.

The following day Brian's dad was busy on the phone arranging for a mechanic mate of his to do a bit of panel-beating on the car in exchange for help with a tax return. Almost everybody in the country had a network of mates with particular skills that could be called on in an emergency. It was not quite a

41

cashless society but for a man whose business was money, John MacArthur was an adept practitioner in the barter economy.

Brian meanwhile, was at the woodheap, resuming his relationship with the mallee roots. By the end of the day, determined they would not get the better of him, he had not only reduced the pile of roots to a dozen or so particularly recalcitrant monsters but had nearly filled the woodshed to capacity, sustaining only minor injuries in the process. His stamina may have been due to an anticipation of events after tea.

The sun was low on the horizon. It was ten to six and Brian was up by the racecourse. There was nothing fancy about it, despite the name. It was a long sandy circular track a mile or more in circumference that had been cut through the bush. It must have been used once for regular horse race meetings, but the corrugated iron shed now empty and rusting, the only evidence of this activity, was slowly being reclaimed by the bush.

In the centre of the circular track was a roughly cleared area, presumably so that the horses on the other side of the track could be seen from the "stand". The only ones who used the course now were a handful of men training their horses in "trotting" in which the "driver" is pulled around by the animal in a lightweight cart, a bit like a chariot race but without the scythes on the wheels.

Conditions were perfect. Not a trotter in sight and not a breath of wind.

The sound of a bike coming up behind caused Brian to swing round.

'Trevor! Good to see ya! Did ya manage the balloon okay?'

'Yep. I've got it!'

Trevor parked his bike against a tree and gently lifted a briefcase from the saddle.

'It's in here. What about you? Have you got the metho and the cotton wool?'

Brian nodded affirmatively and patted the bag slung over his shoulder with a grin.

'And the matches?'

'Sure have.' Brian had carried out a lightning raid on the bathroom and the pantry cupboard while his parents were out checking the chooks for eggs.

Having already decided that trees needed to be avoided, the two boys set off across the sandy track, mounted the rail fence and made their way to the cleared interior of the track. The sun had now just crossed the horizon. The sky was beginning to take on the first breath-taking colours of sunset. Everything was perfectly still and silent.

'This'll do,' said Trevor, depositing the case in the scrub. He dropped to his knees and opened it.

Brian put down his bag and took out the other items.

Both boys had been thinking about the launch procedure arrived at the same conclusion. The balloon would need to be partially inflated first before any flame was applied. Trevor did the honours and gently blew in to the mouth of the balloon so that the panels began to expand.

'That's perfect!' said Brian and turned his attention to the cotton wool. He tore off a piece the size of his thumb, rolled it into a ball and with a small piece of cotton, tied it to the wire cross piece, Trevor all the while kept the canopy steady. Brian then poured a capful of methylated spirit and applied it to the cotton wool allowing the fibres to soak up the liquid.

Trevor, watching the process, suggested a bit more spirit. 'But don't get it on the tissue paper!'

Brian rolled his eyes skyward muttering. 'Yes Trevor.'

The moment of truth.

Brian took a match from the box, stuck it and applied the naked flame to the sodden cotton wool bud.

'Now keep it dead straight Trevor, or the whole bloody thing will go up!'

From his vantage position, Brian could watch the progress of the flame. It was looking good, the flame going straight up into the canopy.

Trevor could feel the balloon starting to inflate.

'It's working!'

Brian looked up, and, sure enough, one by one the tissue paper panels were starting to pop out.

'Hang on to it until its good and ready to go!' he said, trying to sound calm.

Seconds later, Trevor was certain. The whole thing was pushing against his hands like some gravity defying basketball.

With mutual consent, Trevor removed his hands.

Lift off!

With surprising speed, the balloon ascended into the early evening sky above them. Twenty feet, thirty feet, surely well over tree height now and rising. And higher yet with the flickering light still visible at its base. After maybe a minute, a gentle breeze high above caused the balloon to drift to the east. The darkening purple sky obscured the canopy. Only the flickering flame betrayed its course.

An external observer would have seen two small boys transfixed in the middle of a clearing in the bush, heads back, mouths agape, staring into space for three whole minutes.

Now the spell broke.

'EEEEEHAR!'

They screamed, they shook each by the hand and they clapped each other on the back. It had WORKED!

They grinned from ear to ear and could not contain their excitement. The talk was immediately about another, bigger and better one, of different materials and different fuel…until Trevor said,

'Shit, I've just thought of something.'

Brian, still grinning said, 'What?'

'S'pose that thing catches fire or is still alight when it comes down. It's headin' east and there it's tinder dry farmland all the way from here to Esperance.'

As Brian took in what was being said, the smile slowly receded from his face and a look of panic was suddenly in his eyes. It didn't make him long to decide on an appropriate course of action.

'Let's get outta here!' he screamed.

Five minutes later, high above and heading slowly east, a tissue balloon drifted. When the spirit on the cotton wool was exhausted, the flame went out. Slowly, the canopy cooled and the balloon began its descent. It ended up in a tree ten miles away. For many weeks it flapped about in the wind until one day it disintegrated completely, the first hot air balloon ever to be safely and successfully launched from Martinup.

Brian woke to the sound of the six o'clock news on the radio:

'…Fires have raged in the early hours of the morning through farmland to the east of Martinup. There have been reports of extensive damage to property but the situation is now under control. A spokesman for the Fire Brigade said the blaze was probably caused by a discarded cigarette from a passing car and urged all drivers to exercise care, especially at this time of year. And now the weather outlook...'

'Oh my God!' he groaned and pulled the blanket over his head, his worst nightmare had come true.

'Brian! Time to get up! We'll need to walk to mass today because we've got no car remember!' his father called.

'And it's your big day too!' chimed in his mother. 'You are an altar boy now remember!'

From beneath the blankets he wondered what else his Vengeful God could throw at him.

The Incarcerated Priest

Clutching the white surplice and red soutane that he had reluctantly accepted from Father O'Neill the previous Sunday, Brian trailed his mum and dad along the road deep in thought. His anguish was profound. A bushfire! He had started a bushfire that had caused "extensive damage". How much damage is that? A hundred pounds worth? A thousand pounds? Ten thousand pounds? And worse, much, much worse, he could easily have killed someone, all because of his thoughtlessness. Burned them alive in their own homes as they vainly tried to protect themselves from the wall of flame! He could hear the screams! Oh why, oh why did he set off a hot air balloon in the bushfire season? This was definitely a mortal sin. If he died now, he'd go straight to hell. If he could just hang on to dear life long enough to go to confession, about twenty minutes, he reckoned looking at his watch, it would be alright. He could then die in peace, safe in the knowledge that he had escaped eternal damnation.

Then his thoughts turned from matters spiritual to matters temporal. Arson was a serious crime and the police would take a very dim view if they knew what had happened. What if they knew already? What if they had found the balloon, identified it as the cause of the blaze and were in the process of lifting fingerprints? They were on to him and Trevor for sure!

'Naah!' Brian said out loud to himself in response to his train of thought.

'What's that Brian?' asked his mother over her shoulder, but before he could reply, his father said.

'Come on Son, hurry up or we'll be late for mass. We can't have that, can we?'

Brian nodded and continued the mental argument. There was no way a tissue paper balloon could have survived a bushfire and besides that, if it had managed to survive, in a day or two it would have disintegrated with the weather. He heaved a sigh of relief that he had, in all probability, escaped the long arm of the law.

The surplice was beginning to slip out of his grasp. Impatiently he gathered it back up under his armpit.

He was annoyed at the way he'd become an altar boy. It was his dad's fault. The casual conversation that he had had with Father O'Neill last Sunday after Mass resulted in Brian being nominated for the vacant position, an offer gleefully accepted by the priest. Brian was presented with a fait accompli along with the appropriate vestments. His protests were met by John MacArthur saying cheerily, 'Oh, you'll like it son. I quite enjoyed my time as an altar boy. Just try it and see how you get on.' Brian wondered how it was that parents always assumed that their offspring would enjoy what they themselves had enjoyed in their youth. In fact, his father had not been an altar boy at all, but a choir boy, quite a different thing altogether, a role that enabled him to be excused, amongst other things, some very boring Latin lessons. Brian mentally resolved to give it one shot.

Walking to church was a new experience for Brian. The journey took just minutes by car. Now he was able to observe in detail houses along the route that were a blur. Each was different, but in some respects, many were the same: the jaded front lawns, the shaded verandas, the tangled rose bushes from a distant country. But every now and then a house would stand out from the asbestos, weatherboard and corrugated-iron crowd. It would inevitably belong to an Italian migrant who worked hard as a shopkeeper or builder to rise above the desperate childhood poverty of a village in Sicily or Napoli and who now could show the people of Martinup how much had been achieved in twenty years. The style of choice was a Roman villa. Brick-built, sometimes incorporating Doric columns of concrete, these two storey giants gloated imperiously over the neighbourhood. From a balustrade balcony, the owner could savour a generous glass of his own vino and smile with pride that his house with its marble statue of a naked boy child urinating into a fountain scale model in brick of the Leaning Tower of Pisa and granite grotto with a full-colour life-size image of the Virgin Mary would impress the casual observer. Such a house always impressed Brian when he passed one. Indeed, the image would stay with him for the rest of his life.

In the distance, the bell-tower of the church came into view. In the middle distance, the concrete-grey edifice that was the Convent of the Little Sisters of the Poor opened its gates to disgorge a handful of little nuns whose garb matched their convent and whose size matched the name of their Order. In single file they made their way to Mass. From the side streets came a trickle of other parishioners heading for the same destination.

'Get a move on son!'

'Dad, we've got loads of time. Father O'Neill's always ten minutes late anyway.'

Father Francis O'Neill was in the lounge room of the presbytery, a fairly modest bungalow generously shaded by white gums. located just behind the school. It was clear he was a worried man. As he paced the length of the room and back again, he drew heavily on a cigarette, accidentally dropping ash in the process which he quickly dispersed into the carpet with the toe of his shoe.

He had been up since seven nursing a fearful hangover which was only now beginning to dissipate. Father O'Neill had a fondness for the drink. The Saturday night had been spent entertaining himself as usual with Johnny Walker, periodically muttering throughout the evening, 'Well I'll just have another wee one and that will be it.' He stopped saying that at two in the morning when the bottle ran out and he was left with no choice but to weave his way to bed.

He awoke to a dawn chorus of magpies, a splitting headache and no resolution to a worrying situation. The phone call from the Bishop had come out of the blue the previous week. Father O'Neill was to receive a visit from an Envoy of His Grace sometime on Sunday. TODAY! The bishop declined to give further details just saying that there were a few matters that Father Harding would like to discuss with him.

His sixth sense warned him that something was up. This was no casual visit. A phone call to a fellow priest in Perth, an old school friend from Dublin with a good inside knowledge of the Church in this part of the world confirmed his worst fears. The "envoy" was a Jesuit, William Augustus Harding S.J. He was not a messenger from the Bishop at all. He reported directly to the Cardinal and his remit was to investigate parish priests, particularly in relation to financial matters! He was a Vatican hit-man!

Father O'Neill gulped at the thought and fumbled in the packet for his last cigarette before Mass. There was an "anomaly" in the parish accounts. Six hundred and forty-nine dollars had been raised from the Planned Giving program in the last month, but only two hundred and forty-nine dollars had found its way to the Diocesan account. There was a way around it, but he hadn't quite thought of it yet. He lit the cigarette, inhaled deeply and wished he was back in Ireland.

It had all seemed so straight forward when he left Dublin. The usual round of the colonies then home to Wexford perhaps, or maybe even Cork, then a peaceful retirement in Co. Donegal. But it was not just the drink that Father O'Neill had a fondness for. It was the women too. But wasn't it just his luck to be caught in Sydney's King's Cross in the wrong company? Result: a reprimand and a transfer to Wollongong. And then there was that lovely young Mrs Donovan, so recently bereaved and himself only trying to comfort her? Result: transfer to Martinup, Western Australia where he had been these last twelve long years. It had all been a series of terrible misunderstandings but he'd not looked at a woman since.

'And it's not as if I've been idle,' he mused to himself as he stubbed out the cigarette in the ashtray and pulled his black jacket from behind the door. He casually brushed his hair with his hand in the hallway mirror, examined his rather blood-shot eyes and grunted. He turned side-on to the mirror and patted his waistline. Those nuns and that rich food! Pulling the door shut behind him he set off for the short walk to the church to hear confessions before Mass.

Father O'Neill was right. He had not been idle since coming to the parish. The church itself with its impressive bell tower and newly refurbished interior was the result of his efforts. New stained-glass windows, an impressive crucifix dominating the air space above the altar, the mahogany pulpit, all this was his doing. He even catered for mothers with small children They were allocated a room with a sound proof window beside the entrance to the church so that the babies would not disrupt the Mass. (He later changed his mind and moved them to the last three pews and converted the room into a sacristy so that he could make a grand processional entrance.) It was he who had introduced the altar boys and inspired the nuns to create the impressive new vestments for Father O'Neill believed the church should be grand, a glorification of the Lord, a celebration of Christ, an inspiration to the parishioner.

Of course, there was the other side to it. If he could do a good job, they might send him home.

Occasionally parishioners interested in financial affairs like John MacArthur would wonder where the money came from. Father William Augustus Harding S.J. had wondered about it too. He was already on his way.

Brian entered the cramped confessional and closed the door behind him. The fact that the purple curtain on the small opening on the wall was closed told him that the priest was in residence, so he got down on the kneeler and began to read from the text pinned to the wall just beneath the curtain.

'Bless me Father, for I have sinned, it is about a week since my last confession...' (and then the crunch)

'I have committed the following sins...'

'Aah, I have told lies to my mother, and, aah...and I've told lies to my father, and...aah...I've started a bushfire.'

Silence.

Brian wondered if Father O'Neill was so shocked at his admission that excommunication could be the only appropriate response but in fact, the truth was more mundane. Father O'Neill's mind was elsewhere. His train of thought was interrupted by the sudden silence from the other side of the curtain, so he proceeded with the usual absolution and told Brian that his penance would be one our Father three Hail Marys and a Glory be to the FATHER.

On his side of the confessional, Brian listened in astonishment. This couldn't be right. Five prayers would atone for the mortal sin of starting a bushfire? Damage worth thousands of pounds? Attempted murder?

This penance wouldn't take five minutes! Maybe he was meant to say the prayers really slowly. But he supposed God knew best and shrugged his shoulders as the priest concluded, 'Go in peace my son.'

As Brian got up to leave, Father O'Neill whispered loudly through to him,

'Is there anybody else waiting?'

Brian put his head around the door and looked.

He whispered back, 'No Father.'

'Good.' grunted the priest thinking that he would just wait a few more minutes for any late comers.

Brian knelt in a pew near the confessional and said his penance. He got up and made his way to the sacristy at the front entrance of the church where he had left his vestments. His mum and dad caught his eye and smiled at him.

Father O'Neill looked at his watch. Nine thirty. Time to get ready for Mass. He turned the handle on the confessional door but nothing happened. He tried again but still the door would not budge. He rattled the handle. 'What the devil is going on?' he muttered, his Irish brogue suddenly re-emerging. A surge of panic rose in the pit of his stomach, as he realised, he was trapped. And he couldn't just start shouting for help and banging on the door without looking a complete eejit in front of the whole congregation. He had to be discreet. Somehow, he had to attract someone's attention. By straining up hard against the slatted window set in the door which provided ventilation, he could just make out the pews nearby, but there was no one in sight.

Brian entered the open door of the sacristy. Another boy was already there.

'G'day Brian.'

Brian returned the greeting. He had known Peter Haddow for years. Peter had been very quiet at the Convent school, but since moving to the high school had gained some notoriety. Whilst pulling on their red and white regalia they chatted on about the new school, new subjects and the new teachers, mutually agreeing that Mr MacDuff was the worst and Miss Marceaux the French teacher was pretty special.

Then Peter looked at his watch and said, 'I'll need to get that bell rung. Come and see how it's done. It's pretty easy once you get the hang of it.' They both scampered off to the bell tower.

Father O'Neil was nearly beside himself with despair when into his narrow field of view came the familiar figure of "Big Arnie" MacAulay. The bachelor farmer had just arrived at his usual spot near the confessional and was preparing to say his prayers.

'*Psst ARNIE!* ARNIE!'

Arnie looked up and around and finally settled his gaze on the confessional which seemed to be speaking to him.

He uncoiled his bulk from the pew and edged his way along the seat to the confessional.

'Arnie! Can you help me please? I'm stuck in here. The door seems to be jammed!'

'Is that you, Father?'

Father O'Neill rolled his eyes to Heaven, sighed, and allowed all manner of bad thoughts to pass momentarily through his head.

'Yes, it is me Arnie. Can you get me out of here, please? The door seems to be jammed.'

'Right you are Father,' said Arnie as he pulled on the handle.

'The door seems to be jammed.'

'Yes Arnie,' said the priest slowly. He was about to say 'Please be careful' when with a loud CRACK, the door came off its hinges. It was however still suspended in space by the handle firmly locked in Arnie's out sized hands. All heads in the congregation swung around in the direction of the noise. Father O'Neill stepped through the newly created opening looking slightly flustered.

Outside, the bells tolled.

DING DONG!

'Sorry about that Father,' whispered the farmer. 'I'll get it fixed for you,' he said, trying in vain to gently prop the door back into the empty space.

DING DONG!

'Thank you, Arnie,' said the priest as he squeezed between the big man and the end of the pew and scurried, head down, for the safety of the sacristy at the main entrance.

DING DONG!

Father O'Neill let the heavy sacristy door close firmly behind him and said a small prayer to calm his nerves. Oh, it was times like these he could do with a cigarette! He took a deep breath, opened the double doors of the wardrobe and set about donning the stunning vestments in gold brocade and vivid silk stitched by the hands of the Little Sisters of the Poor. When he'd finished, he checked his appearance left and right in the full-length mirrors mounted behind the wardrobe doors and patted down a stray wisp of hair.

Satisfied, he lifted the chalice and paten from their special place on the side table and headed for the door. Outside the bells could still be faintly heard. He turned the handle. It came away in his hand. Father O'Neill stared down in utter disbelief at the piece of metal he was holding. Frantically, he placed the chalice back on the side table and rushed back to the door. The handle had sheared off at the base. He tried in vain to insert it back into the cavity. Trapped again! Twice in ten minutes! This was unbelievable! His wonderful church was falling apart! Conspiring against him! In frustration he threw the useless handle into the bin behind the door.

In a silent frenzy, he scanned the room for anything that could be used as a tool to force the door. Nothing. He pulled open a small part of the curtain. He could see out clearly enough, but the congregation had their backs to him and the sound proof window he had installed for the benefit of mothers with small children, effectively prevented him from attracting even their attention, even though they were just a few feet away.

There was a knock at the door. The bells had stopped. '*It must be the altar boys!*' he thought.

Praying to every Saint he could think of for salvation and trying to sound calm, although his voice still came out as a tiny squeak, he said, 'Come in.'

Brian opened the door. The handle still worked fine from the outside.

'Ah Brian!' said the priest effusively coming straight over to greet the boy. 'Great to have you on board! Brian, could you please have a look outside for something to hold this door open. It's got an automatic closing thing and it gets very stuffy in here at this time of year. Would you mind? There's a good boy!'

'The priest seemed a bit pale and breathless. Must have been really stuffy in there, especially with all that gear on,' thought Brian as he duly scurried off to find a brick from behind the church while Peter dealt with the candles.

'There, that should do it,' said Father O'Neill as he wedged the brick in place with his shoe. 'Plenty of air in there now. Well boys!' he beamed. 'Are we ready?' Brian and Peter nodded back, their faces illuminated by candlelight.

Paul Newton's car pulled up in the car park of St Mary's College. He was uneasy. This was not like Susan. She knew he was coming up to the city after his first week in the country but he had not heard from her for ten days now. He had tried to phone her but the single pay phone in the Junior Common Room was next to useless. Everyone avoided answering it because it invariably meant tracking someone else down to leave a message, Why bother? So, the phone often rang till the caller gave up. But why hadn't she phoned him? She knew he would be at his parent's house. She was his girlfriend, wasn't she?

Crossing the immaculate lawns of the College he headed for the South Wing, an imposing concrete structure on three levels framed and partly camouflaged by native foliage where Susan had a room on the top floor. She had just started her honours in Anthropology and Paul had assumed that perhaps her silence was due to the increased pressure of study. No one was in sight, which was not unusual for a Sunday morning at a student Hall of Residence.

'I bet she's probably flat out,' he thought to himself as he bounded the flights of concrete steps, slowing when he reached the top, slightly out of breath. 'One week in the country and already I'm out of condition,' he muttered. He strode along the dimly-lit corridor to her room, the last on the right and knocked on the door. There was instantly sounds of movement inside. The door opened a fraction. It was Susan in her dressing gown which she clasped tightly to her neck.

'Oh, it's you Paul,' she said.

'Yes, it's me,' he replied his voice betraying a tone of annoyance. 'Why haven't you phoned Susan?'

Before she could reply, a noise came from behind her indicating the unmistakable presence of someone else in the room.

And before Paul's mind could even frame the question, 'Is there someone else in there with you?' the door had slammed shut in his face and a bolt had rattled home.

He stood for what seemed like an eternity staring at the wooden barrier that had suddenly torn his world apart while the words formed and paraded through his mind.

Susan…my…girl…friend…has…got…another…man…in …her…room…

A giggle from the other side of the door caused him to snap.

BANG! Paul's right boot rebounded off the quivering timber with a violence that echoed and re-echoed through the empty corridor.

'Bastard!' he barked with a venom that even surprised himself.

With that, he was off, vaulting down the stairs two at a time, pausing only on the last balcony to hiss 'Bitch!'

The car roared to life, reversed with a squeal of tyres, then accelerated up the driveway out of the college.

Paul didn't stop till he was in the park that overlooked the city. He turned off the engine and wept bitter tears of rage.

'And above all...these three Persons...in one God...lie at the heart...of the Mystery...of the Trinity.'

Father O'Neill was in full flow with the sermon. Brian and Peter were seated side by side on two chairs against the wall behind the pulpit, obscured from the view of most of the congregation. Brian always found Father O'Neill's homilies unbelievable dull but at least being behind him for a change was something different.

'And it is our acceptance...above all...of this Mystery...that lies at the heart of our Faith.'

Brian toyed with his surplice and his mind as usual at this part of the Mass, started to wander. If he was a priest and he hastily added that there was no way that he'd be one, but if he was a priest, then he bet he could do a better sermon than Father O'Neill with his "Mysteries" and his "above all's". What other stupid words did he like to use? Oh yeah, 'ecumenical'...and... 'ecclesiastical'...and...and... 'liturgical'...and what the hell was a paraclete? Some sort of bird, Brian imagined. No, he could do a really good sermon specially at Christmas. Encourage the giving of presents to kids! But sensible presents. Because just look what the baby Jesus got from the Three Wise Men. They knew they were going to see a baby. Even if He was God, surely some toys or even nappies would have been more appropriate. Okay, his mother would probably have appreciated the gold 'cos they were pretty poor, but Joseph would have had to say, 'Thanks a lot for the frankincense and myrrh you fellas, we'd nearly run out!' while he stuffed the lot behind the manger. Three Wise Men huh!

Brian's reverie was interrupted by a terrible smell that seemed to engulf him. The curse of Peter Haddow's flatulence had struck again! He covered his face with his surplice to try to suppress the smell and his own giggles.

Paul slammed the car door shut and began to walk nowhere in particular. His mind was flooded with scenes from the past, of moments frozen in time then replayed in slow motion. He'd been with her for a year and a half. She had given no him no clue… How could she do this to him? How could she… He saw the people in the park, but didn't see them, nor the couples, nor the children playing ball, nor the trees, nor the grass. Deep, deep inside he saw nothing, nothing at all, but Susan. And the questions came back and back and back again… Why did she…Why…WHY?

And so, it went on and on till his mind went blank. He loved her. But he could not go back to her. He would not go back to her even if she begged him! But then his mind was suddenly made up. There was only one course of action. He had a job to do and he was bloody well going to do it. With grim determination, he turned briskly on his heel and headed back to the car parked in the distance.

Father O'Neill went down on one knee then rose and lifted the monstrance containing the newly consecrated Eucharist above his head, expecting to hear the more experienced altar boy ringing the bell as the host was raised. The two boys were kneeling together on the top step of the altar dais. The priest was frozen momentarily in time as Peter motioned for Brian to take action, for the bell lay on the carpet beside the new boy.

'THE BELL…RING THE BELL Peter mouthed silently and clearly nodding in the direction of it, next to Brian's knee. Brian picked it up and gave it a vigorous shake. Nothing. A quick look inside revealed that the clapper had fallen out. Looking quickly around, he caught sight of it at the base of the steps. Father O'Neill, his arms beginning to tire from the weight of the jewel-encrusted monstrance, glanced over his right shoulder and saw Brian scurrying down to retrieve the missing piece of brass. With a sigh, he gently lowered the monstrance to the altar and continued with the Mass. Brian, meanwhile, anxious to do the right thing, had re-hung the clapper on his way back up and in trying to gently lower the bell to the carpet, managed instead to knock it down the steps. Father O'Neill groaned inwardly.

Brian was now a bag of nerves. He had completely forgotten the order of the Mass. He was totally reliant on Peter Haddow. But even worse than that was his sudden realisation that everyone was looking at him and had been since the beginning of the service! He didn't know it but it was a very common phenomenon. He had stage fright. A sick feeling was forming in the pit of his stomach.

The rest of the Mass was a bit of a blur for Brian. With the aid of Peter's nudges and whispers which at the same time made him all the more self-conscious and clumsy, he blundered his way through the water and wine and trembled his way through communion, the silver platter vibrating noticeably in his hand as he held it under the chins of the multitude of communicants.

But Brian's ordeal was not over when Father O'Neill gave his final blessing. A long red carpet stretched before him and to the right and left was a sea of faces of people he was sure he had never seen before, not even his own mother and father who smiled at him as he passed. Eyes cast down, he concentrated only on placing one foot after another. All he wanted to do was make it to the end of the carpet without tripping, sneezing, burping, farting or otherwise making a complete fool of himself. He guarded the flickering flame of the candle he held with his life. It was the longest journey he had ever made. His mind was made up.

This would be the first and the last time he would make it.

The three celebrants emerged from the body of the church to the rising sound of the congregation preparing to depart. Brian blew out his candle emphatically. He was just going to tell Father O'Neill of his desire to quit the altar-boyhood but he was already too late. The priest had swept past him, deposited the sacred vessels in the sacristy and was back out again greeting the parishioners. Dejected Brian followed Peter into the sacristy to disrobe.

'See ya t'morra Brian!' Peter shouted to him as he left.

'Rightio Pete,' said Brian as he divested himself of his regalia and folded the two garments into a neat bundle. What should he do? he wondered. Just leave them here with a note? No that wasn't right. Through the open doorway he could see

Father O'Neill was still caught up with the crowds. His mother put her head around and told him she would meet him at the front. Reluctantly, Brian tucked the bundle under his arm and set off to meet her. *'There had to be a way out of this,'* he thought, then the priest caught his eye and said, 'See you Sunday Brian!' before swirling away in a whirl of green and yellow silk brocade to greet another parishioner.

'How did it go?' asked his mother. You looked good from where we were.'

'Okay.' said Brian the usual minimalist, slightly economical with the truth line with his mother, grateful at least that she and his father had been seated well to the back of the church.

'Where's dad?'

'He's just having a chat with Father O'Neill dear. Here he is now.'

Brian's father, resplendent in his new suit (his "work clothes" he called them) skipped down the steps to join them.

'Father O'Neill says you did pretty well for your first time Brian. Well done my boy. See, I told you, it would be fun!' he said as he patted the boy on the head.

Brian grunted and tucked the wretched vestments back up under his arm.

'Right Mary,' said John MacArthur, smiling as he took his wife's arm. 'Are we set for the long-haul home?'

Brian glumly followed his parents out the gate, pausing briefly to look back at the church where Father O'Neill was still going strong.

Ahead of him, his parents were locked in conversation about his brothers, Roger in particular and how he would get on at University.

Brian, meanwhile was now deep in thought. His curiously lenient penance for arson and attempted murder had led him to other things. Since the priest had told him it was worth just five prayers, then that must be okay with God because the priest was God's servant. Anyway, the main thing was that he had been forgiven his mortal sin. So, if he died now, he'd get into heaven no bother. But what if Trevor died just now? He had done exactly the same thing, so he must have committed a mortal sin too. But he was a Methodist. They don't have confession. They didn't even have to go to Mass every Sunday. So, did that mean that

Methodists can't commit mortal sins? That couldn't be right. So, what happened when they died? St Peter was definitely a Catholic so no way would Trevor get in. So did that mean Methodists went straight to hell? That couldn't be right either 'cos Trevor was a decent bloke. And what about Anglicans? And the Lutherans? Surely there couldn't be separate heavens…?

The theological argument was getting out of hand and Brian's brain was starting to hurt. He lightened up with the thought the cricket would be on the radio from eleven o'clock. It was Australia against the MCC in Melbourne and the Poms were in serious trouble. Brian suddenly realised that his parents, still in earnest conversation had inadvertently left their youngest son well behind.

'Wait for me!' he called out, breaking into a trot whilst grappling with his bundled regalia.

The church was nearly clear. With a sigh, Father O'Neill swept into the sacristy and began to disrobe. His headache was at last beginning to clear. He was looking forward to the tranquillity of the presbytery and the luxury of a strong cup of coffee and a cigarette.

'Good morning Father.'

Father O'Neill spun around to face the tall good-looking stranger in the well-cut suit obscuring the doorway.

'You haven't met me before,' he said stepping forward with his hand outstretched. Father O'Neill caught sight of the silver cross pinned to the stranger's lapel and his heart skipped a beat as the colour drained from his face.

'My name is Harding, Father William Harding,' he said as they shook hands.

'Perhaps we can talk in private,' said the Jesuit as he bent down to remove the brick holding the sacristy door ajar.

Father O'Neill watched in horror as the door swung into place with an audible click. 'Don't shut,' was all he could say in a strangled squeak.

The Glasgow Kiss

'Cup of tea dear?' asked his mother.

Brian was sitting at the kitchen table, his vestments beside him staring into space.

'Yes, please Mum,' he said, trying to sound casual but his face must have betrayed him.

'What's up Brian?' she asked.

Brian gave a deep sigh. He might as well come out with it even if it did upset his parents.

'It's this Mum,' indicating the altar boy outfit beside him on the table. 'I don't know, it's just...well...l didn't like being an altar boy at all. I didn't know what was going on and...l don't want to do it any...'

He was interrupted by his father who had just entered the room struggling to release the knot of his tie.

'Give it a chance boy, you've only done it once.'

'Aw but Dad...'

Brian still wasn't able to admit to the real reason for wanting to quit.

'Now John,' interjected Mary MacArthur (Brian's dad always knew he was onto a loser with his wife when she began with "Now John") 'if Brian feels that he really doesn't want to be an altar boy, I don't think we should force him to do it.'

With his head swinging from left to right, Brian felt he was watching a tennis match as his parents decided his fate.

'Mary, it's good for the boy. It teaches him...' (he couldn't quite think what it taught the boy exactly but the score now was definitely forty thirty)

'John!' she said raising an eyebrow at her husband.

Good deep serve from Mrs MacArthur.

'Kids these days! They don't stick at anything for more than ten minutes! I don't know!'

His voice trailed off in his retreat to the bedroom at the front of the house still grappling with his tie.

That lob is over the line and it's game, set and the match to Mrs Mary MacArthur!

Brian's mother smiled at her boy. Brian didn't know it but there was once a small girl whose parents wanted desperately for her to be a concert pianist. Every day after school she would practise for hours and hours and every Friday, she would endure a lesson from the dreaded Sister Theresa. She passed the exams all the way to Grade Eight. Her first public recital was in the school concert in her final year. Faced by a huge audience, she froze. She couldn't play a note and left the stage in a flood of tears, never to touch the instrument again. Mary MacArthur knew quite a lot about pushy parents and stage fright.

'That's okay, Brian, if you are sure you don't want to do it. But do the right thing. Go back straight away to tell Father O'Neill so that he's got plenty of time to get someone else. Take your bike and by the time you get back, dinner should be ready.'

'Thanks Mum,' said Brian with a smile, bundling the vestments under his arm.

'Don't forget the cricket's on son!' shouted his father from the bedroom.

'Yeah Dad, I know! I'll be back as fast as I can,' Brian called out as the back door slammed shut. Mary MacArthur shook her head.

'Men and boys! They're all the same!' she said and set about preparing the Sunday dinner.

It was just after eleven when Brian freewheeled his bike into the presbytery driveway. Although, the hottest part of the day was still some hours away, the sun had stung his bare skin and with the combination of physical exertion, perspiration now dripped from his brow down his nose. The presbytery by contrast looked cool and dark.

The priest's car was parked in front of the garage.

Dismounting, he pushed his bike up the drive, navigated it between the car and the trunk of the gum tree that dominated the front lawn and parked it against the garage wall. He decided to leave the vestments in the basket on the front of his bike for the moment and made for the front door.

The presbytery was a good-sized brick-built bungalow dating from the 1930s. It had features which came straight from England, like the broad bay window which thrust forward on the right-hand side of the building and the stained-glass panels that surrounded the massive front door. It also had incongruous features, such as the steeply-sloped corrugated iron roof, designed to deflect snow in the old country but obviously of no use in this part of the Antipodes.

Brian mounted the steps to the front door and creaked his way over the dusty wooden floorboards of the verandah.

He reached up to the black-painted iron door knocker in the form of a lion with a ring in its mouth and gave it several loud raps. The front verandah was heavily shaded and it struck Brian that all plants that surrounded the place were native species; the banksia and kangaroo paw, the peppermints and black boys, the red gums and white gums all cheerfully without the need for consistent watering and indeed looking very attractive. *'What a sensible idea for a garden instead of roses and tulips and daffodils and hydrangea,'* he thought.

There was still no answer, so he tried again and waited another minute. *'He might be around the back,'* thought Brian. So he abandoned the front door, skipped down the steps and made his way to the back of the house.

The back was very much like the front, a central lawn walled off by various species of Eucalyptus that gave off a heady mixture of smells. Set in the lawn was a rotary clothes line, a relatively modern innovation that was beginning to replace the line, post and pole method that Brian's mother still employed. Indeed, Mary MacArthur still did the washing on a Monday in the old-fashioned way but was now armed with a twin-tub washing machine rather than the wood-fired boiler. The old copper however, still stood in the wash house at Brian's place.

What fascinated Brian was the sight of, amongst other things, the priest's underwear hanging on the line. Somehow the priesthood and singlets and Y-fronts just didn't fit. Then he remembered he had a brother who was going to be a priest and somehow it suddenly didn't seem so incongruous.

Brian tried the door at the back porch, but there was still no answer to his knocking. Through the side window he could see the priest's outdoor boots on the floor and overcoats on the hook.

He wondered if it was worth seeing if the backdoor was locked. He was just about to try the handle when a voice barked at him from behind.

'WADDA YOU WANT?'

Startled, Brian spun around to be confronted by the beetroot-red face of Mrs Jaworski, the Polish widow from two doors along who took care of the domestic duties in the presbytery. Brian had seen her before at Mass, always saying her prayers at the side door of the church before entering in the old East European way, but he had never spoken to her before. Short and stocky, she wore a faded floral knee-length dress topped by a full-length white apron from under which sprouted brown woollen-stockinged legs that terminated in well-worn once-pink slippers. Her tanned muscular arms held a basket full of newly-washed priestly things still dripping and ready to be hung. She glared at him from under her head scarf.

'Hello Mrs Jaworski,' said Brian keen to prove he was not an evil cat-burglar. I'm looking for Father O'Neill. Is he in do you know?'

'NO. HE NOT HERE. I DUNNO. MAYBE YOU TRY CHURCH HUH?'

'Thanks very much, Mrs Jaworski.' Brian watched a moment as the little woman dumped the washing basket on the lawn, shoved a handful of pegs in her mouth and continued hanging up underpants. She looked back at him.

'Bye now!' he smiled and waved but a grunt was all he got in return. On the way to retrieve his bike, he reflected on the cruel irony that an immigrant to Australia who was very probably well-spoken and eloquent in his or her own tongue should on arrival be immediately condemned to a lifetime of sounding like a Red Indian from a Wild West movie.

The church looked completely deserted as he slowed his bike at the front steps and gently lowered the frame to the ground. He pulled out the vestments. This time he was determined to be rid of them somehow.

No sooner had he entered, he was aware of voices coming from behind the closed door of the sacristy. What should he do? He didn't want to disturb an important meeting. Nor could he just go away. After a moment's hesitation his mind was made up. '*Too bad*,' he thought and knocked on the door.

The instant silence inside unsettled him, so too did Father O'Neill's voice when it came as he sounded either angry or upset. In fact, it was neither emotion. Sheer desperation gave the priest's voice that cutting edge for the two men had been incarcerated for nearly an hour, their only hope being the arrival of the cleaning ladies at noon.

'Yes? Who is it?'

'It's me Father, Brian MacArthur.' He opened the door and put his head around. 'I'm not disturbing you, am I?'

'NO! NO! My boy! Please do come in!' boomed Father O'Neill, bounding across the room to grab the door with both hands whilst sliding the brick into a holding position with his foot.

Brian was rather taken aback by the enthusiasm of his welcome.

'Oh, Father Harding, meet Brian MacArthur, my new altar boy,' continued Father O'Neill flapping an arm towards the boy by way of introduction. His back, for psychological reasons was still firmly propped against the door.

'Pleased to meet you Brian,' said Father Harding coming forward to shake the boy's hand. 'I served as an altar boy too, although it's a while ago now. How do you like it?'

Brian shuffled his feet and nervously stuffed the bundled regalia more firmly under his arm. He could hardly come out with, Glad you asked. It's crap actually. I'm scared out of my skull. 1 haven't got a clue what's supposed to be going on, I drop things and the other altar boy keeps farting.

So instead. he lowered his eyes and said, 'It's okay.'

Father Harding looked as if he was in a hurry. He pulled up his sleeve to glance at his watch. 'I've got to go,' he said to Father O'Neill. 'I have a meeting with the Bishop, then I need to be in Perth to catch a flight to Sydney. I'm sorry it wasn't possible to see the figures and discuss things in more detail, but I am sure His Grace will be interested in what you've told me. No doubt you will see me again soon.'

Brian was impressed. '...catch a flight to Sydney?' he thought. This bloke must be really famous!

The Jesuit shook hands with the priest who was still locked into position against the recalcitrant door, said a cheery farewell to Brian and then was gone.

'Brian.' said Father O'Neill, 'would you mind getting another brick from outside. No, get two bricks please.'

The boy collected two more bricks from the rubble pile. It was an operation not without difficulty as he still had the surplice and soutane under his left arm and wondered why on Earth the two men wanted to have a meeting in a stuffy sacristy on a day like this when they could have been in the nice cool presbytery. 'Father,' he said, when he returned with the bricks and handed them to the priest. who then quickly stacked them along the bottom of the door.

'Yes Brian?' said the priest looking up.

This is it. Come out with it now and be a man or keep your mouth shut and stay a boy.

Father O'Neill by now was cautiously edging away from the door eyeing it off to see if it would budge.

Brian went for it.

'Father, I don't want to be an altar boy, okay, I don't know everything I'm supposed to know and I drop things, and it was only my first day, but I... can't stand...people looking at me.'

The priest smiled. The boy had struck a chord with him. Francis O'Neill was not a shy man. Some, indeed would say he was a loud and boastful man. He enjoyed being the centre of attention, and if he hadn't had the vocation he could have been a successful salesman or barrister or entertainer. He had known since he was a boy that so far as crowds and entertainment go, either you've got it, or you haven't. You are either the showman or the audience. His dad who played the music halls of Dublin long ago had taught him that. Not that there was any connection between that and the celebration of the Mass of course.

'My boy! Of course! It's not for everybody. Give those things back to me and I'm sure someone else will enjoy doing the job!'

Lost for words, Brian handed over the slightly crumpled red and white bundle of cloth. It seemed a moment of profound significance that should have been recorded for posterity by the flashing of cameras. Brian, for the first time in his life had said "no" and the weight on his shoulders lifted just as surely as the uncomfortable bundle from beneath his arm had gone. He was free.

'Thank you, Father, thank you very much,' he mumbled as he bolted for the door.

'See you next Sunday Brian,' called the priest, still eyeing off the door and wondering what the Jesuit had made of his explanation of the state parish financial affairs. Incarceration had in fact been a mixed blessing as all the relevant paperwork was in the presbytery.

Brian was full of the joys of life when he greeted his mother in the kitchen then bounced down the passage to the front room.

'Well son, did you see father O'Neill?' asked John MacArthur from his favourite leather armchair.

'Yes, Dad. I am no longer an altar boy.'

'Hum,' grunted his father with no further comment and continued with his book.

'The cricket should be on,' said Brian.

John MacArthur glanced at the mantelpiece clock above his head.

'By golly, you're right son. Turn on the radio.'

Brian crossed the room to the mahogany-encased monster that dominated the furnishing on that part of the wall and turned on the switch. The tuning dial illuminated and the whole thing gently hummed. It would take a few moments to warm up.

…comes in to bowl from the pavilion end…and this one is well pitched up on the off stump…and he's driven him beautifully straight through the covers… that's four runs!

'YA BEAUDY!'

Michael Jackson or "Jacko" to his mates was having a great time. He'd done some shopping yesterday so there were plenty of sausages lying about somewhere and because the pubs are shut on a Sunday, he'd also got in enough beer to see him through the weekend. Well, he reckoned two dozen bottles should be enough. It didn't all fit in the fridge so he'd stored the rest in the bath with some cold water to keep them cool. Can't drink warm beer. Only bloody poms drink warm beer. And poofters. Bet they drink warm beer.

But best of all, he had the place to himself 'Bloody poofter!' he muttered to himself as he thought of the meek and mild high school teacher, he was forced to share the house with.

'Bloody high school teachers! Think they're so bloody smart just 'cos they went to bloody university. Bloody pommy bastard poofter!'

Michael was not a local lad. He was from Kalgoorlie, ("KAL" to the natives), an inland town three hundred miles from the coast famous for gold whose survival depended on the water pipeline built at great cost from Perth in the early part of the century. Michael, although quite bright, was lazy. His exam results were, however, good enough for primary teaching. There was a shortage of teachers at the time. Michael figured that teaching was an easy enough job, good money, ten weeks holiday a year and a chance to see the country before heading back to Kal. He hadn't thought much beyond that. He was just glad to escape his domineering family and in particular, his hard-drinking father. At College in Perth, he boarded with an elderly aunt and still unsure of himself in the city, generally toed the line. In Martinup for the first time in his life, he was free.

'...that's wide and he's gone for it...caught...he's gone...caught brilliantly at third slip!'

'Oh, no! We only need...what...another thirty runs to beat the bloody poms! Stupid bastard!'

Jacko stubbed out another cigarette into the already overflowing ashtray perched precariously on the arm of the flimsy sofa and hauled himself up to a sitting position. He was in his usual off-duty uniform of singlet and black football shorts. He did not cut much of a figure in his day job as a primary school teacher either. His wardrobe consisted of two shirts and two pairs of trousers, none of which quite fitted, but he thought he could get away with it by wearing a different tie each day. He had a number of them of which he was quite proud. All of them lurid and ostentatious. He didn't have a girlfriend, which was probably not surprising.

Having reached sitting position, he decided he needed another drink. He stood up, snatched and scratched his substantial hairy stomach that protruded from the bottom of his singlet. He burped then he farted, raising his leg as he did so and wandered off in the direction of the fridge.

The sound of a car arriving outside caught his attention. With beer bottle in hand, he raised the net curtain at the window.

'Oh, no! It's that bloody pommy poofter back again! Just when a bloke was tryin' to relax in peace and quiet!'

Paul Newton got out of the car. He had left the park determined that he would survive this horrific emotional disaster and that his life would change for the better. He had a job and a new life in the country. He knew it was useless to pretend there was any going back but on the long drive down from the city, his mind could not help going over and over his relationship with Susan. Yes, she was, or rather had been special to him, but betrayal like that? No. That can never be right. No way would or could he do that to her. She was gone. She was in the past. A new future awaited him. He just needed to be strong. To grit his teeth and see it through. He had seen worse things before. He would survive. Even though he could not believe it, this was the best thing to happen. It must be. It had to. He had been deluding himself. She was not the girl for him. She couldn't be. Good luck to her and whoever that bloke in her room was. Good luck and goodbye.

And, so the internal dialogue went on and on as the miles passed by and in what seemed a short time, the sign saying "MARTINUP population 5000" swung into view. Now here he was at the barren asbestos and corrugated iron bungalow that was his new home.

Paul had already made up his mind to throw himself into his work. Not only was it the right thing to do, it was necessary for his own survival. Work, work and more work. He would try to be the best teacher he could. Young people depended on him and he would not let them down.

The stale smell of old beer and tobacco smoke and the unmistakable sound of the cricket on the radio greeted him as he entered the kitchen from the back door. His heart sank. This was all he needed.

The kitchen and living room were separated only by a partition, through which he could see the slumped form of his housemate.

'G'day,' said Jacko unenthusiastically over the top of the radio. Paul returned the greeting with the same depth of sentiment and cast his eyes over the mess in the sink and on the kitchen table.

You're back early aren't ya? I thought you weren't comin' back till tonight. Paul declined to reply and started to clear some of the filth from the table.

…It's bowled 'im! Straight through between bat and pad!…

'BASTARD!' shouted Jacko at the transistor radio that stood amongst the forest of beer bottles on the living room coffee table.

'Shit, we've only got ten runs to get! Come on!'

In the kitchen, Paul's anger was rising. '*He didn't need any of this,*' he thought as he threw another beer bottle into the bin. This guy is an animal! With gritted teeth, he wrung out a cloth from the sink and started vigorously wiping down the table.

…just waiting as the new batsman looks around the field…he's ready now… comes in…left arm delivery with a lot of pace…oh it's bowled him! Middle stump! It's all over! An amazing victory pulled off by the MCC. Well, who would have thought it?

'BASTARD! Right! That's enough of you,' Jacko snarled as he savagely turned off the radio, knocking over a couple of bottles in the process, his dexterity becoming affected by the drink. He struggled under the table to retrieve them cursing the English as he did so. For Jacko, anyone who spoke with anything but a broad Australian accent was either English or of a different sexual orientation, (much the same thing to him in as much as they were both beneath contempt). The same applied to all the wops. eyeties, dagoes, abos and all the bloody rest of them that spoilt his great country.

Paul had at last cleared enough of a space to get some work done. He went back out to the car to collect his bag containing clothes and schoolwork which hadn't been looked at over the weekend. When he came back, he found Jacko sitting at the kitchen table with a beer and a cigarette.

Paul tried to ignore him but Jacko would not be put off. This was his home too, so what did he care if this bloody pom didn't drink or smoke. That was his problem. By now the drink had the best of him.

Paul ignored his housemate and sat on the chair opposite with his back to the wall. He began to bring out his school work from the bag at his feet. First the chemistry essays of the fourth years, then the blue first year science text. Jacko said nothing. He exhaled on the cigarette and swayed slightly on his seat.

Inside Paul, the anger was mounting. He had work to do. Important work and he damn well wasn't going to be put off by some drunken yobbo even if he did have to live with him. He tried to concentrate on the first essay.

'Wossa matter with you then?' slurred Jacko over the top of his beer bottle.

No answer.

He tried again, enjoying the baiting game.

'Ya won the bloody cricket, dincha? Why aren't ya out celebratin'?'

Still no reply from Paul whose muscles were now beginning to twitch and tense.

'Sumpin' goin' on with yer missus then eh? Didn't she...'

Jacko never got a chance to complete his lewd suggestion about Paul's former girlfriend. He was wrong about Paul Newton on two important points. First, he was not English. He was born and grew up in Govan, near Glasgow, but rapidly acquired a different speech pattern when the family migrated to Australia when he was just thirteen. To someone like Jacko with little experience of the world, Paul sounded English.

Scots, for reasons best known to themselves do not like being called English.

Second, he was not a "poofter" which aside from being homosexual, had the alternative meaning (for Jacko at least) of being someone incapable of standing up for themselves. Paul had grown into a strong young man who although he generally avoided trouble had never forgotten the brutal fighting he had witnessed in the mean streets of that distant ship-building city by the Clyde. Now he had snapped. Jacko was about to experience the awesome power of a "Glasgow kiss".

The movement was executed at lightning speed. The distance between the two men was just a few feet, or even less as Jacko had leaned provocatively over the table to make his last remark. Paul lifted from his seat and rather than swinging a punch (as Jacko might have expected had he been sober enough to do so), instead launched his forehead straight into his antagonist's nose. Bone met flesh in a sickening crunch.

There can be no escape from such an unexpected devastating attack at close range. The effect was dramatic. Jacko flew backwards in his chair, his face obscured by a red mist. No sooner had he bounced off the floor when he felt the full force of Paul's boot in his ample gut which caused him to double up, followed by another to the kidneys. Paul thought about stamping on his head for good measure, but that was perhaps a bit much.

Paul's trembling hands were by now firmly around a chair which he was fully prepared to use if his housemate chose to continue. But Jacko wasn't going anywhere. He was still on the floor twitching, gurgling and spitting blood onto the lino.

Paul gently put the chair down. He was still white with anger, even though he knew his adversary was finished, but he didn't care. Although part of his rage came from elsewhere, it was now all directed at Jacko. 'Drunken pig!' he spat as he stalked around the prostrate body still wheezing and gasping on the floor, mentally willing it to get up so that he could hit it again.

'Come on, get up and say what you want to say. I'm going to kill you.'

Paul was suddenly horrified at what he was saying. He actually meant it!

He stopped and watched as Jacko blubbered and spluttered in the steadily increasing pool of blood and spilt beer.

'You've broken by doze!' he burbled in the puddle of red and clear liquids, his hands to his face. Paul was still reluctant to feel sympathy for the beast.

'Really!' he said making his way back to the table to resume his work. But after a minute, he had to relent especially when the plea came from the floor.

'Ah c'mon mate. Ya gotta help me!'

Paul sighed, put down his pen and went to get a cloth from the bathroom.

When he returned with a towel, Jacko had managed to haul himself onto a seat.

'I think we'd better get you to hospital,' he said as he passed over the towel. Jacko, his face now covered by the cloth nodded in agreement and struggled to get out of the chair.

The car pulled up outside the main entrance of Martinup District Hospital where the sign said "Accident and Emergency". Paul jumped out to get the passenger door, but Jacko had already struggled out by himself. The towel he clutched to his face was by now mostly red. Blood spatters ran down his shirt and onto his bare legs. Because of the drink and the shock, he was unsteady on his feet, so Paul assisted him up the steps and through the heavy wooden doors.

They were met in the foyer by the crisp white uniform of Staff Nurse Patricia Clelland and her heels echoing on the polished wooden flooring.

'My! My! What have we here? What's happened?'

'He's been in a fight,' said Paul.

'Oh, I see,' said Sister Clelland and tutted disapprovingly. 'Come with me and we'll get some details!'

She strode into her office while Paul waited in the foyer.

Jacko stood miserably at the glass window. He could hardy say 'HE HIT ME' without sounding like one of the eight-year-olds he was supposed to be in charge of.

Sister Clelland could smell the drink immediately.

'Name?'

'Bichael Jackson,' Jacko's voice was somewhat muffled behind the sodden towel.

'Are you a teacher at the primary school?' Sister Clelland was suddenly shocked. Her daughter Jennifer had already come home with some alarming stories about her funny new teacher.

Mr Taylor, headmaster of Martinup Primary School for twenty years was furious.

He had been awaiting the arrival of a certain teacher for nearly fifteen minutes and his car had just arrived.

Word spreads fast in a small town.

'MISTER JACKSON!'

The teacher in question walked with difficulty towards the school principal.

'Mr Jackson. Could you come into my office for a few minutes please?'

Jacko followed his boss into the sparsely furnished room. Mr Taylor motioned for him to sit on the opposite side of the desk.

The headmaster wasted no time.

'Mr Jackson. I believe you have been involved in a fight over the weekend. Is that so?'

'Um, yes.'

'Mr Jackson, have you looked in a mirror this morning?'

Jacko's right eye was half closed and the surrounds were a mixture of blue, red and yellow. Before he had a chance to reply, Mr Taylor fired a more difficult question to answer.

'Did you seriously think you could take a class in this school looking like that?'

Jacko's mouth was beginning to involuntarily open and close like a goldfish.

'Mr Jackson,' the principal continued, 'may I remind you that you are a teacher on probation.'

Jacko managed to get a nod into the conversation.

'And may I also remind you that this school has standards, which I expect every member of staff especially new teachers on probation to meet. You will not, sir, come into this school looking as if you had just come from a drunken brawl. Do I make myself clear Mr Jackson?'

Jacko nodded again.

'Good. You are suspended for two weeks, by which time I hope that your eye has cleared up and you have learnt to behave like a professional. I will be writing a full report on this for inclusion in your file. Good day sir.'

The lesson was nearly finished. Paul stood up from behind the bench.

'Homework tonight...' A collective groan came up from the first-years. He continued...'is to finish reading the second chapter and answer the questions at the end.'

The siren sounded for the end of period two.

'Right. That's it. Off you go! Quietly please!' Trevor and Brian were the last to leave.

'How did you get on with the hot air balloon Brian?'

Brian shot a glance towards Trevor who shrugged his shoulders then looked back to the teacher. 'Ah, we didn't get around to it Mr Newton. See ya!' and with that the two boys scampered off. Paul thought that was a shame as the one he had made when he was about Brian's age had worked quite well. Just a pity about the fire it started when it came down.

He tidied the books and papers on the bench then joined the milling crowd of students outside.

The staff-room was crowded when he finally got there. A queue had formed for tea at the hot water urn.

His mind was awash in the weird events and mixed emotions of the weekend.

He felt a nudge in his ribs as someone behind him said,

'Heard you had a bit of a fracas over the weekend!' Startled, he turned around to be transfixed by the most beautiful eyes he had ever seen.

'Huh?' was all he could manage by way of reply.

'Jacko. I heard you hit him. Sorry, we haven't been introduced. I'm Michelle. Michelle Marceaux. I teach French.'

She offered her hand which Paul shook with difficulty as the space was so tight Paul was rendered speechless for a moment. She was gorgeous.

She motioned to him that the urn was now free.

As he poured the hot water into his cup, she said, 'I can't condone violence of course, then with a broad smile whispered in his ear, 'but he was a complete shit!'

Paul was lucky to contain most of the tea in his cup as he shook with laughter.

'Where do you want to sit Michelle?'

The Unfortunate Demise of Giovanni

Brian trotted around the side of the house, sprang up the steps and tapped on the back-door frame. He stared into the gloom through the fly wire door.

The familiar figure of Trevor's mum emerged from the darkness; her features illuminated by a sudden glow as she drew on her cigarette.

'Hello Mrs Stewart, Is Trevor in?'

She stood in the doorway for a moment, apparently lost in thought.

'Yeah Brian, he's down in the workshop I think.'

'Thanks Mrs Stewart!' He had half turned to go when she asked,

'Brian, is your mum in?'

'Yeah she is. Dad's gone to the bowls but mum decided to stay home. It's a competition or something and she didn't fancy it.'

'Good,' said Margaret Stewart. 'I think I'll go down and see her. I haven't seen your mum for ages.' As Brian headed across the back lawn, she dropped the cigarette onto the wooden verandah and ground it in with her boot. Then she turned inside into the darkness letting the fly wire door bang shut behind her.

The unmistakable sound of Australian Rules football radio commentary was coming through the open door of the workshop. The footy season had just started.

'…that's a tremendous drop-kick into the right full forward pocket and it's BUNTON high above the pack and he should have NO trouble from that distance…'

'Trevor? Are you in there mate?'

Trevor turned from the workbench and reached up for the volume dial of the transistor radio perched precariously on the shelf above his head.

'I didn't know you followed the footy Trev,'

Trevor, not renowned for his sporting prowess, was always picked last for the team. Brian never fared much better. He was usually second last.

'I do sometimes. Me old man used to follow East Fremantle.' For a moment his eyes had a faraway look, then it was gone. 'Look what I've got here.' he said turning back to the bench and vigorously undoing the vice.

'A Boomerang!' Brian was impressed. 'How did you make it?'

'Start with a piece of this,' he picked up a piece of plywood from the bench by way of demonstration. 'Draw the shape.' He indicated a pencil nearby. 'Cut it out with this,' he held up a fret saw. 'That's the hard bit,' he conceded. 'Then you round off one side to make an aerofoil with a rasp.'

'What's a hairy foil?'

Trevor sighed. 'An aerofoil. It's the same shape in cross-section as an aeroplane wing. Does the same job too. Gives it lift as it goes through the air.'

Brian's rather blank expression prompted Trevor to momentarily abandon construction of the returnable flying machine for the role of teacher as he showed Brian the rudimentary aerodynamics of an aeroplane wing in cross-section with a pencil stub and the back of an envelope.

'Oh, I get it,' said Brian who in fact had not got it. He was more anxious to find out if it would work and that would happen faster if his mate stopped teaching.

'Same principle as a gyroscope,' said Trevor enigmatically as he cranked the wood back into the vice. Brian was not to be caught out again.

'Yeah,' was his diplomatic offering as he lowered himself into the old overstuffed armchair in the corner to watch the proceedings.

'It's all out of that magazine, look there by your feet.' Brian bent down and glanced at the front cover.

EAGLE The magazine for boys.

'It's English,' said Trevor. 'Me mum gave me a subscription for it at Christmas. I get it every week from the news agent.'

Brian leafed through until he found what Trevor was working on while his mate turned his attention to rasping an aerofoil. 'whatever that was from' the bit of three-ply.

'Oh, hullo Margaret! This is a nice surprise! Come on in! It's getting a bit chillier now isn't it?'

Mary MacArthur beckoned her visitor enter through the open back door.

'It is Mary. It does get cold here in winter over here doesn't it?'

'It does indeed.'

Margaret Stewart followed her neighbour through the back room to the kitchen.

'I keep forgetting that you're not really used to the cold like us. Come in and have a seat,' said Mary. 'Cup of tea?'

'Yes please. Mary, you wouldn't have an ashtray handy, would you?'

'I think we still have one somewhere. Roger smokes so there must be one…' Mary fumbled in the kitchen dresser, 'Ah there you go…Margaret, are you alright?'

Margaret was sitting quite still and staring into space. Her features were uncharacteristically pale.

She snapped to at the sound of the question and fumbled for a cigarette from the packet.

'Yeah, I'm fine. Just got a few things on my mind.'

As Mary got down the tea canister from the mantle-piece above the fire, Margaret lit a cigarette and continued,

'Things haven't been going too good Mary. It hasn't been easy for me being here, especially since Peter passed away. Trevor's been great, don't get me wrong, but it seems like he is looking after me all the time when it should be me looking after him, do you know what I mean?'

Mary nodded and spooned the tea into the pot.

'I wouldn't be here if it hadn't been for Peter. And Trevor and me wouldn't be stuck in that bloody house if it wasn't for that bloody woman!' Margaret's colour was returning as she remembered the events of ten years past. Mary murmured in agreement as she poured in the boiling water and set the pot on the table.

She knew the tragic story of that "bloody woman" well.

Margaret was Peter's nurse as he convalesced in a Sydney hospital after the war. They married as soon as he had recovered but Peter was never settled in the city. He longed to return to Western Australia. A letter eventually arrived from his cousin, Ted saying that Peter's uncle had died. Ted had been left the farm. As he was alone on the property, the offer was made to Peter that he was welcome to return and take up a share in the farm if he wanted. It was Peter's dream come true.

When the couple and their three-year-old son arrived six months later, they found the deal was off. Ted, a quiet and unassuming chap had taken a wife who did not want the farm shared. Peter had no choice but to take a house in the town and work whenever and wherever he could as an itinerant shearer. But his health was still poor from the prison and the heavy work almost certainly contributed to his early death.

'Anyway,' continued Margaret, 'I got a phone call last night from my sister Jean, she looks after my mum. She's nearly eighty you know. It's quite a big house they've got in Sydney. Jean was saying that it was getting harder for her to manage, so...' her voice trailed off.

'You're thinking of moving back to Sydney?' volunteered Mary pouring the tea through a strainer into Margaret's cup.

'Thanks love. Yeah. I am actually. Does that sound crazy to you?'

'Not especially, would you go back to nursing in Sydney?'

'There's a thought,' conceded Margaret. 'I get a war widow pension of course, but it's always been a bit of a struggle. I suppose I thought about going back in the early days after Peter died but he wanted to be here so badly and then Trevor started at the primary school and I didn't want to rock the boat.'

'That house of yours could be worth a bit now, especially with the paddock.'

'You might be right Mary. To be honest, I hadn't considered any of this 'till Jean's phone call.'

Margaret sipped her tea and gazed at the fire.

'What does Trevor think?'

'I haven't asked him yet. I thought I'd better find out from a friend first if I was talking complete rubbish than have my own son tell me! So, yeah, that's it. I haven't decided for sure one way or the other and I'd have to see what Trevor thought.'

Margaret paused for a moment deep in thought then her face brightened as she looked up at her neighbour. 'He gets on so well with your Brian doesn't he? They're always up to something! Anyway, enough of my problems! How are you? Has that husband of yours tangled with any more kangaroos lately?'

'There,' said Trevor. 'That should do it.' He finished off the rounded side of the boomerang with sandpaper.

Brian put down the magazine and got up to inspect Trevor's workmanship.

'D'ya reckon, it's gunna work?'

'No worries,' said Trevor making for the door with Brian in hot pursuit.

They went to "the paddock" at the back of Trevor's place still black from the fire put through it deliberately the previous October. Removal of flammable material was a houseowner's obligation enforced by the fire brigade to prevent worse conflagrations as the summer wore on. The first evidence of greenery was beginning to show through the blackened stubble.

'Right,' said Trevor brandishing his boomerang. 'Which way is the wind coming from?'

'That way I reckon,' said Brian pointing to the south.

Trevor's first effort was a dismal failure, the boomerang wobbling forward only to hit the ground soon after take-off. After instruction from the maker, it was Brian's turn and his effort stayed in the air longer with a distinct left-hand curve in the flight path.

'Good one Brian! That was definitely turning!'

'I think the trick is to give it a really good flick as you throw it,' said Brian as he trotted back and returned the boomerang to its owner.

'Here we go!' muttered Trevor, determined that his new creation would succeed.

He threw it to the right of the wind as the magazine had said with all his strength. The boomerang was a circular blur heading away from the two boys at speed, climbing all the while and banking to the left.

Around it curved till it was travelling across the boys' field of vision, above tree height and still climbing. As it reached the apogee of its flight, a gust of wind caught it and lifted it high, high above their heads and behind them. For a split second, it paused and then started to descend. It gathered pace rapidly until it was travelling at very high speed in a straight line towards the earth. It was making for Luigi de Luca's chook yard next door.

Luigi and Maria de Luca lived a quiet life in their grapevine-covered bungalow. The front yard and back yard were homes to orange, lemon, mulberry, fig, apricot, apple, olive and almond trees. The dusty soil, crammed now after many years of manure and watered by an ingenious plastic-pipe irrigation system criss-crossing the property, yielded harvests of carrots. peas, beans, tomatoes, melons, pumpkins, onions and potatoes. John MacArthur was a frequent visitor to learn more horticultural secrets from the de Lucas, but not today as all three were competing in the bowling competition on the other side of town.

At the back of the garden, surrounded by a high fence was the chook yard. King of the chook yard was Giovanni, a multi-hued beast of great antiquity whose rule was law. A rooster, although bigger than a chook is a still chook for all that. Had Giovanni ever wondered how he might depart this life which is highly improbable, there is no way he could have guessed correctly. As he stretched his neck and spread his wings to crow, a wooden bolt from the sky smashed into his tiny brain. The boomerang embedded itself into the mud and muck beside the twitching body and all the surrounding chooks rose as one in a cacophony of squawking feathers.

The breathless two boys arrived on the other side of the fence, their fingers grasping the holes in the mesh as their noses squashed against the wire.

'Shit!' said Trevor. 'We've killed Giovanni.'

'Giovanni?' queried Brian looking at his mate.

'Giovanni,' confirmed Trevor in all seriousness still staring through the wire. 'Luigi's prize rooster.'

'Oh. Shit,' said Brian.

'Precisely,' said Trevor. 'Now what are we gunna do?'

Both boys considered the, 'Let's run away and hide,' option, but neither came out with it. They were too old for that. Nor did they consider coming out with the truth to the adults and accepting the consequences.

They were too young for that. It was Brian who came up with the third way.

'Let's get the boomerang out of there and then bury the rooster somewhere. Or better still, just leave it where it is and they will maybe think it died of old age, or maybe a fox got it, or sumpin'.'

'I dumno,' said Trevor who had been toying with option two, 'what if we get caught?'

'No worries!' said Brian, with an air of bravado that didn't quite fit what his stomach was telling him.

'They're playing bowls with me old man. They'll be ages yet!'

'But how are we going to get in? This fence isn't strong enough to climb.'

Brian was in charge now. 'No problem. I'll get that corner post. You keep a lookout for me!'

With that, he was off, fingers clawing into the wire mesh which bent and twisted under his weight while his toes struggled to get a grip on the post behind the wire. The chooks below circled in various directions all keeping one eye cocked on his progress whilst clucking amongst themselves. With effort he was making progress, slowly and painfully and with another heave, found himself straddling the top of the post and wire. With one more heave he dropped into the mud and muck causing another flurry of noise and flying feathers.

On the ground outside, Trevor had been casting his eyes nervously right and left. He didn't like this at all. Then he saw what he had been dreading. Luigi and his wife had arrived home early! Their car had pulled up on the street outside the house!

'Psst!' he hissed to Brian who had by now successfully retrieved the boomerang from beside the corpse.

'They've come back! You'll need to go around the back of the shed. It'll give you some cover to climb back.

The sound of car doors slamming sounded ominously from the front as Brian skidded and slithered his way around the back of the shed sending chooks in all directions in the process. His heart pounding, he scaled the fence post, his exit being a bit faster than his entrance. From the top of the post he dropped to the ground beside Trevor, still clutching the murder weapon inside his shirt. Together they took the paddock boundary, obscured by the shed and the trees that lined the back of Luigi's place. They splashed through the creek that by now had a trickle of water and didn't stop running till they were safely in the bush in front of Brian's place.

Trevor pulled up first and breathlessly turned to Brian.

'D'ya reckon we got away with it?'

'Well I don't think anyone saw us. Oh look! There's your mum.'

Margaret Stewart could just be seen coming down the steps at the front as Mary MacArthur waved goodbye.

'Here's your boomerang mate,' said Brian as he pulled it out of his shirt.

'Nah, you hang onto it for a bit,' suggested Trevor still breathing heavily. 'I'll catch up with me mum. But maybe you'd better have a wash before you go into the house Brian. See Ya!'

As Trevor bounded off down the bush track to catch up with his mother in the distance. Brian looked down at his hands and legs. From kneecap to toe, from fingertip to elbow he was covered in mud, feathers and chook shit.

It was after tea-time when the knock came at the back door.

'I'll get it,' said Trevor and put the plate he was drying on the table leaving his mother at the sink.

He came straight back.

'It's Luigi de Luca,' he said trying not betray any emotion.

His mother wiped her hands on her apron and went to the door while her son carried on drying the dishes but with an ear cocked to the conversation.

'Yes Luigi.'

Luigi stood on the back porch carrying a paper bag. He was a small, balding robust man, who's facial features were largely obscured by a black handlebar moustache. His limbs showed the effects of a lifetime of manual toil either in his native Calabria or on the dusty roads of Martinup where he had worked for twenty years as a Council labourer. He was often at the back door with surplus produce from his garden. This time it was two beer bottles of tomato concentrate that Maria had made and he handed the bag containing them to his neighbour.

'Oh, thank you Luigi. I've only just finished the lot you gave me from last year. It's very tasty. Thank Maria for me too, won't you?'

Margaret Stewart always felt guilty that she had nothing to give in exchange, but Luigi and Maria expected nothing. They knew her circumstances and that was enough.

'You betta look after you chook, Missa Stewart. You know Giovanni. my rooster, yeah? He is dead. Fox maybe, or dog get him.'

'Trevor!'

'Yes, Mum?'

'Go down and check our chooks will you? Mr de Luca says that a fox or something has killed Giovanni.'

'Right Mum.'

He ducked under his mother's arm as she held open the fly-wire door, mumbled a greeting to his neighbour and scurried up the back, supposedly to check the poultry but in reality, to hide his acute embarrassment.

It was just after nine o'clock when Margaret left the kitchen to join her son in the lounge room. Trevor had had his bath and was wrapped up in his pyjamas and dressing gown for the night. He was sitting on the floor in front of the fire.

Margaret helped herself to a glass of sherry from the flagon in the sideboard cupboard then eased herself into the armchair near the warmth and glow of the mallee roots and put her feet up on the cushioned stool.

She took a mouthful and then set the glass carefully down beside her on the carpet Trevor was engrossed in building a model of a Sopwith Camel. The light of the fire danced on his face and tousled hair as he concentrated on fixing the propeller. '*How he looked so much like Peter,*' she thought. But he's still just a boy. Is it right to ask him to leave here? To leave his friends, especially Brian?'

She felt in her pocket for a cigarette and looked around the room. Everything was hers. The armchairs, the sideboard, the coffee table, every stick of furniture in the place was hers, even though sometimes she'd had to do without in order to save up for it from her pension. '*Okay, she hadn't taken too much care about her own appearance,*' she thought as she looked down at the faded fabric of her dress, but she had paid for everything. There were no debts. No one was owed a penny. There was still money in the bank, more than enough to see them through. And most of all Trevor never suffered because of Peter's death. She hoped.

She pulled a cigarette from the packet and paused a moment as she looked at Trevor playing happily by the fire.

Yeah, they had survived.

Margaret stared into the dancing flames and felt the warmth on her bare legs and thought how peaceful and cosy all this was. Was it madness to think of leaving it?

Then she thought again of the long lonely days and nights she'd spent in isolation these last ten years. It had been a nightmare for her here. She was used to the glamour of Sydney, the restaurants, theatres and dance halls. She had nothing in common with the people here. Nor was she getting any younger. What was she to do when Trevor eventually left home? Surely it was madness to stay!

A train whistle sounded in the distance.

Margaret lit a cigarette. She would have to get a removal firm because there was no way all this stuff would fit in Peter's old trailer. And would her old Ford even make it to Sydney?

But it would be an adventure! Margaret was once very adventurous. She nearly volunteered for service with the International Brigade in Spain against Franco's fascists but her parents talked her out of it. Margaret exhaled the smoke and smiled at the thought. Then there was the war. Then Peter. And now Trevor.

'*Right*,' she thought, took another large gulp of Sherry and swallowed it. She took a long drag on her cigarette and blew the smoke towards the flames.

'Trevor.'

'Huh?' The boy glanced up to catch his mother's eye and gently put the model onto the carpet.

'Trevor, how would you like it if we moved to Sydney to live with your grannie and Auntie Jean?'

Paul Newton put down his pen and rubbed his eyes. He leaned back in the chair and shifted with discomfort. In front of him on the kitchen table were piles of schoolwork, each stack representing the work of each of his classes.

All afternoon and into the evening, he had waded through test papers from his first, second and third-year classes meticulously recording the results in his marks book. He would know in future not to set simultaneous tests. It just meant he was bogged down with the paperwork afterwards. Not that he minded all that much. He enjoyed finding out if these young people had learnt what he was trying to teach.

And even the dreaded 3B4 had enjoyed the little biology field trip in the bush last Thursday. Especially Brian Grady. He smiled at the thought, clasping his hands behind his head. If he could get through to those kids, now that would be an achievement!

He sat back up in the chair and surveyed the table top. What was still left to be done? The fourth years were okay, they were basically following the text, but all the other classes were onto new topics.

Suddenly; he had enough. It could all wait till tomorrow. He stood up, stretched, yawned and then moved through to the lounge room.

He walked slowly around the sparsely-furnished room. At least it was clean and quiet and had been this last month since Jacko left. Paul smiled at the thought and shook his head. 'What a strange, strange guy,' he wondered out loud to himself as his mind wandered back to the beginning of the second week of term. Paul had come home to find Jacko in a rage. He had spent two days brooding about his fortnight suspension and then he must have just snapped. All his stuff was either thrown into cardboard boxes that littered the lounge or had been randomly tossed into the boot of his car.

'What are you doing man?'

'What does it bloody well look like I'm doing?' said Jacko as he threw another cardboard box full of colourful ties, coat-hangers and kitchen utensils onto the backseat of his car.

'I'm off mate. Outta here!'

'But where are you going?'

'None of your bloody business!'

Jacko stormed past Paul back into the house.

Paul followed him through the door.

'You are coming back, aren't you? Your suspension's only for two weeks.' Paul was suddenly horrified at the part he'd played.

There was no answer from Jacko who pushed past him with another cardboard box of junk.

'But what about the school? Have you told them?'

Jacko slammed the car door shut and turned to Paul.

'Listen, mate, if you want to be useful, how about giving me a hand with the rest of this stuff instead of all these bloody questions?'

Paul could see that it was useless to try to reason with Jacko, so in silence the two of them cleared the house of Jacko's possessions, speaking only to confirm ownership of the occasional item.

When it was done, Jacko stood inside the open door of his car and offered his hand to Paul. 'No hard feelin's mate.'

And with that he was gone.

When the fortnight was up, Mr Taylor the primary school headmaster frantically rang Paul at the high school to find out what had happened to Jacko, but Paul couldn't help him.

'Strange, strange guy!' Paul muttered again to himself. He wondered how many Australian men were like that. Most of his friends at university were born abroad, and come to think of it; most of his friends at the boarding school in Perth had been either Asian or European. Perhaps here was the best place to get to know a few genuine Australians.

'Beer!' he said out loud with a smile. Jacko in his haste had uncharacteristically forgotten his stash of Swan Lager beside the fridge. Paul had from time to time helped himself, figuring that Jacko owed him.

Paul opened the fridge and pulled out a frosted bottle then rummaged in the drawer by the sink for a bottle opener. He grabbed a glass from the shelf, poured himself a beer then went out the back door to sit at the top of the wooden steps.

Overhead the southern constellations twinkled in their black velvet bed. Frogs and other invisible creatures of the night held their conversations. Paul was at peace. The past month had been brilliant. He could keep the place clean and tidy, just as he wanted it. With no one to disturb him, the lessons were prepared properly and his classes responded accordingly, well most of them anyway. It had been a monastic existence. No frills, no luxuries, just plenty of time to think and to inwardly heal. Sure, the memories of Susan were still there, but the pain had at last eased. She had her own path to follow. She didn't belong to him anymore.

He took a mouthful of beer and gazed at the night sky. This place was just glorious. He really was beginning to find a new life for himself. He might even decide to stay here for a while, perhaps another year.

A train whistle sounded in the distance.

Paul drained his glass and got up for a refill from the kitchen. The sudden unmistakable roar of a Volkswagen engine and bouncing headlights in the backyard stopped him. The vehicle stopped in the front drive and a car door slammed shut. He peered through the curtains of the back window but couldn't make out who it was until the figure emerged into the light at the back.

Suddenly he remembered who drove a Volkswagen beetle. Michelle!

'This is a pleasant surprise!' he said to her from the back doorway as she emerged into the light.

'Hello Paul! I thought I'd pay you a visit in your new single accommodation!' she laughed from the bottom step.

'Look! A belated house-warming gift. She waved a bottle of wine.

'I thought you were up in Perth this weekend with your boyfriend.' said Paul as he helped her up the last step.

'That bastard!'

'What?'

The two were now in the light of the kitchen.

She bit her lip and closed her eyes for a moment. Paul could see she had been crying recently.

'Come on through to the lounge Michelle. It's slightly more comfortable in there. Well the chairs are a bit nicer to sit on than the ones in the kitchen, put it that way.'

She smiled and followed him through. As she eased herself into a chair, she breathed a deep sigh and offered him the bottle.

'Got a corkscrew Paul?'

'Not for me thanks, I've got some beer. But let me get you a glass of wine.'

He took the bottle from her and struggled to open it on the kitchen sink.

'So what happened in Perth then? he called back to her over his shoulder.

There was no answer. He hurried through with the glass of wine and found her in deep thought staring into space.

'Oh, I'm sorry.' he said, 'I didn't mean to pry.'

She suddenly came to and smiled up at him brushing her hair away from her eyes.

'That's all right Paul. Thanks.'

She took the glass and ran her finger thoughtfully around the rim as he sat opposite her across the coffee table.

'Paul you are very kind. Look, I've been through this drama and dramas like it with, this guy in my head for a long time. Last night I got rid of him like I should have done months and months ago. At the end of the day he was not a very nice bloke and I would like to spare you the gory details. I didn't come around here to cry on your shoulder. I came to enjoy your company. We have only got one life. Am I right?'

He nodded and grinned.

'Cheers!'

She beamed at him across the coffee table and her eyes sparkled as she held out her glass.

As the two tumblers collided, Paul knew he was hopelessly in love.

Brian saw Trevor easing his bike through the front gate of his house. He pedalled faster.

'Hey Trevor!'

Trevor wheeled his bike down to the road and waited for his friend.

Brian called again as his bike slowed outside Trevor's place. 'What happened to you yesterday? I called round twice in the afternoon but there was no one in.'

The two of them mounted their bikes and cycled off together as Trevor answered the question,

'Me and me mum were just out for a drive testin' the old man's trailer to see if it still worked okay.'

Brian looked a bit puzzled as Trevor continued,

'Brian! Brilliant news mate! Me and me mum are goin' to Sydney!'

'Sydney? What are ya goin' to Sydney for?

'Well, me mum comes from Sydney.'

'Oh, I didn't know that!'

Brian paused for a moment, still unsure of what he was hearing then asked,

'When are ya goin'?'

'Easter prob'ly.'

'When are ya comin' back?'

Trevor looked slightly incredulous as he turned to Brian.

'No Brian, we're goin' over there to live, sellin' the house here, we're gunna live with me grannie and me Aunty Jean.'

Brian bit his lip and cycled on in silence as Trevor enthusiastically continued,

'It'll be brilliant in Sydney. There're loads of shops and parks an' picture theatres an' the Sydney Harbour Bridge and TV! Me Auntie Jean's got TV with about three different channels! It's a huge house an' Sydney's a big, big city much bigger than Perth.

As Trevor related the exciting opportunities afforded by Australia's largest city, Brian mentally examined the consequences of this unexpected thunderbolt. He was about to lose his best friend! This was a disaster! But he quickly became philosophical. Such was life. People come, people go. He could amuse himself well enough on his own and there were loads of things to look forward to like Roger coming home at Easter, then again in May for two weeks. And besides he was already friendly with quite a few other boys in his class.

Trevor stopped his eulogy when he realised his friend's mind was elsewhere and voiced a shared sentiment.

'Course I'll miss your company mate,' he smiled.

'Well at least I won't have you gettin' me into trouble anymore.'

'Me!' said Trevor in mock surprise, then he remembered Giovanni.

'Oh yeah,' he said, 'Luigi was over on Saturday night,

and well, I reckon we got away with it. He said it must have been a fox, but I still feel like a real shit.'

'Me too!' said Brian and the two boys cycled on in silence.

Where's My Farm?

The Prince Regent Hotel in Rose Street Kalgoorlie reflected the style of the times when it was built in 1910, a massive brick-built structure on two levels with wooden verandas on each. The upper floor was designed for accommodation but visiting guests were rare these days and the rooms lay idle for most of the time. The bottom floor was for drinking. Serious drinking, although the numbers of serious drinkers had seriously declined of late and were nowhere near the glory days when Kalgoorlie had as many pubs as it had families. It was when the gold fever was at its height at the turn of the century, when some men made fortunes in a day, others lost them gambling on the fall of two pennies in less and most came to find nothing, eventually leaving, their spirits broken.

For the survivors and opportunists, Kalgoorlie was a paradise. Drinking water cost two and six a gallon but in 1910 the town could still boast a swimming pool. Two race courses and a street of brothels made the community unique in Western Australia although the alluvial gold had long since been picked up off the streets and surrounding shrub, the mines still chewed their way through the rich underground deposits of the Golden Mile and attracted men over the years like flies to a honey pot.

Rich as the deposits were, one by one the seams ran out and the mines began to close. The fluctuating price of gold, especially after the war also affected the viability of many operations with resultant job losses. Young people attracted by tales of the city three hundred miles to the west and anxious to avoid the hazardous life in the mines began to drift away. Businesses in the town were inevitably affected and many of the stately hotels closed their doors for the last time.

Despite increasing hardship, the Prince Regent soldiered on serving a small but dedicated clientele. The presence of the betting shop just around the corner was the real reason for its survival. A ladies' lounge with a discreet side entrance catered for the few ladies who wished to imbibe. The saloon bar took up the rest of the space.

Michael Jackson stood in the half open double doorway and tossed his cigarette into the street. He turned on his heel into the bar and let the door swing shut behind him and then surveyed his new universe.

The long room with its leather seating running along the edge was cluttered here and there with assorted tables and chairs still gleaming from the wet cloth that he had just dragged over them. The partially frosted windows, which kept out the prying eyes of angry wives and inquisitive children, cast a dim light over the empty bar.

The ornate wooden-cased clock on the wall registered opening time.

Jacko sighed as he looked up at the massive display of drink on the glass shelves that were rarely requested by the regular clientele but nevertheless required regular dusting: the Italian, Greek and Russian liqueurs, the Creme de Menthe and the Advocate, the Drambuie and the Johnny Walker Black Label, the Tequila and the Cointreau.

He lifted the hatch at the end of the bar, picked up the damp cloth from the sink and continued his daily routine. His head ached from the drink the night before and his mind was still humming with anger from the latest violent argument he'd had with his father. Ever since he had returned unexpectedly, life in the house had been hell. His father had wanted to know what had happened but Jacko had refused to tell him. Mr Jackson Snr, a miner whose job was under threat had called his son a useless waster and a layabout and threatened to chuck him out unless he found work and started paying board.

So now he had a job and he was grateful for its long hours as an escape from the bitterness in the house.

But Jacko knew that this was a dead-end. He would have to get out of this place. Somehow. Somewhere. He only came back to Kal because this was all he knew and he only got this job because he was once a regular and this pub had been his first port of call after two days on the road straight from the walk-out at Martinup.

He couldn't believe his luck when Macka, the owner offered him the work despite the fact that his eye hadn't healed properly. Shoulda seen the other bloke!' was his standing joke to laugh it off. But inside he knew he'd failed. He'd failed to make the grade as a primary school teacher, so he became a barman instead, working with people he understood and who understood him. That was nearly a month ago now. It seemed like much longer. The novelty of serving drinks to his mates had soon worn off. But the feeling of failure never did.

'Give us a middy mate.'

Jacko dropped his cloth into the sink and took a glass from the rack beneath the bar to serve the familiar figure who had just walked in.

'You're lookin' a bit rough this mornin' Jacko, Wassa matter?' On the slops again last night. Eh?' Ha! Ha!'

'Shut it. Mick.' was Jacko's only comment as he watched the foaming beer pour slowly into the tilted glass.

'So, what's it like bein' back in Kal? You've been back a while now eh?'

'S'all right. Here ya go,' said Jacko as he pushed the glass over the wooden bar top.

Mick reached into his pocket and poured a handful of coins and notes onto the bar. Jacko extracted the required amount and rang it up on the cash register.

'So ya didn' like teachin' much?' asked Mick taking a sip of the freezing cold lager and wiping the froth from his top lip.

'Nah.'

'So are ya gunna stay in Kal?'

Jacko sighed, 'Prob'ly for the time bein' and turned to resume work on the shelves.

'Ya know wot you orta do mate?' said Mick leaning back on his barstool, 'why don't ya enlist in the army?'

You're still young enough. There's a war on ya know! You should be fightin' for yer country in Vietnam! Fightin' for Australia mate! Gettin' them bloody commie bastards before they come 'ere. I know I would if I was your age.'

Jacko paused in polishing the bottle of Tawny Port then carefully placed it back on the shelf.

A female voice came from behind him.

'Jacko, can I have a word with you?'

It was Tracey, Jacko's first one-night stand. He'd been avoiding her for a fortnight but now she had obviously found out where he worked.

'Hullo! Wot have we 'ere?' observed Mick swaying lecherously from his barstool.

'In private if you don't mind Jacko,' said Tracey first glaring at Mick and then back to the barman jerking her head to the other end of the bar.

Jacko dropped his cloth in the sink and dutifully followed her mincing miniskirt.

'I'll come straight to the point Jacko.' She perched herself on a barstool and dumped her handbag on the bar.

'I've just been to see the doctor. I'm pregnant.'

'Another middy when yer ready Jacko!' came the shout from the far end of the room.

Brian looked around the silent classroom. This was his third period in a row in the same classroom. Room Ten with its vast expanse of windows on the far side that allowed no passer-by to go unnoticed. The first period had been English with Mrs Martin, his form teacher. Then it was Social Studies with Mr Ludovic. He never seemed too sure either of himself, his subject or his teaching aids. Period two was pure entertainment because by the time he had figured out how to darken the room effectively, how to prevent the portable screen from collapsing and how to make the images of volcanoes show the right way up, the siren had gone.

But this was serious. It was French with Miss Marceaux, a name that had everyone fooled when she had first written it on the board, except of course for Brian Clelland at the front, who pronounced it correctly to the amazement of the rest of them. He was at present scribbling furiously. After just five weeks of a foreign language, Miss Marceaux had given the class a test, and Brian had finished early. He glanced to his right to see Trevor still beavering away then across at his teacher, her head down earnestly at work at her desk, the details of her figure partially obscured by the light from the window behind her.

Brian enjoyed French. It was just like a secret code. In fact it might as well be a secret code in Australia because apart from Miss Marceaux, he had never heard anyone else speak it Indeed. He wondered, who needs to speak French? His dad who had learnt it at school and helped him out with his homework had told him that diplomats speak French he had asked his father what a diplomat was. The reply was that infuriatingly enigmatic "someone like me". Accountants speak French? No, you have to live in a place where they spoke French like France obviously, or…Belgium or… Africa somewhere. So why was the whole class learning it?

Miss Marceaux was still absorbed in her paperwork. She spoke French so that she could teach it seriously. Maybe she was French. She had a very French name. But what about everyone else? He glanced casually around the room. He knew his class well now, obviously some better than others. So, who would need to speak French when they grew up?

Brian Clelland at the front was an obvious contender. But he was very bright and good at everything. His mate Ken Groves next to him was a possibility too. Brian's eye swept down the far side of the room where the girls he knew from the convent school sat, their faces sharply illuminated in the morning glare. Marjorie O'Toole, Kate Kucharski, Susan Cunningham and Rosetta Pollini. Would they speak French one day? Brian doubted it. They'd be lucky to get a job in the bank before being consigned to early parenthood in a distinctly non-French speaking quarter of Martinup.

And the hostel kids who always sat together at school but whose homes were scattered far and wide: Paula Jones, Mary Livingstone, Ken Chappel and Roger Sutherland. A foreign language any use to them? Hardly. As soon as school was finished, they'd be off back to the sheep stations. Sheep were hardly noted for their linguistic ability.

Brian half turned in his seat to get a better view of the class. What about the rest? Mostly local farmers' sons and daughters and the offspring of Martinup blue and white collar workers like Barry Barclay, Susan and Robert Simpson, Gary Anderson, Michael O'Sullivan, Kevin Shearer, Kelvin MacQueen and the flatulent Peter Haddow. Would any of these end up in a French-speaking country? Or become a diplomat?

(Whatever that was.)

'BRIAN!'

Brian's attention was suddenly focussed on the obscure form of Miss Marceaux who had looked up to see him idly gazing around the room.

'Have you finished Brian?'

He shielded his eyes from the light behind her and mumbled, 'Um, yes.'

Well, read over what you've done and make sure you haven't made any silly mistakes or left out any questions.'

She glanced at her watch and called out to the class: Two minutes everyone! Deux minutes tout le monde!' Brian turned his question paper over to discover to his horror that there were two questions worth ten marks each that he had failed to notice.

He also failed to notice unlike several girls by the window. Mr Newton giving Miss Marceaux a shy grin on his way up to the science lab. He had started scribbling frantically. '*La vie en Australie c'est bon parce ce que...*'

When his teacher's voice rang out,

'Stop now! *Arrête*! Papers in please! *Les papiers s'il vous plait!*'

'It's a good life in Australia, isn't it, Michelle? said Paul, his eyes leaving the road for a moment to glance at her.

'Funny you should say that,' she said I set a test question for my first years about why life in Australia is good. They had to write a few lines about it, '*La vie en Australie...*' began Paul hesitantly.

'*C'est bon parce que...* added Michelle. '*les plages sont tres blanc et le soleil...ah...*'

His own schoolboy French had faltered but Michelle ignoring 'blanc was still impressed.

'Very good, Paul, but don't go asking me chemistry questions. She gazed out the window. There was not a lot to see at night. The road seemed to go on forever, the headlights bouncing off the overhanging trees that lined the road and illuminated the tops of the wooden guide posts that warned of sharp drops off the side of the road.

'How far is it to Albany, by the way?'

Paul glanced at his watch.

'Well, we should be there in about one and a half or two hours maybe. This is great isn't it?'

'Yeah, it really is nice to be away from Martinup,' said Michelle as she settled back on the seat.

Paul smiled at her and then switched his attention to the road with its double white lines that twisted and turned its way through the bush. Of course, he had spoken to her at school once or twice been around to see her, but an open relationship in a small country town was not possible. Gossip was rife. He knew what had happened to Jacko, so their affair had been conducted on a clandestine level over the past few weeks.

Paul had been to Albany once before but it was the maths teacher, Charlie Macduff who reminded him about the unspoilt beaches and wild coastal scenery. It shouldn't be a problem with accommodation he'd assured Paul, assuming of course that his young colleague would be travelling alone.

'Charlie MacDuff says there's plenty of secluded beaches around the coast.'

'Well, he'd know all about that wouldn't he?'

'How do you mean?'

'He'd know about secluded beaches because he'd be in the dunes with his binoculars, wouldn't he?'

Paul laughed. There was something refreshingly honest and perceptive about Michelle that he couldn't quite define, but he felt he should defend his colleague who had provided the details for a perfect weekend.

'Oh, he's not so bad,' he volunteered.

'Yes, he is, he's a bloody pervert!'

Paul chuckled and conceded that defending Charlie MacDuff might be a lost cause. He was more interested in what made Michelle so special.

Kids playing games in the cobbled streets and closes and Michelle's tales of the jungles and temples of Cambodia. Their backgrounds could hardly have been more exotically different.

After a while, Michelle said she felt tired and curled up against the passenger door. Paul pulled his tweed jacket over her and they drove on in silence towards the coast.

It was nearly eight o'clock at night before Roger passed the sign announcing that Martinup was thirty miles distant. He had left Perth just after four thirty and it had been an eventful journey, his first major excursion in his Volkswagen Campervan, the ultimate cruising machine. He'd bought it from a mate at college for just $250, some of his savings from the lucrative job he had in the mines up north during the Christmas holidays. The van had its faults of course, like the steering wheel which had a mind of its own and needed to be held in a vice-like grip in order to keep the vehicle on the road. But he had successfully negotiated the heavy traffic in the metropolitan area with only one near-miss and no collisions. And it was a bit heavy on fuel. And it was really slow going up hills. And the brakes were a bit dodgy.

'BUT THESE THINGS LAST FOREVER!' he shouted to himself over the roar of the engine, which although located at the back seemed just as loud in the front. Roger opened the window and took a deep breath before closing it half-way again. Another minor eccentricity of his Volkswagen Campervan was the primitive heating system. Pipes feeding what was supposed to be warm air from the engine to the dashboard tended to deliver instead mostly hot gases. Roger had learned in the course of the journey to alleviate the toxic fumes by opening the window to the optimum amount so that the freezing air allowed in would prevent death from asphyxiation but was insufficient for a case of acute hypothermia.

He turned on the overhead light and examined his reflection in the mirror. His beard was coming along nicely and his hair was nearly the right length for a ponytail. He wondered what his new girlfriend would think of that. With one eye on the road, he pulled his hair back behind his head to get the effect but abandoned his efforts in favour of concentrating on the road as the van wobbled violently when the tyres momentarily made contact with the gravel.

'Michelle, your surname, Marceaux, are you French? I mean, your English is absolutely perfect.'

Michelle laughed. 'Sort of. My dad was French, but my mum definitely wasn't. I was born in Cambodia.'

'Really?' Paul would never have guessed that. It suddenly made sense, the jet-black hair, the wide eyes and the smooth, slightly olive skin.

'Yeah, my mum's Cambodian, my dad worked for a big French company in Phnom Penh after the war.'

'So, are all your family here now?'

'Most of them except for some cousins I've never met. Dad could see things were going badly wrong even in the early fifties so he arranged for everyone to go first to Singapore and then to Sydney. He still works for the same company but he's talking about retiring.'

'So, no thoughts about him returning to France then?'

'No. Not really, he likes the lifestyle here too much although I'd like to go sometime.'

'And I suppose, Cambodia is out of the question?'

'Absolutely. My mum misses it occasionally but she knows she's well out of it. There's a big Cambodian community in Sydney so she's got plenty of company. Let's face it, this place. Australia saved all of us,'

She turned to him.

'What about you, Paul? You haven't got an Australian accent, have you?'

'No, that's quite right. I don't sound like Jacko!'

'Ha! That shit! Whatever happened to him?'

'God only knows, but anyway, no, I was born in Scotland.'

'Well, you could have fooled me, I've never heard you say, "och aye the nooh", isn't that what people in Scotland say?'

'No,' laughed Paul, 'I don't say that and nor does anyone else in Scotland. I don't even know what it means.'

'No, I was born in Govan.'

'Where the hell's that?'

They spent the next hour or more chatting about their respective childhoods: Paul's in a tenement a short distance from the dockyards where the giant ships that sailed the empire were built and launched.

He shivered as he fiddled again with the sliding controls of the heater. The white cotton Indian kurta he wore over the two T-shirts and his blue denim flares did little to keep out the cold. If anything, his bellbottomed trousers seemed to be funnelling the draught coming from unseen gaps below the door straight to his nether regions.

Deciding that he might as well die from the engine fumes as freeze to death, he wound up the window and thought of his girlfriend. He had wanted her to come down too so that she could meet his parents but she had important assignments to finish over Easter. And maybe it was best that she didn't meet his parents yet. She was a bit controversial. This would be the first time back in Martinup for Roger since he had left the high school nearly five months ago. How he had changed in that short time!

As he rounded a bend, the road straightened and he could just make out in the dim headlights (which were supposed to be on high beam, another eccentricity of his vehicle) what looked to be a car off the side of the road and a man next to it waving him down. Thinking at first it might be an accident he took his foot off the accelerator and gently applied the brakes, coming to a halt off the road behind the stationary vehicle.

The man approached the driver's side of the van. Roger turned off the engine and wound down the window. The stranger was a middle-aged aboriginal, his yellow teeth accentuated by his black skin and the red woollen hat he had pulled over his head nearly obscured his eyes completely.

His speech had patterns common to all Australian aboriginal languages where no distinction is made between voiced and unvoiced consonants so that "t" and "d" were interchangeable, as were "k" and "g", "p" and "b". 'G'day mat. Ginye gimme a lift ta maadinup? Me morderis run oudda bedrol.'

'Yeah, sure!' said Roger leaning over to open the passenger door.

When the stranger appeared at the other side, he asked through the open doorway,

'Ya don't mind, if me family come along doo?'

As he spoke, a half-dozen other aboriginals emerged from the darkness of the bush just outside the scope of the van's feeble headlight.

'Nah 'course not!' laughed Roger as he heaved himself from the driver's seat and trotted around to open the sliding passenger door to allow the men, women and children of the "family" to clamber into the van.

'Hey! Is that a guitar you've got?' he said to the last man aboard,

'Yeah. D'ya wanna few songs on the way?'

'Sure, why not?' said Roger as he pulled the sliding door to with a bang and resumed the pilot's seat.

The lights dimmed as the van's engine spluttered and roared into life.

'Hey Jacko!' yelled Mick Stone. He had been at the bar the whole day apart from the occasional fifteen-minute excursions to the baker's shop to put on some more weight or to the betting shop to lose some more money. Now he was holding court at the end of the bar with a few of his mates.

Michael Jackson had been going about his business with little enthusiasm, putting away glasses and emptying ash trays before he looked up in response to his customer's call.

'Yeah?'

'Hey Jacko, come 'ere a minute. I gotta joke for ya!'

Jacko stepped through the bar hatch, stood back from the group and lit a cigarette while Mick launched into his story.

'It's this bloke, see, drivin' down to Norseman on a really dark night.

'He's only got a couple of miles to go when these two abos jump out of the bush to wave him down for a lift. So, before he knows it, BANG! HE'S hit the both of 'em! One hits the 'roo bar and goes flyin' off into the bush an' the other one comes SMASH! Straight through 'is windscreen an' ends up on the back seat.

'So, he stops the car goes lookin' for the first one but he can't find 'im. An' then he looks in the back of 'is car an' this other abo's dead! So he thinks: '*Bloody hell! I've killed him. What am I gunna do? Betta just give meself up!*' So, he drives on to Norseman an' he gets to the police station an' he says to the sergeant,

'Sergeant! Sergeant! Something terrible has happened!'

So, the sergeant says, 'Just calm down sir and tell me about it.'

'So he gets out 'is notebook an' the bloke tells him the whole story while the sergeant's scribblin' away.

Then the bloke says, 'What's gunna happen now, Sergeant?'

'An' the sergeant says, 'Well, I reckon we'll do the one that went through your windscreen for Breaking and Entering and the other bugger for 'leaving the scene of an accident!' Ha!'

The collective roar of mirth engulfed Jacko but he remained expressionless and exhaled the smoke from his cigarette.

'Wassa matter with you, Jacko? No sense of humour or sumpin'?' Mick was peeved that his joke was not appreciated by the entire company.

'Heard it before, Mick,' he said as he lifted the bar hatch to continue his duties. His mind was elsewhere.

'WUT'S YORE NAME MAT?' enquired Roger's new co-pilot over the roar of the engine.

'ROGER, ROGER MACARTHUR,' he shouted back, leaning over to offer his right hand while his left kept a firm grip on the wheel.

'AHM, PEDER GRADY, THAT'S ME MISSUS JESSE AN' MA BOY BRIAN AN' 'IS SISTER PATSIE AN THAT'S ME COUSIN JIMMIE ANDERSON AN' 'IS DAD MICHAEL. WE'RE ALL GON' TA ME UNCLE NORMAN'S FUNERAL IN MAADINUP T'MORRA.'

Peter Grady paused for a moment to catch his breath. This thing was noisier than his own car even when it had lost the exhaust.

'D'YA WANT SOME OF THIS?' he shouted, offering Roger a half-full flagon of Penfold's Tawny Port.

Roger declined, so he offered it to the others in the darkness behind where it rapidly disappeared.

'SO, WHUT'S YORE JUB RUDJAH?'

'I'M A STUDENT AT UNIVERSITY IN PERTH.'

'WHUT'S A UNA…VER.'

'UNIVERSITY. IT'S LIKE A BIG HGH SCHOOL WHERE YOU STUDY DIFFERENT THINGS.'

'LIKE MATHS?'

'YEAH, AND LOTS OF OTHER THINGS.'

Singing had started in the back. Peter swung around to join in for a minute with *"Slim Dusty's"* classic, *"Pub with No Beer".*

'WE LIKE OUR MUSIC. BUT AH DIN' LIKE MATHS MUCH. SO WHUT DO YA STUDY AT UNIVER…?'

'I'M DOING ENGLISH, HISTORY AND ANTHROPOLOGY.'

'WHUT THE HELL'S THAT?'

'WELL, STUDYING YOU BLOKES FOR A START.'

'WHUT? US NOONGAS?'

'YEAH, AND OTHER ABORIGINAL PEOPLE LIKE THE ARUNTA AND PITJANJARRAH AND…' 'REALLY?'

Peter Grady sounded surprised. Indeed, he was shocked that after generations of abuse and neglect, his people should suddenly be considered worthy of study. As Roger explained in more detail about linguistics, kinship groups, totems and initiation rites, his eyes widened. He stared at this young long-haired *"wadjallah"* telling him more about his own people than he knew. It was astonishing enough to be picked up in the first place by a white man because they usually accelerated off at the sight of a black face, but to be told all this...

He suddenly felt a twinge of suspicion. Was this young bloke just winding him up?

'YO'RE NUT PULLIN' MA LEG, ARE YA RUDJAH?' he demanded.

'NO, NO! I'M DEADLY SERIOUS! I ONLY JUST STARTED ANTHROPOLOGY BUT IT'S TAUGHT ME A LOT ABOUT ABORIGINAL PEOPLE AND LOTS OF OTHER PEOPLE ALL OVER THE WORLD.'

Peter Grady was convinced. He turned in his seat to the interrupt the singing with an announcement.

'HEY, YOU PLOKES! RUDJAH HERE IS AT UNI...WHUT IS IT AGAIN RUDJAH? OH YEAH, UNAVERSITY STUDYIN' US NOONGAS! THAT'S GOOD, HEY?'

The welcome this news received was honest enough but Jessie Grady had a contribution to make. She crawled forward into the space between the two front seats and demanded of Peter,

'WASSIS NAME?'

'RUDJAH.'

'HEY RUDJAH! WHERE'S MY FARM?'

'EH?' Roger didn't have a clue what she was talking about.

'NAH, I MEAN IT. HOW YOU WHITE BLOKES HAVE GOT FARMS AN' STUFF AN' WE HAVEN'T? SO WHERE'S MY FARM?'

Peter could see she'd had a good bit to drink so he told her to shut up and helped her into the back with the others and joined in with the country and western session leaving Roger alone in the front.

Roger drove on in silence. He had just been asked a question he could not answer. He conducted an imaginary question and answer session with Jessie.

'You don't have a farm Jessie because the white man owns the land.'

102

'Who says so?'

'The white man says so.'

'But how come, when we were here first?'

'Because the white man thinks he's better than you are and he's got the guns and the law to prove it.'

'Is that right? Can that ever be right?'

'If it's not right, how the hell do you go about putting it right? Start giving the land back to the aboriginals when the bush has been cleared, the animals they used to hunt are gone, the creeks dried up and the people themselves lost all sense of dignity and forgotten the ways of the past? Could he ever imagine a local cocky giving up his farm? To aborigines?'

Peter Grady put his head around.

'YORE NUT GUNNA TELL THE CUPS ABOUT THIS, ARE YA?' he asked as he waved the nearly empty flagon towards Roger. In 1967, it was still illegal for native Australians to consume alcohol. In fact, they were not even allowed to vote; effectively not even considered to be citizens of their own country.

'NAH. BUT DON'T GET TOO PISSED OR YOU'LL MISS THE FUNERAL TOMORROW AND HEY PETER, WHERE DO YOU WANT TO BE DROPPED OFF?'

The van had just rumbled past the sign announcing the town.

Peter looked through the passenger window.

'HERE'LL DO,' he indicated a dirt track off the main road surrounded by bush.

Roger pulled over and left the lights on and engine running. He hopped out to pull open the sliding door.

The various members of the Anderson and Grady clans dropped out one by one.

'Mind your guitar,' he said to Michael Anderson as he helped the old man down.

Then he turned his attention to Jessie Grady as she prepared to jump. She grabbed his hand when she landed awkwardly and pulled him towards her.

'Yer nodda pad ploke fer a white fella!' she laughed and clapped him vigorously on the back.

Roger felt honoured indeed.

'What about your car Peter?'

'Ah, no worries mate. Whun o'me cousins'll pick it up sometime. Least no pastard's gunna pinch it hey?'

'HA! See ya!'

Roger shut the rolling door and stood to watch the group disappear into the bush.

A question kept repeating over and over again in his mind as he resumed the journey. Where's my farm? Indeed. Where *is* my farm?

Drug Addicts and Communists

Mary MacArthur drew back the net curtain on the kitchen window and peered into the darkness.

'I think that's him now.'

John MacArthur looked up at the clock on the mantelpiece and sighed.

'Just look at the bloody time. His tea will be cold by now.'

Brian meanwhile, had bounded out the back door at the first sound of the engine and was already in the glow of the headlights as the motor shut down.

'Roger!'

'How goes it, little dude?'

Brian was swung into the air then hastily put down as Roger realised his little brother was not so little any more.

'Hey, you're getting really heavy, little man!'

'And your hair's getting really long Roger!'

'Yeah. It's cool, isn't it? Hope mum and dad don't mind too much.'

John and Mary MacArthur approached, their features obscured but their silhouettes clearly visible in the feeble light over the back door.

Mary greeted her third son with a kiss on the cheek and a remark about his hair length. John offered his hand and some advice about a special offer from the local barber. Roger smiled, shrugged and nudged his younger brother.

'So, this is it?' asked John MacArthur as he walked the length of the VW campervan that now dominated his driveway, pausing only to give the back tyre a perfunctory kick.

'Yep. This is it. She's a beauty, isn't she?'

'Hm. Yes well you'd better get it off the driveway so that I can get out tomorrow morning. Put it on the back-lawn son, but go easy because it's taken me ages to get that grass in shape.'

Roger duly obliged. Mounting the driver's seat and with engine roaring, he lurched the van forward and back while his father, arms flailing, navigated in the headlights like ground crew at an airport. John MacArthur's shouted instructions went largely unheard by the driver but at last the vehicle was adequately positioned on the lawn.

'Hey Mum!' said Roger as he clambered down. 'Am I sleeping in my old room?'

'Yes. I thought Brian could sleep in the lounge room floor while you're here.'

'Well, this van is plenty big enough, there's sleeping bags and a mattress, so Brian would you like to sleep out here instead of the lounge room?'

The huge grin on Brian's face immediately confirmed his acceptance of the unexpected alternative sleeping arrangements. A glance at his mother indicated parental approval, but only in the event of the provision of additional bedding material she warned, such as could be found on the lounge room floor. Brian needed no further instructions. He was off to make a nocturnal nest for himself in the back of the van while Roger and his parents made for the kitchen for cups of tea and a belated lukewarm meal for one.

In the cosy darkness of the back of the van with its heady engine smells of oil and petrol, Brian snuggled in to the ample warmth provided by the bedding. As always on his mother's insistence this was sufficient to withstand a substantial snowfall, a highly improbable event even in the most severe Martinup winter, which at the worst could only provide a light covering of frost on the back lawn. It was not long before the heat became oppressive and he was obliged to start discarding some of the heavy woollen blankets.

Through the stillness of the night he could just make out the sounds of conversation from the kitchen. His eyes, accustomed now to the darkness, wandered around the interior of the van, straining to make out the details of walls and ceiling. What a wonderful bedroom this was. A mobile home. *'What fun it would be to go camping in this,'* he thought. *'To travel! To see new places and meet new people and then to just move on again when you wanted!'* When he was old enough, he wanted something like this, not a fuddy-duddy old caravan that his father was

106

talking about getting. '*Yes, travel,*' he mused. '*Up north maybe or even right around Australia!*'

His thoughts turned to Trevor who with his mother had no doubt spent the evening packing. He had dropped in to see them after school, but they were so engrossed in difficult decisions about what must go and what could be dumped or given away he made a polite early exit. Trevor was in charge of the work shed while his mother was steadily going through each room clearing the ten-year accumulation of detritus. The bulk of the furniture had already gone with the removal van a week ago. The pair of them were reduced to eating meals from a card table and sleeping on two mattresses on the lounge room floor surrounded by a sea of cardboard boxes.

He tried to imagine what it was like for Trevor to completely move away from the place where he was born, and start all over again on the other side of Australia, but he couldn't. His home had always been Martinup and he could only guess at what life would be like somewhere else. Perth was just conceivable, but Sydney might as well be on another planet.

The murmur of voices from the kitchen grew distinctly louder and Brian heard his father say: 'Oh, for God's sake Roger!' Then things went quiet. In the stillness, his thoughts returned to Trevor. Did he envy him? Not really, he decided. Sydney was big and exciting right enough, but this place with the bush, the night sky and the silence, this place was home and he dreaded the thought of being forced to leave it. His mother had once suggested boarding school in Albany and he had fought tooth and nail against the idea till eventually his parents relented. But one day he knew he would leave. One day he would travel far away from Martinup…

The back door slammed shut with a violence that interrupted his reverie. The crunching of boots sounded across the gravel and the van door cracked open. Roger put his head around squinting to make out his little brother in the gloomy interior.

'Hey Brian, you don't mind if I come and join you for a bit, do you?' he asked brushing a long strand of hair behind his left ear.

'No, 'course not!' said Brian heaving himself upright against the van wall behind the passenger seat using a pillow to brace himself.

Roger heaved the sliding door shut and climbed into the driver's seat.

'The old man is really giving me the shits at the moment,' he said as he fumbled in the pockets of his jacket slung over the back of the seat.

'What's going on?'

Brian was keen to understand the conflicts that his older brother was having with their father. It gave him a chance to understand a bit more of the grown-up world. Roger had so many opinions about lots of things that seemed to be in direct conflict with those of his father. The two of them couldn't always both be right. For his part, Roger had found that the "Swinging Sixties" had not made a big impact on Martinup and controversial well-argued ideas were not John MacArthurs notion of a fun night at home around the fire. His little brother's eagerness to listen was a welcome relief from the feuding in the kitchen.

Roger had at last found what he was looking for. He opened the metal tobacco tin and carefully inspected the contents. He took out the cigarette papers.

'Ah, it's always the bloody same isn't it? It started with the usual bit about the hair and the clothes, which is cool, I can handle that. But the next minute he's onto the bloody Vietnam war and what a great job Australia is doing fighting the communists! So, I said that's crap. And then mum's getting upset because she thinks he's saying I should get a haircut and fight for my country like he did against the Japs…'

'What are you doing, Roger?'

Brian was propped over the passenger seat watching his older brother carefully sticking together three cigarette papers to make one large one which he then spread out on an old map on his lap.

'I'm rolling a joint little dude.'

Silence from the back of the van.

Roger gave a deep sigh. Now don't you start on me too little man.'

He carried on with the delicate operation of sprinkling tobacco the length of the enlarged paper. Without taking his eyes off the proceedings, he continued without pausing for answers from his wide-eyed younger sibling perched over his left shoulder,

'The nuns at the school told you about drugs didn't they? Drugs. Bad Right? Take drugs. You die. Right? Well, I bet they didn't go on about booze and fags and aspirin. They're drugs too. Right? And opium and cocaine and heroin are really dangerous drugs. But this…'

He held up what looked to be a small pill capsule between thumb and forefinger for his silent audience of one in the darkness behind him.

'…this is marijuana, cannabis, hashish…or in this case hash oil…'

As he spoke, he prised it gently apart and sprinkled a few drops on the line of tobacco.

'…yeah, it's a drug but it's been used as a medicine for over two thousand years…'

Having deposited the capsule safely back in the tin, he massaged the oil into the tobacco.

'…So when people start going on about drugs, they conveniently forget or more probably they don't even know that this stuff does not cause addiction and has not caused a single death in its entire history…?'

Roger now commenced the delicate operation of rolling the joint on the folded map perched on his knee.

'…and some people still use it as a medicine and in some parts of the world it's more common than alcohol…'

'Does it give you a trip then?'

Roger shook his head slowly as he finished off the joint with a piece of torn-off cardboard from the map.

'No Brian. That's stuff like LSD, acid. That's nasty stuff. This is totally different.'

'So, what does it do then?'

Roger wound down the window, lit the twisted end and sent a trail of blue smoke into the night sky.

'It makes you relaxed, that's all little dude.'

Brian was prepared to accept his brother's explanation for his illegal activities and pulled some blankets around himself as the chilly night air suddenly made itself felt in the back of the van. If Roger said it was safe, then it must be safe.

'So why are you so against the Vietnam war Roger?'

Roger inhaled deeply on the joint and carefully ejected the smoke clear of the van.

'Because it's not our war little dude. We shouldn't even be there. The only reason we are there is because Australia is trying to suck up to the United States of America.'

'So why is America in Vietnam?'

'Because they want the world their way. They don't like communists. In particular they don't like Communist China.'

'So, are you a communist Roger?'

'I could live in a commune, yeah, I suppose that could make me a communist.'

Brian was now totally confused. His favourite brother turning out to be a drug addict was one thing, but a communist. The nuns and his parents had used the word in the same context as "mortal sin", Satan and "eternal damnation".

Roger could tell from the silence behind him that his off-the-cuff comment had caused consternation but he was getting tired. The explanation could wait for another day. The hash oil was beginning to have an effect.

He would sleep well tonight.

'I'm off to your bed now little dude. Sleep well in mine okay?'

In the silence of the night that followed Roger's departure, Brian fell into a deep sleep and dreamt of his brother on a platform sporting a green cap with a red star. His arm was around Chairman Mao. Both of them were laughing loudly and smoking huge joints in front of thousands of adoring communists waving little red capsules of hash oil.

The sun burst through the low grey cloud with a brilliance that almost blinded them. They both pulled down the shields to protect themselves from the glare.

The happy couple were exploring the famous south coast near Albany. They had set off after breakfast for Frenchman Bay which the Italian owner of the rather shabby hotel on the waterfront assured them was a sight they should not miss on their honeymoon. Although Paul winced a little at the deception, they were unknown in the town and the weekend so far had been sheer magic.

When the car rounded the last bend, Michelle could not contain a gasp of wonder at the panorama that stretched before them. It was a scene of unparalleled natural beauty. The sea, framed left and right by massive purple headlands of a size that could be only guessed at, sparkled in the distance like multiple moving strings of diamonds. In its midst, islands of varying sizes and distances from the shore lay scattered dozing in the warmth of the morning sun. The bay stretched in an enormous arc that encompassed at least half of their field of view and below, far, far below at the end of the narrow winding road that took them through blue-green rolling hills of heather-like scrub that reminded Paul so much of the highlands of Scotland lay their destination: Frenchman Bay.

Paul glanced at Michelle. He marvelled at the way she always managed to look radiant, no matter what she was wearing. Even his tatty old jumper looked like high fashion on her, Michelle had not anticipated the Albany chill factor. The winds from the south came straight from the Antarctic.

'What do you think of this Michelle?' he asked nodding ahead.

'Oh, Paul, it's just magnificent. It's so…so perfect. It's like we're the first people to ever see it. Did you notice how few cars we've seen on the road? If this was Sydney, the place would be mobbed. These hills would be covered in houses and shops and restaurants…'

'Even sleepy old Perth is going the same way,' Paul admitted. But this place hasn't changed since I, was a kid. This was one of the first places dad took us not long after we arrived. It was supposed to be our big "Discover Australia holiday", but we only managed the south west and didn't see most of that anyway. Well here we are.' He indicated the sign for "Frenchman Bay Caravan Park and Tea", on the left and pulled the car in to the deserted parking area.

'Fancy a cup of coffee, Michelle?'

'Later,' she said hopping out of the car and slamming the door. She leaned over the roof and grinned at him. 'I want to see this beach you've been going on about. And I don't want to see any bloody whaling station either.'

Paul smiled as he locked the door. Michelle had been fascinated to hear from their Italian host that Albany boasted the last remaining land-based whaling station in Australia. When he told her his childhood recollections of visiting it, she changed her mind.

The Cheynes Beach Whaling company was still a viable business, employing many young men from the town. Three "chasers" and a spotter plane roamed the Southern Ocean in search of the lucrative sperm whale. An explosive charge on the harpoon tip quickly dispatched the mammals, some up to fifty feet in length and weighing as many tons. Their bodies would be towed back to the whaling station before being pumped full of compressed air and anchored. The tethered carcasses were easy pickings for sharks and the seas around the station often ran red with blood.

When the time came the dead whale would be hauled up to the flensing decks. This was what the visitors came to see. Tartan-shirted young men in black shorts and wellington boots skated through the red gore of the wooden decks each armed with a flensing knife, a long-curved razor-sharp blade mounted on a wooden handle. This weapon would remove blubber as thick as a man's forearm in a few strokes. Within minutes the beast would be reduced to a gory mass of blood and sinew. The blubber, carved into square chunks would then be propelled across the deck like a puck in a game of hockey and encouraged through a hole to the boiling vats below. The cameras would flash, and for those without a camera, post cards of half-flensed whales were available in the visitor centre.

As a thirteen-year-old, Paul Newton had stood with the rest of his family on the visitor's deck. The stench of cooking whale meat stung his nostrils and stayed in his clothes for days. The roaring and hissing of the steam-driven saws that slowly cut through flesh and bone and the clanking of the hooks and chains that tore the beast below him apart filled him with a mixture of fascination and revulsion. He vowed then that he would never return.

'Wait for me!' he called after her but Michelle had already disappeared down the concrete steps leading to the beach.

Paul followed the steps through the thick bush that had not changed much since the coming of the white man, through stands of peppermint and she-oak until he caught sight of her on the beach below. By the time he reached her, she had taken off her shoes and was encouraging him to do the same. Together they walked hand in hand through the snow-white sand flecked here and there with foam and piles of seaweed.

Continuous rolls of surf came in great surges from the emerald and turquoise bay, lapping and snapping at their bare ankles as they walked, locked together in conversation.

'Isn't this place so wonderful Paul? I mean, where else in the world can you get scenery like this and a beach to yourself? It's just gorgeous!'

Paul smiled and nodded in agreement. From the day his family arrived, Australia had been a source of fascination and delight. There was only one thing that concerned him.

'Pity I can't say the same about some Australians,' he mused.

'Oh? What do you mean?'

'People like Jacko. Racists. Petty people. Small-minded bigots. The ones who reckon that Australia belongs only to them and everyone else should go back to where they came from. You haven't experienced any racial prejudice since you've been here have you Michelle?'

She shook her head.

'No. But then maybe I had a pretty sheltered childhood in Sydney!'

'Here's something you maybe didn't know,' said Paul. 'This country once had a thing called "The White Australia Policy". That was the attitude to migrants back in the thirties. The name says it all doesn't it?'

'Never.'

'Yep, 'fraid so. If you and I arrived here then, I would get in and you wouldn't. Simple as that. That's a frightening thought isn't it?'

Michelle nodded and fell silent for a moment. She had never considered before the darker side of her adopted country. She felt as much a part of it as anyone else, never thinking of herself as in any way different.

'But things have changed now haven't they Paul? Loads and loads of people have come here since the war.'

'Right enough. And hopefully the more cosmopolitan this society becomes, the less chance there'll be for the small-minded ones to have any real power. And I can see the day coming when Australia will have to accept migrants from Vietnam...'

'And Cambodia,' added Michelle.

'And all the rest of Asia. I want to be clear about this because I'm not saying all Australians are bigots,' said Paul earnestly. 'What gives me inspiration and the knowledge that this country is in good hands is my own classroom. Have you got Brian MacArthur and Trevor Stewart in your class by the way?'

Michelle paused for a moment then nodded. They were the two boys who always sat near the door.

'Uh huh.'

'I'll use those two as an example. Here we've got a couple of white Australian boys born in a little country town in the bush who are really keen to learn. If you've got people who want to learn and accept new ideas, there's no room for prejudice. There's no place for bigotry. Education can really change people. I think teachers do a pretty important job don't you Michelle?'

She looked up at him as he gave her a squeeze.

'I think so too Paul. Shall we go back for that coffee now?'

Hand in hand they strolled back along the beach. The wind had eased and the sun warmed their faces. Paul told Michelle how much he was enjoying life as a teacher despite having early doubts. She felt the same.

Michelle had left Sydney to do her teacher training in Perth simply because she wanted to see more of Australia Before she knew it, she was into the system and her first posting was just taken on as learning experience for a year before she returned to Sydney. Paul asked her if she still intended to go back.

Michelle paused for a moment before answering.

'You know Paul, I honestly can't answer that. Sydney seems such a long way from here. I don't think about it every day if that's what you mean. But I miss my mum and dad and of course Giselle and Catriona.'

She told him in detail about her two older sisters who had both left home. One was practising medicine in Queensland and the other was a journalist in America. They were both happily married.

When Paul was asked about his own family and how it felt being an only child Michelle suddenly interrupted him.

'Sorry Paul! Look! Can you see who that is?'

A couple had just walked past them on the other side of the beach. The man was middle-aged and balding. It was incongruous because the pretty girl he was with was so much younger. They were locked in deep conversation, oblivious to the two curious observers near the water's edge.

'You know who he looks like?' said Michelle with a smile then whispered into Paul's ear.

He roared with laughter. 'Nice one Michelle!'

Trevor heaved the last bulging cardboard box through the front door and down the steps. He half-carried, half-dragged it over the short garden path before manoeuvring it through the open gate He bent over it, panting and bracing himself for the final lift. With muscles bulging and the strain showing on his face, the last, the very last box was up off the ground and on board the trailer in the last possible space. The suspension groaned ominously. That was it. The trailer was well and truly full. As was the roof-rack, the boot and the back seat. Any more stuff and there'd be no room for the driver and the all-important navigator.

Trevor paused for a minute to catch his breath. He and his mother had been going non-stop for two days. She was over with Luigi and Maria saying goodbye and handing over a spare set of keys. Their chooks had already gone to the de Lucas' which eased Trevor's guilt over the untimely demise of Giovanni. This was the first time he'd had a chance to reflect on the enormity of the occasion. He stood in the road and stared at the empty shell that had been his childhood home. Overhead the "For Sale" sign rocked gently in the wind. A dozen images of the past flashed through his mind. A blurred vision of his father and the swing at the front, his birthday party, his first bike, a Christmas tree in the front room…

A familiar voice drew his attention away to the bottom of the road. He surreptitiously wiped away a tear and drew in a deep breath.

'G'day Brian. I was just comin' down to see ya to say goodbye.'

Brian leaned his bike against the fence.

'When are ya goin'?'

'Just after twelve I reckon. Well as soon as mum sorts out the keys and stuff with Luigi and Maria'

Both boys looked at the ground. It was a moment both had mentally rehearsed but it still came far too soon for ease or comfort. It was never going to be easy.

Brian took the initiative.

'Goodbye mate,' he said and offered his hand.

Trevor took it but was unable to speak. His eyes misted up and he bit his lip to control an unseemly torrent of raw emotion.

'I'm going to miss you, said Brian.

Trevor nodded, drew a deep breath and looked his friend in the eye. He grinned and said,

'I'm going to miss you too.'

Margaret Stewart appeared on the steps of her Italian neighbours' house and her cheery conversation with them was clearly audible. Trevor located the tarpaulin covering of the trailer under a tangle of kitchenware in the boot,

'Bye now Luigi and Maria and thanks for everything.'

She waved to them as she danced down the front path. Brian had never seen her so happy and animated and he had never seen her in jeans. She looked ten years younger!

'Oh, there you are Brian! Look, can you tell your mum and dad we won't be able to see them before we go?'

The trailer is a nightmare to reverse! No wait. Our phone is still connected. I'll give them a call just now. How's it going Trevor?' She shouted over her shoulder on her way up the garden path but she had already disappeared in the gloom of the open doorway before Trevor could mouth a reply so he turned his attention back to the tarpaulin instead.

'Give us a hand with this will ya Brian?'

The two boys struggled with the ancient inflexible canvas, spreading it across the bulging load as best they could.

How long do ya reckon it'll take ya?' asked Brian, as he wrestled with an intractable knot in the rope.

'Four. five days maybe. It's hard to tell. I'm just guessin' from the map.'

'But your mum must know?'

'Not really. She and dad came over by train.

The conversation tailed off. There was not much else to say. When the trailer was secured, Brian collected his bike from the fence.

'Reckon I'll be off now mate.'

'Don't forget to write. You've got my address!' Trevor called out but his friend was fast receding into the distance.

An Outbreak of Conjunctivitis

Brian gave a brief wave over his shoulder to his old friend and headed for home. In the distance, something unusual was happening. A white van was parked outside his house and two men were struggling with something obviously long and heavy. He speeded up for a closer look. By the time he had arrived, the two men had ceased their activities and were pointing to the roofline.

Brian knew immediately what was going on. It was his father and Tom Wainwright from Will Wright's of Martinup Radio and TV Services. On the lawn was a fifty-foot long aluminium-ribbed TV mast wrapped with steel guy wires. The MacArthur's had joined the TV age!

'Dad! TV! That's absolutely brilliant!'

'Well it will be son as soon as we get this bloody thing sorted out.' John MacArthur gave the mast on the lawn a poke with his toe. He was not noted for his technical skills, but in this case fortunately, he was just the assistant.

'No worries John,' said Tom, a ruddy-faced giant of a man with a shock of unruly white hair whose faded blue overalls strained to fit him. 'Soon as I've got that base plate secured, this thing'll go up in minutes. You'll see!'

John MacArthur made a face and shrugged his shoulders.

Brian left them to it and bounded inside. His mother was in the hall on the telephone saying goodbye to Margaret Stewart. He found what he was looking for in the lounge-room. The radio had been displaced sideways by the new technology. There it sat in all its 24"-screen-tapered-spindle-legged glory.

It was a triumph of minimalism. An on/off switch that doubled as a volume control and a dial for ten channels, which was a bit optimistic, since only one was available. Brian was to learn quickly that the two most important controls in fact lay at the back just under the WARNING: DANGER OF ELECTROCUTION label. These were the horizontal and vertical hold knobs. The former when twiddled a bit sometimes halted bizarre distortion from the side. The latter supposedly halted rotation of the picture like an old-time movie out of control. Often, it was necessary to twiddle both, no easy feat when you had to watch the screen at the same time. In the early days, more time was spent adjusting the set than actually watching it.

Mary MacArthur came into the room while Brian was busy examining the intricacies of the space-age newcomer.

'Well Brian, I know your birthday is a month away, but what do you think of the present?'

'For me?' gasped Brian.

Mary laughed. 'Well I hope your father and I can watch sometimes too! We just thought that with everyone else in Martinup getting one, it would be a shame for you to miss out.'

Brian grinned. 'Thanks Mum.' He sat down in his usual chair and imagined watching TV in his very own home. Then he remembered something.

'Mum! Where's Roger?' he called after her as she disappeared in the kitchen.

'He's gone for a walk. He left straight after you went up to see Trevor. That was Margaret on the phone by the way. Did you say goodbye to Trevor?'

'Yes Mum.' But Brian's mind was now elsewhere. Bonanza! The Lone Ranger! The Cisco Kid! They were all within his grasp!

Yet even a boy's imagination was not sufficient to make a blank screen interesting for long, so Brian wandered out to see how the men were getting on with the aerial installation.

To his surprise it was already up! Tom Wainwright perched precariously on the ladder, had just tightened the second set of bolts and his father was holding some of the wires dangled from various points up the mast.

'Can I help, Dad?'

'Yes, son. Take this one over to the fence there.'

Brian was happy to oblige, surprised that Father seemed to know what he was doing. Things mechanical or requiring manual dexterity usually reduced him to fits of raging impotence.

Christmas presents that required self-assembly were a nightmare. Motor cars that misbehaved had their tyres kicked.

But on this occasion, all was calmness and efficiency. One by one the wires on the mast were fitted to the ground and the tensions adjusted to ensure that the towering edifice above their heads did not end up through the roof as the result of a blustery southwestern.

The mast in position and secured, the next job was to drill through the lounge-room window frame and feed through the all-important cable. That done, Tom Wainwright wired up the set, plugged it in and said dramatically, 'Right folks! Let's see what your picture's like.'

Three members of the MacArthur family sank into their chairs simultaneously and watched in open mouthed anticipation as their set crackled to life, but any expectations of instant crystal-clear picture quality faded immediately. In fact there was no picture at all, just static and the occasional flickering distortion. Tom Wainwright, on all fours on the lounge-room carpet beside the set surrounded by pliers, wire-strippers screwdrivers and bits of wire was undaunted.

'No worries, John, just need to turn the mast around a bit. You stay here and give me a shout when you get a decent picture.'

He hauled himself up to his full height and Brian, from his seated position wondered if he had just said he was going to turn the house around a bit, a feat he was surely capable of achieving, should he put his mind to it.

Brian and his mother watched the screen, John MacArthur in a relay position at the front door while Tom Wainwright grasped the base of the mast like a sumo wrestler with a telegraph pole. Slowly the mast began to rotate. Inside, the flickering on the screen intensified then burst into a discernible picture of a symphony orchestra.

'That's it!' chorused Mother and Son. 'That's it!' echoed John MacArthur.

'Thank Christ for that!' muttered Tom Wainwright as he bolted the mast tight and wiped the sweat from his brow. He folded down his ladder and made it fast on to the van. Five more calls this afternoon. This TV business was getting out of hand. Soon everyone would be running around with square eyes. It couldn't be good for you. Kills the conversation. Makes people's brains go soft.

He went back into the house to find all three MacArthurs glued to the screen. He squeezed through and collected his bits and pieces from the floor. Each family member adjusted their position as the sizeable frame of the TV man inadvertently obscured the view.

'I'll send you my account John. Don't get up, I'll see myself out.'

'OK Larry,' said John MacArthur absent-mindedly, without taking his eyes from the screen.

Tom Wainwright shook his head in disbelief as he climbed into the van. He glanced at his watch. He'd be lucky to be home before dark. Martinup was going mad for TV. It would be robots and computers next he shouldn't wonder. He set off down the road in a cloud of dust and in his haste very nearly collided with a heavily-laden car and trailer making an illegal turn in front of him. Tom braked heavily and sounded his horn in annoyance.

Trevor slowly took his hands from his face.

'Mum! Take it easy! We've got 5000 miles to go and we've nearly had an accident before we're out of the street!'

Margaret Stewart laughed and patted her son on the knee.

'Relax Trevor! I'm bound to get better with a bit of practice. I should be a really good driver by the time we get to Sydney. Now where am I supposed to be going?'

Trevor shuddered, trying not to think of the disastrous possibilities ahead and fumbled in the glove box for the map.

Brian looked across at his mother. He had no idea she had an interest in classical music, 'Will I get myself something to eat Mum?'

The midday meal, termed "dinner" in the old Irish way, was usually a semi-formal occasion of table setting and plate laying. Suddenly things were different. The TV had arrived.

'I think there's some cold meat in the fridge Brian,' she said anxious not to miss a beat of Daniel Barenboim's baton or a close-up of a violinist's chin. His father obviously another closet classicist, was similarly entranced by the flickering blue screen and the strains of Vivaldi's "Four Seasons" but sufficiently conscious to shout after him.

'Put things away when you've finished.'

Brian took his two roast beef and tomato sauce sandwiches to his room. Roger's open rucksack lay on the floor amidst a pile of socks and T-shirts. Something on top of the wardrobe caught his eye. It was Trevor's boomerang. He'd forgotten to return it to him. Now it was too late. He took it down and ran his fingers across the curving surface and along the lethal edge that had been Giovanni's last contact with life on earth. He reflected on Trevor's genius and his mind briefly flashed back to past memories. But he quickly put them aside. Time to move on. He shoved the boomerang up his jumper and called through the kitchen door,

'I'm just going out for a walk!'

His mother shouted something incomprehensible which Brian took for parental approval and with the boomerang uncomfortably anchored in the top of his trousers, he took off for the bush.

When he reached the race-track, the site of the ill-fated balloon launch, Brian wrenched Trevor's creation from inside his trouser belt. He was determined to make the thing work. Conditions were good in the cleared area at the centre of the track, a light northerly breeze and not a soul in sight.

His first efforts were feeble, the boomerang doing little more than rebounding off the ground. Time and again he retrieved it, refusing to give up in frustration. Then he remembered Trevor's advice, 'A hard flick at the end of the throw.'

Success! Indeed, outstanding success! The wooden missile arched around then up and back again straight towards him at such a pace he had to dive out of its way to avoid the same fate as Giovanni. Delighted and encouraged, Brian kept going for an hour or more, the frequency of successful flights steadily increasing.

He even managed to catch it from time to time quickly learning that the palms of his hands, not fingertips were the approved method.

Becoming adventurous, he decided to see how far he could throw it. He noticed that the wind conditions had changed. What had been a light northernly was now a fairly strong wind from the north-west. His gargantuan throw was caught by a gust which sent the boomerang far over his head and a good distance into the thick bush that lined the side of the track.

Cursing himself for his stupidity, he set off to find it, mentally marking an imaginary spot where it had last been sighted some distance away.

He followed an imaginary flight path on the ground through the bush, over fallen trees and across thick regrowth completely ignoring childhood warnings of dangerous reptiles, spiders and insects whose homes he now brutally invaded in search of the missing boomerang.

The group of tall white gums just ahead had been his mental reckoning of where the boomerang had landed. He cast his eyes around in desperation. For all his bravado thus far, the bush was a hostile environment and he wanted to be out of it as soon as possible. In desperation he scoured the tree canopy. And then he saw it! The boomerang, apparently none the worse for its record-breaking flight was sitting on top of the tangled branches of a felled white gum.

As Brian waded through the undergrowth to retrieve it, he became aware that he was not alone in the bush.

He could hear voices up ahead!

Thrusting the boomerang up his jumper, he set off cautiously to investigate. Inching his way forward and taking cover behind the larger trees, the voices grew louder and more distinct. They were singing! He could hear a musical instrument…a guitar perhaps. Brian heard the crackling of a fire and could just make out three figures, two seated and one standing. Male or female, he couldn't tell. His curiosity got the better of him. He moved further forward for a better view. Then he realised what he had stumbled across. An aboriginal camp!

From his position crouched behind a tree, Brian could make out perhaps a dozen figures around the fire. An irrational fear began to rise from the pit of his stomach, no doubt inspired by an American western movie he had seen where the cowboy hero discovers a Red Indian campsite and then gets caught and tortured by the savages. He decided to carefully retreat, avoiding cracking any twigs in the process which had been the downfall of his celluloid hero.

A hand grabbed the back of his neck in a vice-like grip. A voice growled from behind,

'Whut have we got here?'

The hand released its grip and pushed him forward.

Brian spun around to see the grinning black face of the aboriginal boy that had tripped him up at school. Brian Grady.

He struggled to his feet and as the aboriginal boy was nearly twice the size of himself, Brian felt obliged to do as he was told. There was clearly no point in trying to make a run for it.

'Come an,' join the paidy white boy!' With a shove in the back, Brian was propelled towards the gathering around the fire.

'Look what ah found! A little ploke spyin' on us!'

The music and the conversation stopped. Brian, sick with fear and his heart thumping, cast his eyes around the unfamiliar black faces until he reached the guitarist sitting on a fallen tree trunk.

'Roger!'

'Brian! What are you doing here? Hey fellas! This is my little brother Brian! Brian meet Peter and that's

Jessie, Michael, Patsie, Jimmie and of course that's Brian. Brian nodded with each introduction, still shocked at the turn of events. Instead of mutilation by wild savages, he was being introduced to them by his own brother.

Sensing Brian's consternation, Roger handed the guitar back to its owner, Michael Anderson and crossed the campsite to his little brother. He put a comforting arm around him.

'What are you doing here little dude?'

Brian breathed a sigh of relief at the comforting presence of his older brother.

'I was just practising throwing this at the racetrack and it sort of got away from me,' he said as he pulled the boomerang from under his jumper.

'Hey, that's really neat! Where did you get it? Can you throw it?'

'Trevor made it. He forgot to take it with him and yes, I can throw it a bit.'

'Sit down Brian. Make yourself comfortable,' said Roger indicating a boulder by the fire.

Michael Anderson started singing "*Michael Row the Boat Ashore*" and the rest of the company either joined in or resumed their conversations while the flagon of port was passed around. Brian shoved the boomerang back inside his jumper and seated himself on the rock.

'Roger!' he whispered to his brother who leaned his head towards him.

'What are you doing here and how come you know these people?'

Roger replied cheerfully, 'Oh, I gave them all a lift last night into town. There was a big funeral this morning, so they're all having a party now. I bumped into them when I was out walking, so they invited me to join them.'

Brian shook his head in amazement. White people just did not communicate with aboriginals the way that Roger did. They shunned them. They looked the other way. They pretended they didn't exist. They put them in reserves outside the town. They didn't give them lifts. They certainly didn't receive and wouldn't dream of accepting invitations to parties with them. But here was his brother, completely at home right in the middle of it.

'Hey Rudjah, D'ya want some of this?'

The port bottle was passed to him and he took a generous swig before offering it to his little brother.

'Try some of this Brian, but go easy little dude. That's real firewater!'

Brian gingerly took the heavy flagon and raised it to his lips. He had never tasted alcohol before. A mouthful of the fiery-sweet red liquid scorched his tongue and burnt its way to his stomach where it exploded. The involuntary fit of coughing that resulted caused Roger to grab the half-gallon bottle for safekeeping and thump his younger brother on the back.

The enthusiastic back-slapping dislodged the boomerang from beneath Brian's jumper. It tumbled onto the ground in front of him. Brian Grady seized on it.

'Can you throw this?'

'Uh huh.'

'Can ya' show us?'

'Yeah go on Brian!' urged Roger. 'I'll come and watch!'

'We'll come too!' A handful of the Grady clan followed the trio through the bush leaving the Andersons in charge of the fire.

The surreal scene that followed set in the centre of the racetrack was certainly unprecedented in Martinup and probably in the rest of Australia too. A thirteen-year old white boy teaching his older brother and three local aboriginals how to throw a boomerang. The shouts and whoops of laughter carried through the bush. Kookaburras, crows and magpies took to the air in the tumult of bodies that dashed here and there through the low scrub attempting to anticipate the flight of the erratic wooden missile.

Roger persuaded his brother to show them again how it should be done. Brian obliged. It was a perfect throw and a perfect catch. When the yells of delight subsided, a thought came to him. Something he must do. Something he felt it was only right to do. He turned to Brian Grady and offered him the boomerang.

'This is for you. Take it,' he said. 'It's a present.'

The older boy's face broke into a broad grin as he accepted the gift. It was the first kindness he'd ever been shown by a wadjullah.

'C'mon Brian. Time to get back home,' Roger put his arm around his younger brother.

'See ya later, fellahs!' he called but they were away in the scrub alternately laughing and applauding each other's efforts at making the boomerang return.

'That was a really nice thing you did, Brian.'

Brian shrugged his shoulders. He wasn't quite sure why he had done it. It was a spur of the moment decision. And even though it wasn't technically his to give away in the first place, he knew that Trevor would have approved.

But now he was feeling distinctly unwell. The burst of physical activity had agitated the contents of his stomach. He was rapidly beginning to learn that fortified red wine can have a disastrous impact on one so young. His cheeks grew pale. A sweat broke out on his brow. Nausea swept over him in waves. He was finding it difficult to keep to the narrow track through the bush.

Ahead, cheerfully oblivious to the situation, Roger loped on, his hair swinging over the collar of his black duffel-coat. Lost in thought and whistling, '*Blowing in the Wind*,' he suddenly became aware that Brian had fallen behind. He turned and called out. To his great embarrassment, he soon located his brother crouched on all fours just off the track being violently sick.

'Roger! You're coming to mass this morning aren't you? It's Sunday after all.'

Mary MacArthur's voice carried clearly from the kitchen through the open door of Brian's bedroom where Roger was just emerging from a deep sleep.

He screwed up his face at the thought of it and pulled the hair away from his eyes.

'Yeah, right Mum,' was his unenthusiastic reply as he dragged himself out of bed.

'I think Brian must be still asleep in the van. Can you make sure that he's up and ready too?'

As Roger had mentally if not spiritually converted from Catholicism to Buddhism but had not quite got around to telling his parents, the whole exercise of going to mass, Easter or not, seemed a pointless exercise. But it wasn't worth it making a stand just now. Relations with his father were at an all-time low and his mother would not be too impressed either.

A happy thought came to him as he pulled on his black jeans. The hash oil in the van! A surreptitious joint before proceedings might make the Liturgy more interesting!

Inspired by the thought of an interesting sermon for once, Roger pulled on his military-style shirt and knotted his best silk psychedelic tie around his neck. He completed the outfit with black desert boots and duffel-coat, tidied his hair roughly in the wardrobe mirror and bounded out to the van where his younger brother was indeed still fast asleep.

'Time to get up Brian. We've got to go to mass!'

'Huh?' said the prostrate form in the sleeping bag.

Roger was busy fumbling through his jacket for the tobacco tin.

'You told me you didn't believe in going to mass any more,' said Brian sleepily, struggling to raise himself on one elbow.

'Well all religions have their relevance Brian and we do need to be tolerant,' said Roger hastily sticking cigarette papers together on his knee. 'And it is Easter you know,' he added, sprinkling a line of tobacco the length of the papers.

'I'll need to get into my room. All my clothes are there,' said Brian, slowly putting on his slippers and dressing-gown.

'No problem Brian. I'm dressed already. I'll just wait here in the van till everyone's ready to go.'

'Don't you want any breakfast?'

'No, I'll have something when we get back from mass. How are you feeling this morning by the way?'

'Bloody awful,' groaned Brian as he struggled out the sliding door and onto the frosty lawn.

Shuffling from the van in his nightclothes, Brian was puzzled by his favourite brother's slight inconsistency on the matter of Faith, but as a thirteen-year old he certainly had no choice in the matter. There was no way he could get out of going to mass. At least he wasn't a bloody altar boy anymore!

Father O'Neill was in top form. His sermon on the meaning of Easter, the implications of the Resurrection and the significance of Everlasting Life had Roger's drug-fuelled brain in overdrive. He sat smiling and nodding through the entire homily grasping hitherto hidden meanings and making associations with Faiths in no way connected to the Church of Rome. Every now and then he let out a slight gasp whenever the insights and revelations got really, really deep. A whispered affirmation of 'Yeah man. Right on!' usually accompanied a particularly profound insight. His father was fast asleep as usual at the end of the pew but he did get occasional quizzical looks from his mother and younger brother who were seated on both sides of him.

As the crowds poured out at the end of mass, Father O'Neill was quick to pounce on the MacArthur sibling he had not seen since Roger's departure for university.

'Roger how are you my boy? Great to see you!' boomed the priest pumping the young man's hand.

'Nice sermon Father,' said Roger trying to appear normal.

'Thank you, my boy. I do try to say something meaningful especially on such an important occasion on the church calendar. Are your eyes alright Roger? They look very red and swollen.'

'Probably too much TV Father,' laughed Roger nervously, the first feelings of paranoia striking in the pit of his stomach.

On the way home, Roger faced further interrogation from his parents.

'Yes, your eyes do look red Roger. And you haven't been watching TV. Maybe you should go to the doctor when you get back to Perth.' said Mary MacArthur twisting around in the passenger seat.

Roger's paranoia level increased.

'It's probably just conjunctivitis, Mum.'

'You can't be too careful as far as your health's concerned son. What time are you going back to Perth this afternoon?' asked John MacArthur eyeing Roger in the rear-vision mirror.

Relieved that the conversation had moved from the state of his hash-enhanced eyes, Roger replied,

'There's no rush to get back, Dad. Probably after four.'

'Well, we have a bowls competition that should finish at three, so we'll be back in time to see you off. There might be something good on the TV.'

'Right, Dad.'

Roger's paranoia level dropped but it would not stay that way for long.

The car rounded the corner into their street.

'Hullo. What's this? What are the police doing here?'

At the sound of his father's words, Roger sat bolt upright in his seat. Sure enough, dead ahead outside the house was a police car! His worst fears were confirmed! They were on to him for sure! Someone must have grassed on him! A fine for the possession of dangerous drugs! A criminal record! A PRISON SENTENCE! HE WAS BUSTED! RUINED!

He desperately tried to remain calm despite the cold sweat beginning to appear on his forehead. He wiped his hands nervously on his jeans and swallowed hard. He desperately hoped that country cops, inexperienced with drugs would not recognise his give-away red-rimmed eyes. But they were sure to search the van and the hash was still in his jacket pocket on the seat! Brian, beside him could sense what was going on, but there was little he could do.

John MacArthur pulled up the car in the drive and got out. Two uniformed policemen were checking out the van.

'Morning Donald. Everything alright?' asked John MacArthur cheerfully. He knew Constable Donald Finnegan from the club.

'Morning John, Just interested in this van. Is it yours?' Constable Finnegan directed his question at Roger.

His father answered the question for him.

'Yes, it is. This is my son Roger.'

'Would you have the registration papers for it?

As he spoke, the other officer inspected the exhaust and the back tyres.

'Um, yes, I think so. They're in the van. I'll just get them.'

Roger was lying through his back teeth. The papers were on his desk at college but it was the excuse he needed to get rid of the evidence. His shaking hands fumbled with the keys. Once inside, he located the tobacco, ripped it open, prised out the tiny capsule and pushed it lightly into the back pocket of his jeans.

Alighting from the van he announced to Constable Finnegan that he was mistaken, the papers were in Perth.

'That's a pity. You don't happen to know how old this van is do you?'

'Ah no, 'fraid not,' replied Roger, making his way towards Brian who had been standing apart from the proceedings.

Whilst the two policemen and his father were locked in conversation, Roger edged close to brother.

'Get rid of it!' he whispered, pressing the hash oil capsule into the boy's hand.

Brian looked down in horror at what he'd just been given. Drugs! His fingers quickly closed over the evidence. He looked up to find out if the two policemen had seen anything suspicious. They hadn't. He quietly turned on his heel. His mind was in a panic. Where was he to put it? What was he to do with it? Hide it? No, that was far too dangerous. By now he was out of sight behind the garage. Roger's words flashed through his mind...this is...hash oil...used as a medicine for over two thousand years...does not cause addiction...makes you relaxed...'

Then he had the answer. A stroke of genius. He swallowed it and strolled back casually to join his brother.

The two policemen had started to wander off down the drive with John MacArthur leaving Roger looking rather pale and shaken by the van.

'Yeah John,' said Constable Finnegan. 'Having looked at it, I am not convinced a van like that would suit my daughter. But you know what kids are like. Once they've set their heart on something...'

'Don't I know it! Roger just bought it off a mate of his because he liked the look of it and he had the money. He tells me it drives okay, just a bit slow on the hills and a bit heavy on fuel.

But he tells me they're pretty reliable and well, you don't want Jane in a Ferrari, do you?'

The policeman laughed. 'Bloody hell no! By the way, has your boy Roger got some kind of eye infection?'

By now the three of them had reached the police car parked at the front of the house.

'Yeah, his mother and I noticed it this morning. Must be some kind of conjunctivitis. Brian will have it next.'

'It's funny that it? Jane gets it from time to time too. She had it this weekend. She seems to get it every time she comes home from Perth,' said Constable Finnegan taking off his cap and getting into the car.

John MacArthur had an explanation.

'Must be a bug going around. Are you going to be at the Tennis Club wind-up party tonight?'

'Probably. You know the police mate. Always into a good piss-up if there's one on the go! Will you be there?'

'No. Mary and I are at the bowls this afternoon. Big competition against Albany so we won't be out tonight.' 'Good luck! See you around mate,' said Constable Finnegan as the police car wheeled around in a cloud of dust and cruised off into the distance.

As he started back up the drive, John MacArthur heard Roger distinctly whisper, 'You did WHAT?' But he knew he would never know the contents of that secret conversation as he looked up at his two youngest sons smiling angelically at him from the top of the driveway. He would never know about that and a lot more besides.

Whilst his parents grappled with the intricacies of the lawn of the Martinup Bowling Club against intense competition from their Albany rivals, Brian watched TV. It was an afternoon to remember. 'The Ten Commandments' followed by a Charlie Chaplin silent movie. Everything was in full colour and the sound was three dimensional. Every piece of dialogue, every image was full of meaning and totally unforgettable.

All the while, his brother chain-smoked muttering, 'Five joints worth, five joints worth!'

When Roger had departed, Mary discovered that Brian had indeed contracted his older brother's conjunctivitis and John discovered a huge patch of oil on his back lawn.

131

A New Day Dawns

Morning. Dawn on the Nullabor Plain. Trevor hauled himself upright on the front seat and grappled with the blankets that trapped his legs. He yawned and stretched then glanced at his mother still fast asleep under a pile of assorted bedclothes on the back seat. She'd driven for the best part of ten hours until almost at the point of total exhaustion, they'd pulled off the road at a lay-by somewhere short of the South Australian border. They shared the parking spot with two enormous trucks which had pulled up sometime during the night. Neither Mother nor Son had heard them.

Trevor rubbed his eyes and in the dim light tried to make out the time. It was 5.30 and dawn had not yet broken but the first rays of light were beginning to appear in the eastern sky.

Gently, he eased open the door handle. The inevitable noise it made still insufficient to arouse his mother. He paused for a second to look at her peaceful face framed by long wisps of light brown hair flecked here and there by touches of grey. Trevor had never thought of his mother as beautiful before. But she clearly was. She looked so peaceful and content. She was going home. And so was he in a way even though he'd never been there. The idea gave him a thrill of excitement. Time to explore.

He pushed the car door open enough to ease his legs out and rummaged on the floor for his shoes and socks. Then he pulled the rest of himself through the doorway and gently clicked the door shut. He stretched again and shivered. The desert air was chilly but he was prepared to brave it for a while in his jeans and T-shirt. This was totally new territory for him. Of course, he'd read about the famous Nullabor Plain but it was quite another thing again to be standing in the middle of it. Geography for real. The realisation of missing school added to the sense of adventure.

132

The Nullabor Plain, he mused to himself as he scanned the horizon. Sure enough, not a tree in sight as the name of this impressive geographical feature implied, just mile after mile of knee-high scrub.

Behind him was the long straight road west to Norseman, Kalgoorlie and ultimately Perth. Ahead was the long straight road east to Adelaide, Melbourne and eventually Sydney. He was only guessing as he became too tired to navigate accurately the previous night, but he reckoned that they were only a quarter of the way, if that.

The vastness of the island continent of his birth suddenly struck him. Communities of the same country lived here and there, enormous distances from each other, most of the members of each never meeting physically in their own lifetimes, yet all of them still claiming to belong to the same nation. How could it be that people in Sydney were the same as those in Perth? Or were they? Trevor began to realise that he was one of the privileged few to find out.

Indeed, the adventure was of greater significance the more he thought about it. Here he was, travelling to a world-famous city of a size he couldn't yet imagine. To get there, he had to experience the sheer vastness of the desert that makes up most of Australia. Then through the miles and miles of sheep and cattle stations, through wheat farms, vineyards, towns, cities, mining areas and industrial complexes, valleys, rivers, coastal roads and mountain ranges. Then one day they would get to Sydney. He hoped. But so far, so good.

Trying not to disturb the total silence, Trevor walked slowly away from the car, past the trucks and their sleeping drivers, off the road and into the scrub. From the desert floor, he watched the sun come up.

It rose as a great ball of light, directly over the road to the east, forming as it did so a surreal image the like of which he had never seen before. A blood-red ball was emerging vertically from a black horizontal line against a background of graduated colours running from fiery yellow to warm turquoise.

Trevor stood transfixed. This was nature reduced to total awesome abstract simplicity. And he was the only observer of this wonderful event. In the complete silence of the desert, he drank in the tranquillity of those precious moments.

Then in the distance far behind him, the sound of a vehicle could be heard approaching. Turning, he could just make out the pin-pricks of head lights through the gloom. It would take another ten minutes before the vehicle roared past him in a cloud of fine pebbles and dust. He watched its tail-lights being swallowed up in the glare of the newly-risen sun.

'Asseyez-vous s'il vous plait!'

Brian had been having a bad morning. The test results had come back from "fart breath" MacDuff. Brian couldn't believe it. He'd failed algebra 35%! It was little consolation to him that a lot of others had failed too. Trevor hadn't. He'd got 74% but that was immaterial now because he was gone. Perhaps that was the real cause of Brian's depression, but he wasn't prepared to admit it. But even Miss Marceaux inadvertently reminded him of his best friend's departure.

'Where's Trevor?' she asked, making to hand back his test paper to an empty seat.

Then she remembered.

'Oh of course, he's gone to Sydney, hasn't he?'

'What did he get miss? He'll want to know and I'll be writing to him soon.'

She paused a moment then decided it was a fair request.

'You can tell him he got 68% Brian. A bit better than you I'm afraid,' she said handing Brian his paper.

Brian turned it over and groaned 35%! Again! Twice in one day and he'd never failed anything before.

He was so lost in despair that he failed to notice the class had already started. The rest of them already hard at work and he didn't have a clue what he supposed to be doing. Meekly he put his hand up to ask, trying not to sound too pathetic.

'Good morning, Father!'

Father O'Neill glanced up from the letterbox where he was fumbling for his mail.

'Oh, good morning Mrs…ah Mrs Clancy.'

The priest looked a little distracted as he rapidly sorted his mail.

'Fine day again for this time of year, Father?'

'Yes, yes indeed, Mrs Clancy I'm sorry, you must excuse me. I've got some urgent business to attend to, I'll see you later.'

His next-door neighbour watched the black figure of the priest scurrying up the drive and wondered why he was acting a little strange. He was usually bubbling over with conversation.

Father O'Neill burst through the back door and dropped the pile of mail on the table except for one letter. He knew the seal on the front. It was from the bishop. This was the communication he'd been dreading. He drew a deep breath and opened it. Wondering aimlessly around the kitchen, he read its contents. His worst fears were confirmed. He was to meet with the Bishop in a week's time and furthermore, he was to bring with him all financial documentation related to the parish for the last ten years! He was facing an actuarial inquisition!

The priest put the letter gently down on the table, his hands clenching and unclenching involuntarily.

'Shit!' he said through his teeth.

Brian made the long journey home alone. He'd had a rotten day. Apart from his two failures, an English test had been announced for Thursday which was when a Social Studies assignment was due in and Mr Newton had suddenly informed the class they could expect a test on "Magnetism" on Friday. It was all getting too much for him. How was he supposed to cope with all this stuff? At least when Trevor was around, they could joke about the absurdities of life at the high school, the hopeless teachers and the bullies. And they could help each other out with tests and assignments. Brian was good at English and written things while Trevor was better at Science and Maths. They made a good team.

He passed by Trevor's house the "For Sale" sign flapping forlornly in the wind. He was inclined to feel sorry for himself, to relive a thousand incidents from times gone by. Then he changed his mind. There was nothing to be gained by living in the past, he decided and sped down the hill for home.

Mary MacArthur knew there was something wrong the minute her youngest son appeared in the kitchen.

She guessed a possible reason for his melancholia.

'Tea Brian?'

'Yes, please Mum.'

'Are things getting you down a bit Brian?' she asked, taking the tea caddy down from the shelf.

Brian nodded.

'Did you get your result from the Maths test?'

'Uh huh.'

'And'

'35%'

'And what about French? You had a test in that too didn't you?'

'Uh huh.'

She looked at him quizzically. He grudgingly divulged the result.

'35%'

Mary knew that the heart of the matter had still not been reached but she saw a way in which Brian could come to terms with things.

She poured him his tea then poured a cup for herself and sat down opposite him.

Brian, you know I trained to be an accountant like your father, but decided one accountant in the family was enough, don't you?'

He nodded and she continued,

'Then of course your oldest brother decides that's what he wants to do!' She laughed then got to the point.

'What you don't know is that I failed some important exams in my first year. I was devastated. I thought, *I'll never be able to do this subject. It's too hard for me. I should never have taken this course. I should just give up now.* Then a friend gave me some important advice. The best advice I could ever get. Love your subject, even if it's horrible, change the way you think about it. Pretend that it's the most wonderful, fascinating thing in the world. Convince yourself it's true. Why not? Other people think that way about it! Why not you? So anyway, I followed the advice. I got stuck into the study. I forced myself to enjoy every minute of it. I made myself believe that double ledger accounts were the most exciting thing in the world. It worked. I passed. In fact, although he doesn't want it known, I got better marks than your father! I should be the accountant around here!'

'Really Mum? Is that true?

She smiled and sipped her tea. What she hadn't told Brian was that her mother had died in that year and study had helped her come to terms with the grief of the loss. Furthermore, it was her own father who had given the advice.

Brian rose from the table.

'Mum, I'll get some wood chopped and then I'm going for a walk in the bush okay?'

'Of course, son. Then after tea you've got homework I suppose?

'Yeah, a bit.'

Mary smiled. He'd forgotten about the TV. She had already made mental rules for herself and her husband.

That addictive one-eyed monster in the lounge room had to be curtailed.

A half an hour later, Brian was alone in the bush. It didn't look so weird and wild any more. In fact, he felt quite at home. The further he walked, the more he thought. So, he failed, he reasoned. So what? Maybe he just wasn't any good at French. What did he need French for anyway? Or Algebra? Mr MacDuff was a crap teacher anyway. But that was just the point wasn't it? Other people passed. So could he. Why not? What he needed to do was take his mother's advice. Become enthusiastic. Make these things become enjoyable, He could do that. That was what he was at school for wasn't it? It could be a load of fun. Why not?

Brian's mind was made up. He was going to hit the books in a big way. He was going to study, study, study. He wanted to be really, really, really good. No way would he fail another exam. If others could do it, then so could he. With that affirmation, he turned on his heels and headed for home.

The banging on Roger's door nearly made him fall off his seat. All was otherwise quiet at the College. Scattered throughout dark blocks of buildings, lighted windows showed the presence of students of law, commerce, science, arts and medicine wading through the seemingly endless paperwork of their courses.

'Hang on a minute! I'm just coming!' he called as he uncoiled himself from the narrow desk heaving with half-open books and piles of lecture notes. He navigated his way over the floor, an obstacle course of discarded clothing and half-finished essays.

'Oh, it's you Suzie,' he said to her with a smile through the half-open door. He gave her a quick kiss and motioned her in warning her of the mess.

'Thanks Roger,' she said as she navigated the assault course on the floor to the bed while he found his way back to the chair.

'What can I do for you?' he asked, leaning back in his seat, his face half-framed in the light from the desk lamp.

Suzie pulled the long-tangled mass of red hair away from her face and rummaged in the pocket of her well-worn overalls, the bulk of which exaggerated an otherwise slight figure. She retrieved a crumpled tobacco pouch and pulled out a packet of cigarette papers.

'I was wondering if you could take a group of us to the demo tomorrow in your van.'

Roger had completely forgotten the Vietnam war protest march in the city he'd casually agreed to attend. That was two weeks ago and a lot had happened since then.

He breathed a heavy sigh. 'I'm sorry Suzie. I've got to give an anthropology tutorial tomorrow. Not only that, I've got two history essays to hand in by Friday and an English assignment that's overdue by a week. I'm way behind with my work. What about you? How's the thesis going?'

She concentrated on rolling the cigarette.

'Oh, it's going okay. My supervisor is away up north on a field trip, so there's no rush.'

'Well, I'm afraid I'm just a humble first-year student Suzie.'

'So, are you coming to the demo tomorrow?'

'Suzie, you're not listening to me. I can't. I'm too busy.'

Suzie fell silent. She gazed around the cluttered room, the walls adorned with posters: a burning American flag, "*Ché Guevarra's*" far-away look, Kitchener's pointing finger. She blew a stream of smoke into the room.

Roger turned back to his essay, but he couldn't concentrate.

'Have you got an ashtray, Roger?'

He fumbled around his desk and reached over to the bed with it. Deciding that he might as well join what he couldn't beat, he started to roll a cigarette himself.

Suzie studied her sandals and toyed with one of the silver bracelets around her wrist.

'I've started yoga classes,' she said casually.

'Oh?' said Roger, his mind still half engaged with examples of patrilineal societies.

'He's a gorgeous guy.'

'Ananda.'

'Sorry?'

'Ananda Vishwanath. He is taking the yoga classes. Says my technique is pretty good for a beginner. Do you want to come along to the class?'

'Not really Suzie. Yoga's not my scene.'

'That's a pity. Will you be coming to the CND meeting on Friday?'

Roger inhaled deeply on his cigarette and paused. He exhaled the smoke as he replied,

'Suzie, I'm not getting through to you, am I? I'm behind in my work. I can't afford the time. In fact, I should be working right now.'

'Roger, I thought you were committed to this. It's important!'

Roger's patience was at an end.

'Yes, it's important. Yes, I am committed to it. But this...' his hand swept over the crowded desk...comes first. I'm sorry Suzie.'

'That's okay,' she said quietly, her bracelets jangling as she butted out the cigarette.

'Well, I'll be off then.'

He saw her to the door and made to give her a parting kiss, but she was gone. A muted 'Bye' floated up the stairwell over the clatter of descending sandals. He closed the door firmly and with his back against it, let out a deep sigh.

'Brian! There's a program about dinosaurs on the TV!'

Mary MacArthur put her head around her son's door. Brian looked up from the narrow desk crowded with paper and books.

'Are you still doing your homework?'

Brian leaned back in his chair and rubbed his eyes.

'Yes Mum. What time is it?'

'It's after nine o'clock. Do you want to see this program?'

He stretched and yawned, covering his mouth with his forearm as he did so.

'Not just now Mum. There's still some things I need to do for science and I'm supposed to read part of this novel for English.' He held up a dog-eared copy of "*Kidnapped*" for the benefit of his mother standing behind him.

She took it from him.

'I read this when I was at school,' she said as she flicked through the pages.

'I think you'll enjoy it.'

She gently balanced the paperback on the overcrowded desk.

'Anyway, I'll let you get on with it, but don't stay up too late. You need your sleep too you know.'

'Yes Mum,' he mumbled, his attention now drawn to a diagram of an electromagnet which he figured should be easy enough to make.

Mary smiled to herself as she made her way back to the lounge room and its flickering blue light.

'He's not still doing his homework is he? Can't think what's got into the lad,' said John MacArthur glancing up.

'He's obviously not missing Trevor then. He mused and turned his attention back to the screen.

It was just after a quarter past eight in the morning when Paul Newton closed the laboratory door. He had spent the last half hour preparing magnetic and non-magnetic materials for the first years to test, bottles of iodine for the second years to spill over each other, film strips for his two third year classes to enjoy and reading material to enthral the fourth years. And he still had time in a free period at the start of the day to make up the magnetism test for next week. At last he was feeling really on top of things.

He whistled quietly to himself as he made his way through the still largely deserted walkways and corridors of the school to the staffroom, his usual early morning ritual. There were always absentee notes, pamphlets, announcements and documents of all sorts in relation to his classes that needed to be collected and dealt with first thing every day.

With his mind still lingering on Michelle and a glorious weekend, he waved a greeting to the lone figure of Brian MacArthur sitting on the bench outside Room Ten, but the lad didn't notice. His nose was buried in a book.

The staff room too was almost deserted, save for a handful of cleaning ladies and a solitary Home Science teacher he didn't know too well. They nodded and smiled at his greeting.

As he leafed through the wad of paper, he had just retrieved from his pigeon hole, he became aware of a presence beside him and the aroma of a familiar perfume.

'Hullo Michelle! I didn't see you there.'

'Paul,' she whispered moving closer to him.

'Did you hear about Charlie MacDuff? Her eyes darted around the room but it was clear there was no one in earshot.

'He's gone!'

'Gone? What do you mean gone? Gone where?'

'Who knows? But I know who he's gone with. Alison MacDonald.'

'What, Alison MacDonald from the primary school, the friend of your flatmate Maria?'

'That's the one. Maria told me last night that Alison and Charlie have been having an affair since the beginning of term. Charlie's wife found out over the weekend and now they've both done a runner.'

'So, it was him we saw on the beach! But Charlie MacDuff? Having an affair? With Alison MacDonald?

'What he must be, what, in his fifties? And she can't be more than…!

'Twenty-two,' offered Michelle. 'That's what struck me too. She's far too old for him.'

It took Paul a second integrate that one and he tried hard to control his mirth.

'Very cruel Michelle!'

Bloody true though,' smiled Michelle sorting through her paper work. 'The primary school's doing well isn't it? Two members of staff doing a runner in one year.' She was going to add that at least the high school had lost only half a staff member, but contented herself with.

'Why anyone in their right mind would fancy Charlie MacDuff is beyond me.'

Paul had found something.

'Well, well.' 'Would Mr Newton please take Mr MacDuff's first year mathematics class room six period one?' he read out from the yellow slip of paper.

'And guess what I've got, period four.' Michelle waved another yellow slip.

'Hey Brian! Have a look at this!'

Brian wandered over to the cluster of boys. Michael O'Sullivan was holding court with an unusual object.

'Bet you can't guess what it is,' he gloated, passing it around for inspection.

'It's a little metal saucer,' volunteered Kevin Shearer, turning the thin, smooth disc over in his hand.

Michael O'Sullivan shook his head. Roger Sutherland examined it and suggested a large medal that had the surface rubbed down.

'No,' smiled the owner confidently.

Brian took it, but could offer no explanation at all.

'You'll never guess,' smirked Michael O'Sullivan, 'so I might as well tell you. It's a penny or at least it was a penny. I put it on the track and that's what you get after a train's run over it.'

The siren sounded for period one.

'You can keep it if you like Brian. I've got plenty at home.'

'Thanks, Mike. I might try that myself.' Brian shoved the strange disc in his pocket, grabbed his books and joined the throng heading for Mr MacDuff's maths class.

Paul faced the two lines of familiar faces outside room six. He waited for the whispering babble of obvious questions to die down. The devil in him longed to announce the truth.

Ladies and Gentlemen, I regret to inform you that your regular teacher has been having an affair with a woman half his age and has run away. Don't be alarmed. Things like this happen sometimes.

He bit his lip. Michelle was a bad influence.

'Girls, come in quietly...OK boys.' They trooped in, still muttering and gossiping.

Paul followed, composing himself. He kept it diplomatically simple, standing in front of the class to announce.

'Mr MacDuff is not here today, so lucky you, you've got me. In fact, you've got me for two periods in a row haven't you?'

He took the audible groan as a compliment and began searching through Charlie MacDuff's desk for clues as to what had been going on.

By the end of the period, to Brian's amazement, Mr Newton's ad hoc lesson in algebra made sense. A spark of self-belief re-ignited inside the boy.

'Roger! What you doing here?'

Suzie, dressed in her trademark overalls but now sporting a pair of heavy leather boots and a thick woollen hat opened the door. She seemed pleased to see him.

'I've changed my mind. I'm coming to the demo.'

'That's brilliant!' She gave him a spontaneous hug.

'That's really excellent!'

'Suzie,' he said gently taking her arms from his neck, 'I want to make it clear that I can't be involved in this to the same extent that you are. If I'm to get into Law, I need a good pass this year. So today is a one-off, right?

'Sure, sure,' she said, then added eagerly, 'So we can use the van?'

'Yes, I'll drive the van for you.'

'Brilliant! I'll round up the rest of them. We'll meet in the car park in about twenty minutes. Okay?'

'Okay.'

Roger trotted down the stairs while Suzie scurried off down the corridor in the opposite direction. As he wandered through the grass still wet with the early morning dew towards the car park next door dominated by the presence of the campervan, Roger reflected on his late-night decision to attend the demonstration. Could he afford the time to be doing this? Why was he doing it? Sure, he didn't believe in the War. Someone had to make a stand, someone had to protest against something that was clearly wrong.

But it was really because of Suzie that he was now standing in the cold. Was he in love with her or was he deeply infatuated by someone who was so different, so inspirational, so educational compared to anyone else he'd ever met? He'd learnt far more from her about real issues than anything his lecturers and professors could offer. And what about her? Did she love him? Or was she just using him?

His thoughts were interrupted by the tramping of feet behind him.

'Roger!' called out Suzie leading the ragged group of placard-carrying hippies across the car park.

'Roger, this is Marion, Archie, George, Phil and Marco.'

Roger struggled to catch each name as they were called out. George stood out, literally. He was a giant of a man in jeans and a heavy black woollen sweater and his handshake caused Roger some discomfort. Marco too was distinctive for his stature. A tiny man with the dark complexion of Southern Italy, his "*mafioso-like*" appearance enhanced by dark sun glasses.

143

What they all had in common was hair. Lots of it. Frizzie halos, shaggy manes, pony-tails and shoulder length tresses. The placards they all carried, hastily constructed from pieces of pine, cardboard and felt-tip pens bore the usual slogans like, TROOPS OUT NOW! and STOP THE WAR!

Suzie stepped towards him.

'I've got one for you too Roger,' she said handing him a placard saying, "YANKS ARE PIGS!" Roger pondered this provocative statement about the true nature of Americans but put it in the back of the van anyway. After all, it was a protest.

'Right. Everyone in!' He pulled back the passenger door. They piled in one a time, beads jangling and placards clashing. When George had wedged finally himself in and Suzie had ensconced herself in the front passenger seat as navigator, Roger pulled the door to and clambered in to the driver's seat.

The van's engine roared into life and the campervan trundled out of the car park and up towards the university. Approaching the lights at Winthrop Hall, Roger indicated left.

'NO! RIGHT!' screamed Suzie over the noise of the engine.

The driver deftly hauled the van over from the wrong lane narrowly avoiding a collision in the process and set the van on the navigator's course.

'I thought the demo was in the city! we're going the wrong way!'

'The official demo's in the city. We're going to the unofficial one in Fremantle.'

'so, the police don't know about it?'

'NOT YET!' she shouted with a laugh.

'BUT THAT MAKES IT AN ILLEGAL MARCH DOESN'T IT?'

'SO WHAT? THE WHOLE BLOODY WAR IS ILLEGAL ISN'T IT?'

'HOW MANY ARE GONG TO BE THERE?'

'AT LEAST A HUNDRED, MAYBE MORE.'

Roger fell silent, concentrating on driving the sluggish van through the hectic traffic of Stirling highway and trying to ignore the choruses of "We Shall Overcome" that had started in the back.

'SO, WHERE IS THE MARCH GONG TO?' he asked without taking his eyes off the road.

'TO THE WAR MEMORIAL OF COURSE! I MEAN IT IS THEIR BIG DAY, ISN'T IT?'

Roger paused trying to think what she meant by "Big day"?' Then he remembered the date. April 25. Anzac Day. The national day of commemoration for the war dead.

HA! WE'LL SHOW THOSE WAR-LOVING PIGS WHAT WE THINK! IS PERFECT! THE PEOPLE RISING UP AGAINST IMPERIALIST BASTARDS! WE'LL SHOW THEM WON'T WE GUYS?'

A cheer went up from the back, but Roger didn't hear it. He was staring dead ahead. His mouth had suddenly gone very dry and a deep feeling of foreboding was welling up him.

The Divine Miss Henderson

Fremantle, the sleepy sea-port of Perth kept itself to pretty much to itself and like ports of cities the world over clung tenaciously to its separate identity. Its reputation after the war as a heavy-drinking town had waned as the merchant seamen calling in at the harbour diminished but the old two-storey pubs with their ornate cast-iron balustrades remained. The US Navy was a frequent visitor, the warships bringing much-needed business. The American sailors were generally welcomed as comrades-in-arms in the fight against communism that raged far to the north. The town also boasted the State's biggest branch of the RSL, the Returned Servicemen's League. Most of them were now attending the eleven o'clock Anzac Day service at the town's war memorial.

'PARK VAN OVER THERE ROGER!' Suzie indicated a spot at the top of Queen Street.

'IS THIS WHERE MARCH STARTS FROM?' he asked as the campervan edged into the kerb.

'NO, BUT IT'S NOT FAR. THERE'S A RALLY FIRST AT THE TOWN HALL. EVERYONE OUT!'

They tumbled out the door in good spirits, sharing anecdotes of previous demonstrations. Roger, it seemed was the only one with reservations about this particular march, but he didn't show it. To him it was the height of folly to hold an anti-war protest in the centre of arch-conservative Fremantle on Anzac Day, but what the hell? He consoled himself with the thought of only being young once and trotted off after them armed with his "YANKS ARE PIGS" banner.

It was not long before other long-haired placard-bearing demonstrators joined them, overtaking from behind and trickling in from side alleys. They were late and along Adelaide Street was evidence of those who had arrived before them. Buses, vans, motorbikes and scooters with psychedelic livery and "BAN THE BOMB" slogans lined the pavement. Already the invaders were experiencing the displeasure of the handful of locals not attending the commemoration service. Old women turned away in disgust, young men suggested loudly that they all should get a haircut or a job or both while old men just stood and stared. The protesters ignored them all and pressed on eagerly towards the town hall where snatches of a megaphone-enhanced voice punctuated by wild cheering could be heard.

'Hurry up Roger! The speeches are always brilliant!' Roger duly increased his walking pace to keep up with Suzie who was ahead of him pushing her way through the crowd.

Fremantle town hall towered above in snow-white ornate grandeur providing a curious contrast to the tattered, scruffy, multi-coloured rabble gathered at its steps.

From a limestone wall enclosing a modest garden at the front of the building, a protestor harangued the crowd with his megaphone. Suzie strained on tip toes to see him. Roger, being much taller had a better view of the fiery orator. Clad in an ankle-length Afghan coat that swirled around him as he spoke, he glared at the crowd through orange-tinted round wire spectacles. His habit of sweeping the megaphone in all directions to cover his audience had the unfortunate effect of making only every fourth or fifth word comprehensible.

'AMERICA...FORCED...ILLEGAL...PEOPLE   OF VIET...FREMANTLE...NOT SUPPORT...' he bellowed.

Roger, Suzie and the rest applauded anyway. He was preaching to the converted. At the end of his tirade he grinned, obviously pleased with his efforts, then launched himself dracula-like to the ground and handed the megaphone over to another activist of similar appearance who seemed to be in charge of the march.

His words however, were drowned out by the eruption of spontaneous shouting and cheering. The crowd had taken on a life of its own. It began to move along the High Street, taking Roger and Suzie with it. Roger, on the edge of the surge, glanced back and could see Phil and Marion crowded in behind him and could just make out occasionally the diminutive figure of Marco. Of "Big" George and Archie there was no sign. He shouted to his companions and they returned a thumbs up. Roger tried to guess at the size of the multitude. It was certainly more than Suzie's anticipated one hundred. The figure was at least twice or even three times that, spreading across the High Street, a human torrent carrying everything before it. Oncoming cars had no alternative but to dive for the pavement or be caught, stranded like islands in the flood of tramping bodies who were beginning to make themselves heard.

Chants started in sections of the crowd. Typically, 'TWO-FOUR-SIX-EIGHT-WE-ARE-NOT-A-PUPPET-STATE!' alternating with, 'ONE-TWO-THREE-FOUR-WHAT-THE-HELL-ARE-WE-FIGHTING-FOR?'

and from time to time for variety, a colourful alternative to 'hell' was shouted. Roger found it difficult not to accidently step on the sandals of the marcher in front and was frequently clipped by a "PEACE NOW!" banner behind him. Suzie had her own chanting agenda of "TROOPS OUT!" which occasionally caught on in the immediate neighbourhood until something more acoustically attractive presented itself.

The marchers then faced their first opposition. Ahead was a police car straddling the road. The lone officer called to the advancing mob that the march was illegal and that they were to disperse immediately. The protesters were in no mood to listen. They surged past the car with the policeman trapped inside frantically radioing for help.

The lone patrolman was not yet aware that support was almost in position. At the top of the High Street just three hundred yards away, fifty policemen in riot gear were hastily forming up in two ranks. In assistance, were two mounted officers diverted from duty at the nearby on-going memorial service, the march's destination.

Roger had just passed the stranded police car when he heard the sound of breaking glass. Looking back, he caught a glimpse of the shattered windscreen and a protester jumping on the bonnet of the patrol car while the policeman cowered helplessly inside the stricken vehicle.

Events started to move quicker. The mood of the crowd suddenly switched from joviality and good humour to anger and fear. The chanting became sporadic. The pace of the march increased but the marchers were no longer in step.

Television cameras in position for the memorial service swung round to catch a breaking news story.

A bottle shattered on the pavement beside Roger. More missiles followed coming from the right along with screams of abuse from those who had been attending the memorial service but who had now broken away to confront the outrage that violated their sacred ceremony. They vaulted the wall surrounding the memorial, first a couple then crowds of angry men in suits with medals on their chests and hatred in their faces. Screaming abuse, they ran straight at the oncoming march.

Violent scuffles broke out on the right flank and demonstrators were hurled to the ground in the fury of the onslaught. A stone, the size of a man's fist caught Suzie a glancing blow on the head. She collapsed. Roger stood over her against the crush of bodies that came from all sides. Screams and yells of pain and abuse filled the air. Panic spread like wild-fire through the front ranks of the demonstrators.

Seeing the attack on the march by the ex-servicemen and fearing an all-out blood bath, the order was given to send in the mounted officers. The first police horse cut a clean swathe through the right flank of the march. Women screamed and men tried to protect themselves from the wheeling beast with its flying iron-shod hooves and its truncheon-wielding rider in their midst. The second mounted officer was not so fortunate. His animal reared up hurling the unfortunate rider to the bitumen with a sickening thump. The policeman lay still on the road while his mount kicked and reared about him. All the while Roger struggled to keep the panicking crowds and now a crazed horse away from his stricken girlfriend.

The police ranks following at the double, behind the horses clashed with the disintegrating front line of the march and drove straight through it causing a crush in the middle ranks of the demonstrators. Anyone attempting resistance was immediately hurled to the ground, arrested and handcuffed. The scuffles between the servicemen and protesters were quickly broken up by the police but the fury of the restrained ex-servicemen remained unabated. What had been a protest march was now a complete riot. The demonstrators progressively panicked throughout the length of the march, dropping their banners and falling over each other in the race to flee back up the High Street. Sirens sounded in the distance.

All the while the TV cameras from their vantage point on the war memorial caught the best of the action. Roger saw a fleeting window of opportunity. A break in the crowd gave him the chance to pick Suzie up.

Phil and Marco were still behind him protecting Marion who had been hit in the arm by a bottle.

'Let's get outta here!' he screamed at Phil and with Suzie on his shoulders and his companions bringing up the rear, he sprinted down a side-street leaving the mayhem behind.

It was still a good half mile to where the van was parked and Suzie's weight on Roger's shoulders was soon beginning to tell. She began to stir.

'Roger,' she mumbled. 'Put me down or else I'm going to throw up all over you.'

He gently lowered her to the ground. Phil caught up with them with Marco and Marion just behind.

'Let me have a look at her,' he said. 'I'm a medical student.'

'No time for that now!' urged Roger. 'Run for it!'

In the street behind them, the battle raged. The police had broken up the march but had not quelled the conflict between demonstrators and ex-servicemen. No sooner had Roger spoken when a group of men at the end of the street spotted them and gave chase.

'Come on!' Although still groggy, Suzie managed to half run, half stumble, dragged along by Phil on one arm and Roger on the other.

After an eternity, the van appeared in front of them. Roger bundled them into the back without ceremony.

'Where's George and Archie?' shouted Marion.

'Don't know! They're big enough to look after themselves!' Roger shouted back hurling himself into the driver's seat. The van roared into life and Roger swung it around. Something clattered into the side of the vehicle and bounced off onto the street. Roger glanced in the wing mirror to see an angry group of men, fists waving in anger receding into the distance.

As the van pulled into Stirling Highway, two police cars and an ambulance with lights flashing and sirens wailing shot past them in the opposite direction.

Roger concentrated only on getting as far away from Fremantle as he could but by the time the van passed through Claremont, shock set in. His hands, although gripping the wheel till his knuckles were white started to shake involuntarily and beads of sweat appeared on his ashen features.

The tranquillity of the college car park was restored when Roger turned off the engine and assisted in the disembarkation of the walking wounded. Suzie looked pale but Phil was reassuring in his appraisal of her condition. She should be fine but if nausea or headaches set in, that was a different matter and she'd need to go to hospital. Marion, assisted from the van by Marco, seemed to have come through with cuts and bruises.

Looking pale and exhausted, they all decided to go their separate ways.

Suzie looked at Roger. She gave him a big grin and an enormous hug. 'You're a hero!' she whispered in his ear.

'Bloody hell! Mary! Quick! Come and look at this!'

Mary MacArthur hurried down the corridor to see what was upsetting her husband. Brian was in his room absorbed with schoolwork and didn't hear the commotion.

It was the seven o'clock news. The newsreader droned on from the pages he held in front of him, occasionally looking at his imaginary audience.

'...thirteen demonstrators were arrested in Fremantle and will appear...'

'What's going on?'

'...able to bring you pictures of the demonstration in Fremantle...'

'Would you believe that these anti-war protestors marched on the Anzac Day services? I mean, would you believe it?' John MacArthur was so intent at conveying his outrage to his wife that he took his eye off the screen and almost missed the interesting bit.

'Isn't that Roger?' asked Mary in alarm.

Sure enough, the unmistakable form of their son could be seen lifting Suzie onto his shoulders amid the mayhem of battle.

Roger stared glumly at the TV scenes of the Fremantle riot. He saw himself on the small screen and although he looked like a hero, he was as frightened as the rest of them. The TV room was almost empty apart from a handful of Asian students who took time off their studies every evening to catch the news. Most of the other students had taken advantage of the Anzac Day holiday leaving the college even quieter that night than usual.

The telephone outside the room shattered the silence. As was the custom, Roger, being the most junior student in the room answered it. It was his father. Periodically holding the phone away from his ear, Roger participated in a rather one-way conversation.

'Yes, Dad.'

'Yes, I know Dad.'

'No Dad, but…'

'Yes, Dad.'

'OK, Dad.'

'OK, Bye Dad.'

Roger gloomily returned to the TV room in time to catch a graphic shot of George and Archie being pinned to the ground by two burly policemen.

'It's from Roger,' said Mary ripping open the envelope.

'Well, what's he saying?' grunted John MacArthur from his bowl of porridge.

Mary quickly scanned the lines.

He says he understands why we were upset and admits that in hindsight it was a mistake to demonstrate against the Vietnam war on Anzac Day.'

'Humph!' was John MacArthurs monosyllabic comment to his breakfast.

Mary went on, 'He says he's had a couple of poor results on his assignments but he's determined to put in a better effort. And…he's asking if it's alright to come down in the August holidays so that we can meet his new girlfriend Suzie. 'Oh, that's nice. Excellent!' exclaimed Brian eager to be re-united with his favourite brother in just a few short months. 'Well as long as he doesn't park that bloody oil-can on my lawn again. I've had to dig the whole bloody lot up and he'd better not start protesting around here, I'm telling you,'

Mary smiled at her youngest son. At least he wasn't getting into trouble. But Brian didn't notice his mother's attention or his father's tirade. He was too busy bolting down his breakfast, eager to get to school. Mr Newton's magnetism test was on that morning and he was ready for it. In fact, he was really enjoying most of his studies. Only one cloud lay on the horizon. Maths, now by far his worst subject, double period of it first up and to make matters worse, a new teacher no one had seen yet. Mathematics. Even the very sound of the word conjured up images of the evil-smelling MacDuff. He shuddered at the thought.

'Good morning everyone. I'm Miss Henderson. I'll be taking you for maths from now on.'

Brian's jaw dropped as his interest in mathematics immediately soared. It was nothing to do with a sudden discovery of the exquisite intrinsic qualities of the subject, its rigorous logic or the elegance of a well-turned argument. Nor was it the instantaneous appreciation of the perfect simplicity of a right answer or a wrong one.

It was Miss Henderson. She was…beautiful.

He sat spellbound, hanging on every word while the properties of the number line and the uses of algebraic equalities and inequalities were explained by the voice of an angel. Light and reason flooded through the turbid explanations left by "fart breath" MacDuff, becoming a distant nasty memory.

So overawed was he by this divine creature with the long golden hair that whatever she asked him to do, he did it with passion in double quick time. If she needed an answer, he was first to give it, sensible or not and he basked in the warmth of her praises if his earnest reply fell into the former category and reddened with embarrassment if it did not. If there were books that needed to be handed out or collected, Brian was the first to volunteer. Exercises to be completed? No problem. Brian was always first to finish. Homework from last night? Here's mine Miss Henderson,' he'd say handing it over with the enthusiasm of a retriever dropping a stick.

As the weeks passed, Brian became a star in Miss Henderson's maths class. When his new teacher commented in the staffroom on the performance of the little lad who sat alone at the front, Paul Newton said that he too had noted a distinct improvement in young MacArthur. Michelle Marceaux concurred. The lad had definitely come on leaps and bounds recently.

But a thirteen-year-old boy can only be diverted by the delights of academia for so long. One overcast and dull July afternoon, Brian was packing his school bag at the end of a long day in which he had demolished Mr Newton's chemistry test and succeeded in translating an obscure French poem from Miss Marceaux which the rest of the class couldn't do. His hand fell on an unusual object at the bottom of the bag. He wrenched it out from beneath the stack of books. It was Michael O'Sullivan's train-flattened penny. Turning it over in the palm of his hand a glint came to his eye. Why not? he thought and with a grin shoved it into his shirt pocket.

At home, he told his mother over a cup of tea of another easy test, of the strange French poem he'd mastered and of course gave her the usual eulogy about mathematics and a certain teacher.

Mary was becoming seriously impressed with her youngest son. In just a few months he had acquired maturity beyond his years. He was so cheerful these days and so willing to express himself. What a difference from the taciturn youngster at the start of the year! High school was clearly doing him some good. The boy was really growing up she thought to herself as Brian shouted through the back door that he was just going for a ride on his bike and would be back in time for tea.

Brian headed through the bush towards the railway line. Trevor and he had been there before to watch the trains thundering by but being at least a mile away from home, it was not a place he frequented.

The heavy skies cast a gloom over the bush. He passed through a deserted clearing which served as a car park and apparently a meeting place for local lovers (according to Trevor at least), but Brian's objective was further on through the bush.

The rough path took him out of the bush and on to an earthen embankment. He dropped the bike at the foot of it and scrambled to the top. Below him lay the railway tracks. He looked at his watch. The train from Perth was due into Martinup at 4:15. He had ten minutes. He drew out the strange disc from his shirt pocket. So, this was what a train did to a penny. Fumbling in his trouser pocket Brian found his test piece and dragged it out. A brand new twenty cent piece. Scrambling down the embankment, he placed the coin squarely on one track then retreated behind the brow of the hill to wait.

At precisely 4:13 the track started to rumble and a piercing whistle announced the arrival of the train from Perth. As soon as the clattering carriages had cleared leaving a sudden eerie silence, Brian was clambering down to see the result of the experiment.

It didn't take him long to find it. The silver coin had been enlarged to a disc nearly three times the original size. It worked! Pleased with his effort, he stuffed it away in his pocket. A bolt with a rusty nut encrusted to it lying beside the track caught his eye. What would a train do to that? he wondered. There was only one way to find out. Brian delicately balanced the ancient piece of ironmongery on the rail then clambered back up the hill.

He didn't notice that a car had pulled into the car park, some fifty yards away through the bush. If he had, he might have recognised Mr Newton's distinctive vehicle. Paul and Michelle were in deep conversation. They often came to this secluded spot for peace and privacy after school, safe from the prying eyes and gossip of Martinup. Paul suddenly fell silent and his face took on a far-away look.

'What is it Paul?'

Paul Newton was a sincere man but intimate speeches were not his forte. Momentarily lost for words, he eventually managed,

'Michelle, I've got something important I want to say...no wait...I've got something for you...'

He fumbled in the breast pocket of his jacket.

'...I mean...I'd like you to have this...' he said handing her a small black box.

She opened it. The diamonds on the gold ring inside sparkled against the black velvet lining even in the gloomy light inside the car.

Brian's attention was caught by an unusual sound coming from the track, a sort of a hum that was getting progressively louder. It sounded nothing like a train. He peered over the embankment. Indeed, it was not a train. Approaching twenty-five miles an hour, top speed for its diesel engine, was a one-man track inspection vehicle. Brian recognised the driver. It was Barry Dawson, a young man the same age as Roger who had left school early to join the railway. As he gazed around the bush that lined the track, he was blithely unaware of what was about to happen. Impact with the unseen object on the line up ahead was just seconds away.

The front wheel of the rail car made contact with the bolt and flew into the air. The rest of the vehicle followed, part of it plunging sideways off the track in a cloud of granite chips and dust, hurling the driver into a grass-filled ditch. The car banged, shuddered and screeched to a halt in a shower of sparks, the back half straddling the tracks, the front wheels firmly embedded in the granite chips alongside. The engine coughed then stalled.

A horrified spectator made a run for it.

'Will you marry me Michelle?'

'Yes, Paul, of course I will.'

'What the hell was that?'

'I don't know. It came from the railway track.'

'We'd better go and see.'

As the newly-engaged couple leapt from the car simultaneously slamming the doors behind them, they failed to notice a small boy on his bike going hell-for-leather through the bush in the opposite direction.

'HIGH SCHOOL TEACHERS AVERT RAIL DISASTER' read out John MacArthur from the front page of the "*Martinup Courier*" as the family relaxed in the kitchen on Friday night after the evening meal.

Brian concentrated hard on stirring his tea.

He continued, 'Prompt action by two local high school teachers on Wednesday afternoon last averted almost certain disaster on the Martinup to Perth railway line. Paul Newton (24) and his fiancée Michelle Marceaux (23), both teachers at Martinup High...'

'Those are your teachers aren't they Brian? And did you say "his fiancée" John? So they're engaged, are they? That's nice. You didn't tell me that Brian!' interjected Mary.

Brian quietly sipped his tea He nodded.

'Will I read on?' asked John MacArthur over the top of his glasses.

'Of course, dear. More tea Brian?'

The boy shook his head and mumbled, 'No thanks Mum.'

'...both teachers at Martinup High School discovered that a track inspection vehicle had been derailed at a spot about a mile from Martinup. The driver, Barry Dawson (19) of Spencer Road

Martinup was thrown clear in the accident and sustained only superficial injuries.

Realising that the vehicle was too heavy to shift, the two teachers, with Mr Dawson, alerted the police and the station at Martinup of the hazard lying on the track.

The Albany train due shortly into Martinup station was then stopped until the track could be cleared with specialist lifting equipment.

Rail authorities and local police spokesman Constable Donald Finnegan praised the actions of Mr Newton and Miss Marceaux. Constable Finnegan said that had it not been for the two teachers, Martinup would have witnessed a train disaster on an unprecedented scale. He added that the cause of the derailment of the track inspection vehicle was still unclear but the police would be continuing their investigations.'

John MacArthur lowered the newspaper.

'Well Brian, looks as if you've got two heroes for teachers. Are you all right son?'

Brian's face had turned a distinct grey. He nodded.

'Fine,' he mumbled as he gulped down the rest of his tea. He made some excuse about homework and bolted for the door, the phrase '...police would be continuing their investigations' running sickeningly through his head.

'He's been very quiet lately hasn't he Mary?'

'Yes,' she said. 'I've noticed. Just over these last few days too. He can be a funny lad sometimes.'

Brian knelt in a pew near the confessional not far from Big Arnie' MacAulay, the giant bachelor farmer. Father O'Neill was late as usual so Brian had plenty of time to think. Indeed, he'd been thinking non-stop for nearly three days about his part in the greatest train disaster in the history of Martinup. Nearly. He shuddered again at the thought. *'How many innocent lives had he endangered? How many people would he have killed if his teachers hadn't stepped in to save the day? How many years would he have to spend in prison for multiple murder? Your Honour, honestly, I saw it flatten a twenty-cent piece so I just wondered what would happen to a twelve-inch bolt... I just didn't think...'*

Then he realised he'd been through all this before. All the agonising about the bushfire he'd started. All that worrying and moaning, all that guilt and anguish, all that fretting and anxiety about the damage he'd caused. And what happened eventually? Off to confession and forgiveness with only an Our Father, three Hail Marys and a Glory be to the Father to say for penance. And that was it, all over and done with. Thank God for the Catholic Church! But what if Father O'Neill hadn't heard him properly? What then? Was he still forgiven for starting the bushfire? He couldn't answer that one, so he decided he might as well throw it in again to be on the safe side. And the drugs. Mustn't forget about that. It was bound to be a sin even if it wasn't written down in the Bible. After all, this was his immortal soul on the line here and there was no point in taking chances. If he could just make it to the confessional without an earthquake or a lightning strike on the church, he just might make it. Where was Father O'Neill?

The parish priest was at the front of the church deep in conversation with John MacArthur. Those who passed them on their way into mass might have caught snatches of conversation, '...Simple balance sheet is all you need...explanation of revenue generated...'

The priest, hand gripping his chin, nodded gravely at John MacArthur's every word. He seemed to be getting wise counsel.

He suddenly broke away from the conversation, his hand now on John MacArthur's arm.

'John, you've been a great help. I'll speak to you again about this. I must hear confessions now. Thanks.'

'No problem Father. Anytime.' John MacArthur followed the priest up the steps. He was still none the wiser as to what the priest was up to, but it was no business of his at the end of the day.

Brian was still in deep thought when the black figure of the priest breezed past and installed himself in the confessional. Big Arnie MacAulay nodded to Brian to go ahead.

Brian squeezed into the darkened confessional, knelt down, made the sign of the cross and addressed the purple curtain.

Father O'Neill listened intently from the other side.

'...last confession was two months ago and these are my sins. I've started a bushfire. I've taken drugs. And I've de-railed a ...'

Big Arnie MacAulay glanced up as he heard a distinct whisper from the confessional.

'You did WHAT?'

Brian spent the rest of that Sunday saying prayers, so many in fact that he had to borrow his mother's rosary beads to keep track of them. Of course, he'd forgotten to mention about the alcohol, but that could wait for next week, just in case he didn't have anything worthwhile to confess by then.

It's a Pig's Life
Down on the Farm

Roger sat on Suzie's bed. This time it was just a minor argument in what had been a tempestuous relationship.

'Suzie, you said you'd come. What's going on now?'

His girlfriend was impatiently sorting piles of paper on the floor under her desk. She looked up at him from the mess, pulling back the tangled expanse of red hair from her face.

'Roger, I do have to work sometimes you know. Remember you were going on about having to study? Now it's my turn. I'm getting desperate. I've got my supervisor on my back. The thesis is way behind schedule and he says the work I've done so far is poorly written and badly documented. That's great, isn't it? He says I'll have to rewrite most of it. I cannot afford the luxury of a week off in the country.'

'So why not take it all with you? There'll be space to work and there'll be plenty of peace and quiet. Dad will be at work during the day and Brian's got a job on a farm, so he won't be there either. I'll be working too. Mum would love it, especially to see me studying because she's convinced I never do.'

Suzie was still not persuaded that what she really needed was a week in the country, in Martinup of all places.

'For god's sake Roger, Martinup, Martinup! It's got...' She struggled for words. She had never been there, but she'd heard the name and her imagination clearly showed a lonely horse in a dusty, deserted street tied up outside the empty saloon, flicking its tail angrily at a swarm of flies while crows circled overhead. She struggled to describe this place, knowing that she was fairly safe with: 'It's got nothing. There's nothing there. Roger! It's the end of the earth!'

Roger immediately thought of the drive-in movie theatre, but knowing a mention of that was hardly going to enhance his argument, agreed with her instead.

'Precisely. Nothing. No distractions. Peace. Tranquillity. Nothing to do but study. Perfect. We can encourage each other to work.'

Suzie paused in her frantic paper shuffling on the floor and reflected on the possible merits of the idea.

'So, your mum and dad wouldn't mind if I wasn't very sociable?'

'Of course, not and they'd be quite happy with me working I can tell you that.'

'But it would mean I'd miss two yoga classes and a CND meeting.'

'See what I mean? What you need is a break from all that stuff. That's why you've gotten behind in the first place. There's more to life than yoga and CND.'

'Humph.' Suzie struggled to her feet with a pile of paperwork and dropped it on the desk. She eased the chair back over the rest of the mess and sat down with a serious question.

'Does your mum cook vegetarian?'

'Well, she cooks vegetables.'

'You mean she boils them with salt then puts in some baking soda to get a bit of the colour back?'

Roger could hardly deny his mother employed the good old-fashioned Irish culinary principles so far as vegetables were concerned, but he was sure some accommodation could be reached.

'Yes, but if you wanted to do your own thing in the kitchen, I'm sure she wouldn't mind.'

'And there'd be a room where I can work?'

'Yes, you'll be in Brian's room, Brian and myself will be in the van. I'll work in the back room next to yours during the day.'

'Pardon?'

'I'll work in the back room during the day.'

'No. What was that bit about you being in the van with Brian while I'm in my room? Why aren't we in my room? Or the van for that matter? Aren't we sleeping together or something?'

Roger cleared his throat. 'Well, my folks are a bit sensitive about sleeping arrangements Suzie.'

'Oh for God's sake Roger! I am on the pill you know. It is 1967 not 1867.'

Roger leaned back against the wall with a deep sigh. He'd done his best. She could take it or leave it. Suzie frowned and fiddled with the strings of wooden beads around her neck. After a minute she straightened up with a decision.

'Okay Roger. I'll come with you to your hick town. I'll give up my yoga for a week and the CND. I'll give up sleeping with you for a week. I'll give up "*civilisation*" for a week. Just so long as I get my own space and some peace and quiet. Right?'

'This is your room Suzie,' said Mary MacArthur turning on the light for her guest's inspection. Suzie put her head around the door. It was smaller than she had expected from the rest of the house.

'That's fine.'

Now is that desk big enough for you because you can always work on the kitchen table.'

'It's ok. Mrs MacArthur.'

'Or there's dad's office at the front. He won't be there during the day,' volunteered Roger from behind.

'No Roger. This will do just fine. Honestly.'

Suzie gazed around the four walls of the space that was to be her's for the next week. She stifled an involuntary shudder. '*Monastic existence? Study break? More like solitary confinement,*' she thought. 'Well I'm off to bed now. Make sure the back light's off when you go to the van won't you Roger?'

No sooner had Mary MacArthur disappeared than Suzie had an urgent request.

'Roger! I've looked in the bathroom and there's no toilet!'

'It's outside,' said Roger cheerily. 'Come on I'll show you.'

'Outside? What do you mean outside?' she demanded in an urgent whisper following him across the back room and into the darkness.

He turned on the back light to illuminate the small brick building behind the house.

'Oh for God's sake!' exclaimed Suzie. 'A bloody outside toilet! I thought that went out with Charles Dickens!'

'That's just the way it goes around here. This is the new toilet. Dad's just got it built. We used to use that one.' Roger pointed down the end of the long path where a dilapidated brick and iron structure snuggled against being engulfed by an enormous fig tree.

At least this one flushes,' he continued. 'The old one was on the pan system. A truck would come around once a week to take away the full pan and replace it with an empty one.' Roger failed to notice in the darkness that Suzie had developed a green colour on her cheeks. 'It was only a problem when visitors came and filled it up too quick. Then we'd have to try and not use it till Thursday came. Wednesdays could be very tricky sometimes. Are you okay Suzie?'

Suzie swallowed hard and assured him that she was fine. She would know in future not to ask questions about sanitary arrangements past and present in Martinup. Her worst fears of life in the country were being confirmed. With a deep breath and a firm conviction that she did not require the toilet this evening she told Roger she was off to bed. He trotted off happily to the van. Over a generous spliff of Thai gold, he regaled his younger brother with the gory details of the Great Fremantle Riot.

Suzie found it difficult to sleep in the bed overloaded with ancient woollen blankets. She tossed and turned but every direction and position she tried was impossible. In the end she gave up and stared at the ceiling. The light of the moon illuminated half the bedroom wall, the shadows creating eerie patterns on the brickwork above the wardrobe. Her eye caught a sudden movement in the gloom. Immediately she was bolt upright, hand stretching for the light switch, blankets falling to the floor. It was what she thought it was alright. Her scream was loud enough to awaken Mary and John MacArthur in the front bedroom. Roger Macarthur heard it clearly in the van and struggled to put his jeans on in order to investigate. Brian MacArthur was rudely awakened from a deep sleep by his elder brother's foot in his face.

Roger arrived on the scene to find his father balancing unsteadily on the desk dispatching a harmless spider, albeit the size of a saucer with his slipper, while his mother gave directions. Suzie sat up in bed clutching the blankets to her mouth, mentally refusing to accept their assurances of the innocuous nature of the beast. A spider was a spider and there was no way a spider that size was not at the very least a child killer. Brian had clearly lived a charmed life in that room. When the MacArthurs had departed, she eased herself back into bed and tried to sleep. She had barely drifted off when the noises in the ceiling started.

'What was that all about?' asked Brian sleepily as his older brother returned to the van.

'Oh, it was just a spider,' said Roger casually.

'Suzie's not very used to things around here.'

'Oh yeah,' said Brian sleepily. 'I should have told her about Albert.'

Brian shivered in the early morning air. He was standing on the forecourt of the petrol station on the main road out of town. It was eight o'clock. He wondered at his own sanity at agreeing to this. Of course, it was his father's idea. 'Fancy working on a farm for a bit during the August holidays Brian?' was the innocuous sounding suggestion. Brian had never worked on a farm before. In fact, he had rarely visited one. And now this farmer friend of his father had offered the young MacArthur a job for a week. The monetary incentive was sufficient to entice him. But how was he to get out to this farm? Not a problem, his father had assured him, 'I'll get Kevin Archer to give you a lift.'

Brian had never met Kevin Archer the farm hand in his life.

A well-beaten up Holden utility pulled up noisily to a stop beside him. A tanned thin-featured man of about thirty leaned over to open the passenger door.

'You Brian?' he wheezed, the ash from his cigarette falling onto his faded jeans as he spoke.

Brian nodded and the driver beckoned him to get in. Brian climbed in over the piles of empty Malboro packets and oily machinery parts that littered the floor.

'Ah don't worry about that shit. Just kick it out of the way. I'm Kevin.' He screwed the cigarette onto his lip and offered Brian a hand that looked as if it had been tattooed with oil and dirt.

'Ever worked on a farm before, Brian?' he asked as the battered vehicle accelerated away in a noisy cloud of dust and smoke. Kevin had the casual style of driving common in those parts, one arm out the window, the other loosely draped over the steering wheel. A well-worn brown leather hat on the dashboard behind the wheel seemed to partially obscure his view of the road, but he didn't seem to care. Perhaps it was a case of anything he couldn't see would be run over and anything he could see might be avoided, Brian wondered. "Might" being the operative word because they hadn't even got out of town and Brian was already feeling the tension. This bloke really drove fast.

'Ah, you'll get the hang of it,' said the driver casually flicking his ash out the open window.

'How long have you worked on the farm Kevin?'

'What this one? About three years. Nah, I've been on farms all my life. Ever since I left school. "*Real*" farms. Sheep stations up north mate. Measure 'em in square miles not bloody acres like down here.'

Brian nodded sagely trying but failing to comprehend farms that size.

Kevin continued his lecture on agricultural matters.

'Sheep, mate. Nothin' to 'em. Thick as bricks. Stupidest animals on earth. Unless ya count chooks. Pigs though. They're smart. Gotta watch the bastards. They'll eat ya if ya give 'em half a chance ya know.'

Brian looked across at the river in disbelief.

'Knew a bloke once who had his face eaten off when he fell over in the pig-pen. They thought he was there to be eaten if he was on the ground I s'pose. Moral of the story is don't fall over in the pig-pen. Still, you won't have much to do with the pigs. That'll be my job. I think old McIntyre wants you to do a bit of tractor driving. Driven a tractor before?'

Brian glumly shook his head. This farm job was shaping up to be a total nightmare.

'Ah, it's a piece of piss. You'll pick it up no sweat. You'll see.'

Suzie entered the kitchen wrapped in a dressing gown. Her hair was a complete mess and her face was puffed and swollen. The black areas under her eyes gave her the appearance of having spent the night in a boxing ring. John MacArthur had left early for work. Mary MacArthur was collecting potatoes from the shed. It was Roger who greeted her cheerily from the breakfast table.

'Suzie! Sleep well?'

She leaned heavily on the back of a kitchen chair.

'No, Roger, I did not sleep well. That bloody bed is the worst bed I've ever slept, no tried to sleep in. I was up all night turning the light on to see if there were any more of those bloody spiders and what the hell was that noise going on in the roof?'

'Oh possums.'

'Possums?'

'Yeah,' said Roger. 'They come in from the bush sometimes and nest in the roof.'

'Well that's just bloody brilliant Roger! Well no way am I spending another night in that room with bloody spiders and bloody possums. You and Brian can sleep in that zoo if you like but I'm going in the van tonight.'

Roger held up his hands in submission but his attempt to placate Suzie was cut short by his mother coming through the back door with a light-hearted greeting for her guest.

'Good morning Suzie! Sleep well? Bacon, sausage and eggs okay for you, for breakfast?'

'So, you're young Brian, eh? Your dad and me are old mates. Same battalion ya know. That was a long time ago. Kenny McIntyre was the third generation of his name to farm "Ballantrae". He was in his late fifties and his broad shoulders betrayed a slight stoop from the years of heavy toil. He was a busy man. There was a farm to be run and in particular a harvester that needed the attention of himself and Kevin. The boy could sort out the mob of sheep he'd brought in from last night but hadn't had time to attend to.

'Brian, see that mob of sheep in the pen over there? Sort out the ewes from the wethers into the two pens at the side for me.'

With that he was off to the machinery shed in earnest conversation with his senior farm hand.

Brian wandered over to the wooden pens in the distance behind which a hundred or so dark grey merinos bucked and scampered. He mounted the rail and stared at them. 'Ewes from the wethers,' he muttered to himself over and over again. He knew that an ewe was a female sheep and that therefore a wether was...

But they were all identical. Every face looked the same.

Roger retired to the back room to spread out his books on the table and started to struggle with a half-finished essay. Suzie had volunteered to help Mary with the washing-up. It was the first opportunity for the two of them to have a real conversation and Mary was keen to find out more about her son's girlfriend.

'I'm sorry about the breakfast this morning Suzie. Roger didn't tell me you were a vegetarian.'

'It's no big deal. I'll fix my own meals from now on if that's okay with you.'

Mary shrugged her shoulders. 'Sure, why not?'

'So, are you quite happy being a housewife?'

Mary paused in the washing up water. She'd never been asked such a question before.

'Um, yes,' she said, slowly depositing a dripping plate on the rack.

'Didn't you ever wish you had a real job?'

'Well bringing up four boys is a real job, I can assure you.'

Suzie tossed her hair over her shoulder as she placed a newly dried plate on the stack behind her. She still had not got her point over.

'Yes, I know, but I suppose women didn't get opportunities for real careers back in your day, did they? I mean there are loads of women studying at university now but there couldn't have been that many say twenty years ago?'

Mary bit her lip, remembering her fellow female students on graduation day, most of whom went on to have distinguished careers.

Suzie carried on, oblivious to the awkward silence that had developed.

'Have you read some of the books on feminism that are coming out? They're excellent. It's fine that women broke the chains that tie them to the kitchen.'

'I don't feel I'm chained to the kitchen,' retorted Mary.

'Well of course, you've still got Brian at school haven't you? But when he's left home what are you going to do?'

Suzie knew nothing of Mary MacArthur's social life in Martinup, of the neighbours who frequently visited the house for a cup of tea and a chat. The Bowling Club. The Tennis Club of which she was Treasurer. The Wednesday night card evenings. The Church. The Friday afternoons when she worked at the Library. And the dinners that John would be invited to that she would have to attend. She couldn't wait for Brian to leave school! Suzie's arguments may have relevance to some women, but to Mary MacArthur, they were fatuous nonsense.

Suzie was now in full cry.

'Women should be free to follow their lives, not be slaves to men.'

Mary MacArthur winced noticeably as the last pan was extracted from the sink. She wasn't a slave to John.

'And men. So unreliable aren't they? You just can't depend on them for anything can you? Women need freedom from stifling relationships don't you think? I mean, freedom to be themselves.'

Mary MacArthur bit her lip as her young guest raged on about how men were responsible for all the wars of history and how men always assumed, they were intellectually superior to women and how women were always denied opportunities in life by men. When at last the tirade ended, Mary dried her hands on the kitchen towel, and looked her young guest straight in the eye.

'I have never heard such a load of rubbish in all my life.'

'LOOK UP ITS ARSE BOY!' came the helpful shout across the farmyard. Brian hid embarrassment and duly inspected each ovine backside discovering in the process the way to separate ewes from wethers.

'You should have heard what she said to me! All that reactionary crap about devoted wives and loving families and the joys of parenthood. Suzie was still fuming hours after her encounter with Mary MacArthur in the kitchen. Roger had suggested a walk in the bush as a break from study which for him had been going well, but his girlfriend working in the bedroom had found it difficult to concentrate. Roger struggled to keep up with her as she strode aggressively along the path. And he found it hard to understand why she was so upset with his mother.

'C'mon Suzie. Your mum must have been like that too!'

Suzie shot him angry look.

'For your information Roger, my mother knew exactly what she wanted out of life. Once she had gotten rid of that no hoper of a father of mine, she made a life for herself. She was a journalist, mate, not a bloody housewife! Look Roger, I'm getting fed up of this place...'

Roger stopped her in mid-sentence with a hand on her arm. He motioned with his head towards the rope like object that straddled the dusty track ahead of them. As Suzie's eyes adjusted to the mottled light falling on the path, the rope moved. A dugite, newly emerged from hibernation had sensed their presence. Its small arrow-shaped head with its black flickering forked tongue slowly rose and turned towards them. Although venomous, the dugite had an undeservedly notorious reputation in those parts, being more of a menace to poultry and small children than the two healthy and agile adults now disturbing its slumber in the afternoon sun but it was still a beast that was not to be trifled with.

'Just keep still,' whispered Roger, but Suzie was quite incapable of going anywhere. Her heart pounded but her limbs were frozen solid with fear. Roger too was rooted to the spot. They watched in motionless trepidation as the brown-skinned reptile uncoiled itself across the track. For a heart-stopping moment, it paused and seemed to be considering its options. Then it turned and made for the safety of the dry undergrowth. Sluggish at the end of winter, its four-foot long undulating body moved in rhythmic muscular slow motion leaving behind its characteristic track in the sand.

When the tip of its tail had disappeared, the spell of the snake had still to be broken. Both Suzie and Roger were transfixed, staring at the marks on the ground where the animal had been, scarcely able to believe it had been there in the first place.

It was Suzie who first broke the spell, her fear transformed to fury.

'THAT BLOODY DOES IT ROGER! I'M FED UP TO HERE WITH THIS BLOODY PLACE! BLOODY SNAKES! BLOODY SPIDERS! BLOODY POSSUMS! BLOODY OUTSIDE TOILETS! 1 WANT TO GO BACK TO PERTH *NOW!*'

The sheep finally sorted, Brian wandered back across the yard for his next chore. Farmer and farm hand were still battling with the recalcitrant harvester which was apparently refusing to start. The two men were hard at work on the engine and had little time to supervise or educate the town boy in the ways of farming.

'Brian, I want you to feed a dead sheep to the pigs. It's loaded on the back of the Ute up there by the pens. You'll need to cut its belly open first otherwise they won't eat it. You can use this.'

Kenny McIntyre, covered in dirt and grease fished in the pockets of his outsized overalls and handed Brian a large pocket knife. All that was visible of Kevin Archer were the bottoms of his legs and all that could be heard of him was muffled swearing coming from somewhere beneath the machine.

'Have you got it yet Kevin?' Kenny shouted into the bowels of the engine.

Brian let them get on with it and headed for the pig pen.

He found the deceased Merino on the back of the utility. With difficulty, he forced down the bolts that held up the back tray which then swung down with a clang against the body of the vehicle. Already the pigs were starting to take an interest in proceedings. The presence of humans near the pen usually meant food. They squealed and snorted and rubbed themselves against the wire mesh of the fence.

Brian tried to ignore them as he grabbed the legs of the dead sheep and tugged. Nothing happened. He had quite underestimated the weight of the animal. He tried again, this time exerting all his strength. The sudden movement of the sheep caught him off guard and he fell to the ground with the sheep on top of his chest. This seemed to delight his porcine audience whose squeals had now turned to screeches as they bucked and whirled at the activity just outside their boundary.

Shocked at the sudden turn of events and partially by the dead sheep on top of him, Brian hauled himself upright, cart-wheeling the carcass onto his legs. He struggled to his feet and reached for the knife in his pocket. The blade clicked into position. For a second, Brian ignored the cacophony from the pig-pen. He had never done anything like this in his life before. His first attempt was useless. The blade barely scratched the skin. Shutting his eyes and numbing himself to grim reality, he drove the blade into the belly and dragged it upwards. The hiss of escaping gas with its stench of decayed intestines, kidneys and other internal organs nearly took his breath away. The pigs reacted differently. The smell of food sent them into a frenzy. They hurled themselves against the fence threatening to bring it down. They screeched and screamed and fought. They bucked and kicked and chased each other around the pen.

Pale and trembling, Brian turned his attention to how he would get the dead sheep into the pen. At first, he tried to lift the beast up to it over the fence but it was too heavy for him and the fence was too high. He dropped it back on the ground spilling a few vital organs in the process, further inciting the pigs to riot as they spotted meaty morsels just beyond their grasp. Brian thought about pushing the carcass under the fence but quickly decided that was too dangerous as the larger ones could easily force their way through any hole that he made. There was only one thing for it. He would have to open the gate and drag the beast in. Kevin Archer's words echoed through his mind as he dragged the dead animal, intestines trailing towards the gate. *'They'll eat ya if ya give 'em half a chance ya know...Knew a bloke who had his face eaten off when he fell over in the pig-pen.'*

He unlocked the gate and braced himself. This had to be done quick. Bloody quick. Bloody pigs. Bastards. He took a deep breath, grasped the hind legs of the carcass and mentally rehearsed the operation. When he was ready, he kicked the door open and charged into the pen screaming every obscenity he could think of and a few more besides. The pigs scattered momentarily. He had only a split second to hurl down the carcass and make his escape. As they charged back towards him, Brian failed to notice the rusty nail protruding from a piece of wood lying on the ground. It pierced the sole of right boot and sunk into his flesh. Yelping with pain, he still had the presence of mind to remain on his feet and hurl himself out the gate, slamming it thankfully shut behind him. The pigs were by now falling over themselves, ripping and tearing the carcass to pieces. Brian watched the frantic orgy from the safety of the wire mesh. It was only then that he started to shake and become aware of the acute pain coming from his foot.

'What's happened to you then?' enquired Kenny McIntyre pulling his shaggy grey head from the engine interior. Brian explained about the nail in the pig pen. The farmer drew a deep breath and scratched the white stubble on his chin. 'When's the last time you had a tetanus injection?'

Brian shrugged his shoulders.

'Hey Kevin!'

The farmhand dragged himself out from under the harvester.

'Kevin, you'd better get this boy to hospital. I'll carry on here. See ya t'mora, eh?'

'Not if I can help it,' thought Brian grimly to himself.

The parting between Mary MacArthur and Suzie was frosty but polite. Roger had persuaded his girlfriend to at least have a beer before she left Martinup with its conservative thinking inhabitants, quaint sanitary arrangements and unique wildlife forever. He parked the van outside the Commercial Hotel on the main street. It was late afternoon. The lounge bar was empty and the saloon bar visible only through a hatch in the wall contained a handful of the usual serious drinkers to hear the horse racing on the radio.

'Beer, Suzie?' asked Roger from the hatch. His girlfriend looked up from the cheap plastic topped table where she had ensconced herself in a room optimistically large for the number of inhabitants of the town who actually drank there. Even Friday and Saturday nights saw the place only half full at the best of times.

She cut a lonely, if not colourful figure in the drab emptiness of the lounge bar.

'Yeah, alright,' she said unenthusiastically whilst rolling a cigarette. 'But I don't want to be here too long Roger. Ok?' She felt uncomfortably exposed in this backward town. This was just not her scene at all and the sooner she got back to the sanity of the city, the better.

The door flew open and a familiar voice called across the room.

'Susan! What are you doing here?'

Startled, Suzie looked up as Paul and Michelle walked over to her table. Paul was shocked to see his ex-Girlfriend in Martinup of all places.

'Oh hi,' was the modest reply to the greeting. Her level of discomfiture had suddenly soared. Now she suddenly remembered why she felt reluctant to come to Martinup. This was where Paul was teaching. Feigning nonchalance, she fumbled with her matches eventually lighting her cigarette and almost setting fire to her hair in the process.

'Michelle, this is Susan.' Paul's voice betrayed a hint of triumphalism. Roger appeared behind the standing couple with two glasses of beer.

'Hi, I'm Roger,' he said by way of self-reflection as his girlfriend seemed momentarily lost for words. '*So you're the shit that was in her room that morning,*' thought Paul as he smilingly introduced himself and his fiancée.

The couple accepted Roger's offer of a drink. Suzie suddenly excused herself for the toilet. Roger asked Paul what he did for a living.

'Really?' You wouldn't happen to teach my little brother Brian, would you? Brian MacArthur?'

Mary MacArthur tore open Roger's letter.

'That's marvellous! Wonderful news!'

'What is it Mum? asked Brian from his cornflakes, his foot still tender from the incident on the farm a week ago which had conveniently confined him to barracks for the duration of the holiday. It could have been a miserable time for the lad, but TV had saved the day.

'What's up? Has he got a haircut?' asked John MacArthur straining to hear the news on the radio bearing more tidings of grief for Australian troops in Vietnam.

'He says they've split. She's run off with someone else.'

Lord of the Manor

Number twenty-six Regent Gardens, a brick-built detached Victorian villa stood in a leafy tranquil suburb of Sydney about a mile from the bustle of the city centre. The shade cast by the mature stands of oak and maple softened the building into its surroundings and protected the fragile lawn from the afternoon summer sun which was now low in the sky. The foliated barrier provided privacy from the neighbours and partially blocked the harshest sights and sounds of the distant city.

Trevor stared down at the garden below from the balcony outside his room. How his life had changed in six months!

He couldn't believe it when he saw the house as their battered and dust-covered car and over-loaded trailer finally pulled up the gravel drive. Although exhausted from the five-day journey, he was overwhelmed by the sight of his new home. It was like something he'd seen in the movies. It was certainly nothing like anything in the west. He had no idea that his granny and auntie Jean lived in such opulence.

Bad news awaited them. Margaret knew her sister Jean and her elderly mother were not in the best of health, but Jean was worse than expected. Despite the best of care in a nearby hospital, within a week of their arrival she was dead. Although pleased to see her youngest daughter again despite the troubles in the past and of course delighted to meet her grandson for the first time, the strain of it all proved too much for granny and she passed away a month later.

His mother coped remarkably well under the circumstances, but then she had never been particularly close to her family. Trevor knew she effectively severed all links when she followed his dad Peter to the west, determined to make a go of it. Back just in time as it turned out to say goodbye, she made the funeral arrangements and dealt with the legal business calmly and efficiently as if she did that sort of thing every day. Trevor was deeply impressed. What a change from the sad, dejected, chain-smoking heavy drinker he had known for most of his life! It was like living with a different person! Now she was back in Sydney in her old childhood home, which would soon belong to her once the Estate was finally settled, and life suddenly had meaning. The future held promise. She'd resumed her nursing career with ease, made new friends and last night she was even talking about taking up golf! What a woman!

He looked at his watch. She would be home soon. He turned back into the house through the lace curtain that surrounded the French doors.

Although months had passed since the funerals, they still lingered in his memory. They had an oddly familiar quality about them. Trevor was too young to remember his own father's memorial service, but the feelings of loss and grief were familiar ones to him. In a way they had been with him all his life and even though he shared the feelings of the other mourners, he didn't know them. Indeed, he hardly knew his aunt and grandmother. His mother had rarely talked to him about them and it was as if these two strangers had waited for the right moment to go, leaving him and his mother an incredible legacy.

He wandered along the corridor. The polished wooden floors, the faded wall-paper and the gilt-framed oil paintings made the house look more like a deserted art gallery or museum. But it was neither of these things. It was very much his home and not only did he feel he had been there a long time, he felt older than his tender thirteen years. He was the guardian of an estate now. The responsibility of maintaining the family property had largely fallen once again to him and he felt quite at ease, not just with being "man about the house", but now "man about the mansion". His mother needed him more than ever, especially as she often worked difficult hours.

The mirror caused him to pause. He'd grown in the last six months and put on a bit of weight too, but what did he look like in this school uniform with its blue blazer and yellow trim? With its breast pocket badge of the red cross of St George and its gold braided motto "per ardua et fides?" What would his old mate Brian make of this? He remembered the time when he had to patch his own school trousers and wear the same shirt for a week because it was the only one, he had.

And what would Brian make of his academic-gowned teachers that were called "masters"? He remembered "fart-breath" MacDuff. No chance of him mastering anything, least of all teaching mathematics. And Latin? That was even more weird than French. At least there were a lot of people still alive who spoke French.

And what about sport that was called "games" which meant "football" but which really meant "rugby"? This was a totally incomprehensible game to a lad from the west and Wednesday afternoons inevitably meant additional bruises for his collection. He wondered if the "game" should be renamed "give the new boy from the bush another kicking".

But he loved it all. It was so different here. He loved the hustle and bustle of the city. When his mum had time off work, they'd go to the movies and indoor bowls, to the all-night amusement arcades and when the weather was right, to the beach at Bondi. Because his mum was so happy within herself, they were probably closer together now than they had ever been. The only thing he missed was a mate to share his new life with. Brian would love it here. He should write to him. He promised he would and there sure was plenty to tell his pal. That would have to wait till after tea. His mum had asked him to cut the front lawn when he got home from school, which was no big deal. In fact, it was great fun. They had inherited a monster of a self-propelled lawnmower that could do the job in minutes. Well, thirty-minutes he conceded and he needed to get his finger out if he was to catch "Bonanza" on the TV. He scurried off to his room, tearing at his tie which seemed to have invented its own knot.

He was just lacing boots when he heard his mother's car in the drive. It was a new one of course, bought for them by granny just before she died. Trevor agreed with his mother that granny's *largesse* could well have been motivated by her desire to see the end of their old banger. "It does rather lower the tone of the neighbourhood", she had confided to Trevor one day thinking he was someone else.

'Hello Trevor!' Margaret called out cheerfully from the front hall hanging her red cape on the hook.

'Hi Mum!' he shouted back pulling an old jumper over his head.

Margaret Stewart took off her white cap as she sprinted up the stairs. Her crisp blue and white nurse's uniform flattered her figure and with her hair tied back and her rosy cheeks, she could easily have passed for a woman ten years younger.

'Trevor?' she exclaimed poking her head around the door, a huge smile lighting up her face. 'Great news!'

'You've been promoted?'

'No. It's better than that.'

'We've sold the house in Martinup.'

No, not yet but the solicitor rang yesterday and apparently someone is interested, so you never know. No, it's much more exciting that, I've met someone. Someone really, really nice.'

'Who is she?'

Margaret beamed at her only son.

'Not she Trevor. He. His name is Tom. Dr Tom Kennedy. He works on the same ward as I do and he's coming around for tea tomorrow night. He's a really nice man. I know you'll like him and he's dying to meet you. '

Trevor's heart sank. His idyllic world had suddenly been turned upside-down.

Roger turned off the van's engine and stared at the lights of the city from the heights of King's Park. The curving arches of the Narrows bridge were barely discernible in the gloom but the steady stream of traffic in both directions across it clearly defined its upper boundary against the multi-coloured luminescence of the city background. In all directions in the vista laid out before him, unseen and unknown people trapped in their tiny cars pursued their own blinkered courses in life oblivious to the lonely observer in the darkness high above.

He took out a well-worn tobacco pouch and with a paper stuck to his lower lip, began to roll a cigarette.

'Bitch,' he muttered to himself.

The drive from Martinup the previous week had been sheer hell. A strong wind had picked up soon after they left town and the van proved quite difficult to steer, swaying noticeably in the violent gusts. Roger's concentration was sorely tested by his passenger's mood fluctuation. There were violent fits of rage where Suzie cursed everything to do with him, his parents and

Martinup. Then there were periods of sullen silence where he caught her glowering at the dashboard, glaring out the window or shutting her eyes pretending she wasn't there.

Roger could do nothing to placate her and his energy was expended anyway just keeping the van on the road. Eventually, she fell asleep for which he was greatly relieved. She didn't regain consciousness till they hit the first traffic light of the metropolitan area at Armadale.

Suzie's mood despite her repose was still as black as thunder and a stony silence was maintained until the van pulled into the college carpark.

When the passenger door slammed shut and she had disappeared into the darkness with a scarcely audible farewell, he feared he had seen the last of her but he was wrong. A few days later he caught a glimpse of her climbing into a car. He couldn't recognise the driver's face from that distance, but he knew the pair of them were intimate by the kiss of greeting, she gave him. Feelings of rage filled his stomach as the car accelerated away in the direction of Fermentile.

'Bitch!' he said to himself as he lit the cigarette.

What was wrong with him? Why couldn't he accept that she'd gone? Even when the note arrived through his door telling him in no uncertain terms it was over, he didn't want to believe it and when he wrote to his mother with the news, he still didn't want to be convinced it was true.

He breathed a trail of blue cigarette smoke through the open window and into the night sky and drummed his fingers on the steering wheel.

'She was a waste of time and space. She was the one who had disrupted his life for the best part of a year. He was better off without her. There were final exams rapidly approaching and revision was as yet out of the question since he still didn't have a grasp of the last five topics in anthropology. Goodbye to law next year if he didn't get at least a "B" and God help him if he failed completely.' He shuddered at the thought.

'Work, work, work. Study, study, study. That's the only way to go Roger,' he said through gritted teeth. He flicked the cigarette out the window, the glowing butt cart-wheeling through the inky sky and disappearing into the night. He started the engine and pulled the gear stick viciously into reverse. He

178

couldn't resist one more comment as he could never have the last word in any argument with her.

'Bitch!'

The presbytery phone rang catching Father O'Neill in the toilet.

'Bloody hell,' he muttered struggling to retrieve his trousers. Fortunately, or perhaps unfortunately, Mrs Jaworski was on hand to answer it. As Father O'Neill fiddled with his zip he could hear her shouted replies in stilted English down the mouthpiece explaining graphically the whereabouts of the priest to the hapless caller.

'EEZA INNA TOILET!'

'Why, oh why, does she have to answer the *phone*?' he muttered pulling the flush chain and forcing himself through the door.

He found his housekeeper in the hall, washing basket between her legs thrusting the hand-piece towards him with a rather obvious comment.

'EEZA FOR YOU FATHER.'

'Thank you, Mrs, Jaworski. Who is it?' enquired the priest taking the phone from her, his voice betraying a hint of annoyance.

'EEZA BISHOP FATHER.' She waddled off with the laundry basket while Father O'Neill swallowed and loosened his collar as he prepared to take the call.

'Hello your Grace.'

Father O'Neill listened intently.

'Yes, your Grace…uh huh…yes, I understand that your Grace…'

Then his features lightened and a huge smile lit up his face.

'Really! Really! Oh, thank you your Grace. This is wonderful news and I can't tell you how grateful I am that you place so much trust…of course, yes of course. Thank you, thank you your Grace …I'll look out for it in the post tomorrow. Goodbye.'

Father O'Neill put the phone gently and firmly back on the hook then with a grin the size of the proverbial

Cheshire cat on his face and punched the air in delight.

'YESSSS!' he screamed and danced a decidedly unecclesiastical jig in the hall.

179

Mrs Jaworski at the washing line outside with a mouthful of pegs in her face and a basketful of underpants at her feet, paused in pinning a pair of priestly Y-fronts to the line and over her shoulder at the cavorting black figure inside.

'*Priests,*' she muttered as she pulled a peg from her mouth.

The university library was warm and light murmuring of occasional conversation over the low hum of the air conditioning added to the soporific atmosphere of the book-lined avenues. Roger had secured a secluded nest by the window and had been going strong for two hours but the strain was beginning to tell. His head started to droop over the books and notes. It was no good. He needed a break. He jerked himself awake, stood up, stretched, yawned and sauntered down the aisles to the reading section where padded leather easy chairs rather than obscure academic journals and eclectic new library acquisitions were the main attraction for undergraduates. There was one chair free and within minutes he was fast asleep.

A whispered female voice and a tug on his sleeve roused him.

He opened his eyes to a pretty face with delicate elfin features dominated by big brown eyes. Her auburn hair was cut short. He struggled to raise himself to a sitting position. She looked familiar but he couldn't place her. To make matters worse, she knew his name.

'Sorry to wake you Roger. I just wondered if you'd like to come down for a cup of coffee.'

'I'm really sorry,' he said blinking and tidying his hair behind his ears.

'I do know you but I can't place your name.'

She laughed and smoothed her denim skirt as she sat down on the coffee table beside him.

'I'm not surprised if you don't remember me. I was a year ahead of you at school in Martinup and I was only there for the last term.'

'You're Jane, aren't you?' Roger had finally come completely to life.

'That's right,' she said. 'Jane Finnegan the…'

'The policeman's daughter!' Roger correctly interrupted.

She laughed and warned him not to hold it against her. Roger assured her that he wouldn't. He'd already met her father, but that was a long story best told over a cup of coffee and there was no way was she paying for it.

They were in the coffee shop for over an hour. The story of the close encounter with her father of course had to be related.

'…and then I found that my kid brother had swallowed it!'

Jane was in stitches.

Roger was in love.

'Roger,' she said earnestly, leaning over the table. 'I had an ulterior motive in dragging you down here for coffee.'

'Oh yeah?'

'Will you be going down to Martinup after the exams?'

'Yep.'

'Can I get a lift?'

Jane was not just a pretty face. The next day she offered Roger loads of material that she had collected, having studied exactly the same subjects in the previous year. Her grades were good enough for first year Law which was Roger's aspiration, if only he could get the necessary grades in this first year of Arts.

The pair of them became inseparable in the library, in the coffee shop and on the lawn outside.

Every night when the library shut, they were invariably among the last out. Jane took her studies seriously.

Roger would walk her home to her room at the residential college nearby.

The conversation between them never dried up and the more they talked, the more they realised how much they had in common. Tales of a Catholic Primary School education: of short-sighted nuns flatulent visiting priests sent peals of laughter around the darkened campus. Tales of slightly ridiculous fathers had them in tears. Roger couldn't stop laughing at Jane's story of Constable Donald Finnegan having to wear a neck brace for a month because he had shut the patrol car door before he pulled his head in and Roger's reply of John MacArthur being trapped for hours by his tie when he slammed the car boot shut after breaking down on a lonely country road had Jane in hysterics. Every evening it was the same, sharing amusing yarns and anecdotes as if they had both lived in parallel universes.

At the end of the underpass they would kiss and part company, Jane to the right and Roger to the left. As he wandered home alone Roger would muse on the fact that he and Suzie had never laughed together and Jane would wonder why it took so long to meet the right man.

With Jane's help, not only was Roger beginning to come to terms with his own studies, at the same time he was gaining a valuable insight into Law which, if his marks were good enough, he would soon be studying himself.

In the course of just one month, Roger blossomed. He had been a bit of a recluse up till then, his world dominated by Suzie and her demonstrations of one sort or another and knew only a handful of people, mostly disillusioned militants, draft-dodgers and potential drop-outs not surprisingly all friends of Suzie.

Now he was meeting Jane's friends who were liberals instead of radicals and he took on board all manner of opinions and arguments. They all enjoyed red wine and the occasional joint. Music was always a feature of their frequent gatherings. Roger quickly became familiar with the lyrics of Bob Dylan, Leonard Cohen, Donovan and James Taylor and the esoteric ramblings of Ginsburg and Kerouac. All of his new acquaintances had travelled or intended to travel through Asia and India, Afghanistan, Iraq, Iran and places beyond. Some of them were born in those countries. Roger tasted food he'd never seen before. He heard about cities and languages and religions he never knew existed.

But more than all that, he knew he now had one thing that was priceless. He had Jane. He loved her more than she could imagine. She had changed his life.

Paul and Michelle's life in Martinup had changed dramatically too. It had never been the same since the Great Train Disaster (Nearly) was plastered over the front page of the newspaper. Before that fateful day, they had been able to walk the streets of the town unrecognised, save for their students who usually offered a polite greeting.

Now they were local heroes and everyone wanted to meet them. The inadvertent publication of their engagement heightened the public interest and now they could walk openly as a couple without risking the approbation of a small country town. Michelle was able to visit Paul's house in daylight and he was able to freely visit her, the couple no longer having to restrict their relationship to a clandestine nocturnal affair.

In the days following soon after the incident, a walk down the main street by the couple on a Saturday morning with the modest intention of buying some groceries could take over an hour as smiling residents queued up and fell over each other in order to introduce themselves. Paul and Michelle dutifully smiled back like visiting royalty, returning the greetings and handshakes and struggling to remember the scores of names and faces. They received offers to join the golf club, the bowling club, the tennis club and even the croquet club. They were forced to decline most invitations to dinners, barbecues, parties and weddings simply because the marking and lesson preparation would never get done but they were grateful for the attention and ensured every overture was properly answered. It was quite overwhelming. They had never guessed the extent of Martinup's social life.

In time, the frenzy faded and they began to feel truly at home in the town, much more so than any of the other young teachers who saw Martinup as just a brief twelve-month stepping stone in their careers.

Paul was delighted with the way things had turned out but Michelle had misgivings. Never one for keeping her feelings to herself, she raised her concerns over coffee at Paul's house one afternoon.

'This is getting out of hand Paul. I'm getting called Mrs Newton,' even at school, not just in the town.

'Does that upset you? That's what you'll be called this time next year.'

'The thing is Paul, my parents still know nothing. I've told them about you of course but I can't just write and tell them I'm engaged. It doesn't work like that with my folks.'

'So why don't we go across and see them in the summer holidays?'

Michelle smiled. 'Great idea Paul, but I thought of it first. Here's an engagement present.'

She dropped a brown envelope on the table in front of him. He ripped it open and looked at the contents.

Airline tickets to Sydney in his name.

He looked up in astonishment and was about to speak, but Michelle motioned him to be silent.

'My dad paid for mine and after all,' she reminded him, 'you bought the ring.'

He reached over and squeezed her hand. Her eyes twinkled as she smiled. She had no doubt her mother would approve of Paul and of course her dad would be delighted with her choice too.

'Do you like it here Michelle? I mean do you miss Sydney?'

'To be honest Paul, in the early days, I hated it here. Everything was really weird and the people really strange. Remember that maniac Jacko? But then I met you. I know you weren't born here, but you've shown me so much. And it's really nice to know so many people here now. I've never lived in a place like it. Okay, so it's not a city, but folk don't get on in cities, do they? You know what I mean?'

'That's exactly how I feel and that's one of the reasons I love you so much. We think alike. Now I've got a surprise for you, but it's not here,' he said rising from the table.

'Come with me.'

She followed him down the steps bursting with curiosity, but he would not be drawn.

'It's a secret,' he said enigmatically holding open the passenger door. You'll find out soon enough. Hop in!'

The car pulled up outside Trevor's old house, the "FOR SALE" sign still there but looking the worse for wear. Paul leaned over the steering wheel and stared at the bungalow which he'd noticed by chance the previous week. It looked perfect, but what would Michelle think?

'This place has been in the market for months apparently. I spoke to the estate agent on the phone yesterday. The previous owners are in Sydney. The keys are with the next-door neighbours. Do you want to come?'

'You bet!' said Michelle scrambling out the passenger door.

Maria de Luca answered the door, but unable to understand Paul's enquiry, she summoned her husband.

Luigi hurried up the passage. He recognised the couple instantly.

'Hey! You two in the paper, yeah? Big train crash?'

Paul smiled and nodded and repeated the request for the keys next door.

'Sure. Sure!' said Luigi disappearing into the gloom, leaving Maria smiling benignly at them on the doorstep.

'Nice garden you have here,' said Paul by way of conversation when Luigi emerged with the keys. Luigi didn't need encouragement like that. The pair of them spent the next half-hour on a tour of the DeLuca estate, the owner delighting in pointing out horticultural features, some ordinary, some interesting, some downright amazing.

'This is impressive Luigi,' said Michelle admiring the potatoes. 'You've done wonders here.'

'What's the soil like next door?' asked Paul.

Luigi shrugged his shoulders. 'Same as dis place. But you gotta work at it ya know? Plenty water. Plenty shit. Then more shit. Easy. Now over here...'

Michelle tugged Paul's sleeve.

'Paul,' she whispered. 'Let's go and see the house!'

They made their escape but only after agreeing to accept an enormous pumpkin and a bag of carrots.

Paul was the first to comment as he pulled the gate shut.

'The neighbours are certainly friendly. I could learn a lot from Luigi.'

'What a sweet man he is,' said Michelle stowing the vegetables in the back of the car.

'Well, let's see what this place's like then,' he said pushing open the rusting front gate.

'Wait for me!' cried Michelle slamming the car door and sprinting up to join him on the front step as he fumbled with the bundle of keys.

'Well, what do you think?' asked Paul standing in the bare lounge room after the inspection.'

'Can we afford it? Four and a half didn't you say?'

'It's been on the market a while, so they might accept four, but anyway what do you think of the place?' Michelle grabbed Paul's arm and held it close.

'Paul, it's brilliant! I've always wanted to live in a cottage, ever since I was a little girl. There's so much I want to do to that kitchen...'

'And the garden can do with a bit of attention...' Paul added.

'But Luigi will help you with that,' she chimed in.

Paul nodded and gazed around. Look. An open fire. It'll be nice when we get that going won't it, Michelle?'

'Where do we get wood from?'

'Oh, it's all over the place. The local stuff's called mallee roots. They burn really well they're very easy to chop apparently.'

Father O'Neill tossed another mallee root on the fire and poured himself a generous glass of whisky from the bottle on the sideboard. The fire crackled and sparked and threw an eerie flickering light around the room. With glass in one hand and cigarette in the other, he paced the floor of the presbytery lounge room with a huge grin on his face. The grin had been there since just before noon when the post arrived and his facial muscles were now beginning to ache.

He eased himself in the comfort of an armchair and stretched forward to pick up and re-read for the umpteenth time the all-important letter from the Bishop.

Dear Father O'Neill, I write to confirm your appointment… he read out loud before leaping to his feet with

a shout of "YES!" clutching the paper and almost spilling his drink in the process. He composed himself, stubbed out the cigarette in the ashtray and started pacing the carpet again.

At last he was vindicated. He was no crook. He was a genius. Now the Bishop could finally see that, although His Grace did take some convincing. But that was it. Some people can understand how to make money and some people can't. Bishop de Canio obviously fell in the latter category.

He took a big gulp of whisky. 'Oh yes.' The Bishop understood now. He finally understood how a struggling parish like Martinup could have renovations and innovations that cost thousands without incurring unnecessary increases in donations to the church. But that had been his down fall hadn't it? Well nearly. To pretend the sums of money coming in *were* donations! And of course, that hiccup one month when there was a shortfall in funds set the alarm bells ringing. That was to be expected because others were clearly suspicious of his achievements and were waiting for their chance. Bastards. Those scumbags had always had it in for him. Ha! That paltry sum was *nothing* compared to the amounts he was used to dealing with.

The Jesuit understood what he was up to. No doubt he played a big part in the final outcome. Maybe they would meet again one day. He quite liked Father Harding. And John MacArthur, the accountant, had given him invaluable advice as to how he should present his case.

Anyway. He had proved his point and now he was rewarded. And what a *reward*! His gaze fell on the airline tickets on the coffee table. He went over and inspected them again. There was no mistake. Ansett Airlines flight to Melbourne. Father Francis O'Neill. No doubt about it. He was leaving Martinup forever.

The priest drained the glass, burped and headed for the sideboard.

Trevor had plenty to think about as he walked behind the mower backwards and forwards across the expanse of lawn. It was therapeutic. The grass soft underfoot, the engine drowning extraneous sound. It helped him think.

He had smiled at his mother when she told him the news, but she knew him so well it was doubtful if he had adequately disguised his reticence. Well it was a shock. His mother never had a boyfriend before. But then, it was hardly surprising in Martinup for obvious reasons. Now she was a different person and this was a big city full of eligible bachelors. It was almost inevitable that this would happen. Maybe that was why she was so keen to come here. No, that was unfair. And certainly untrue. Besides, who was he to stand in his mother's way? She had as much right to happiness as he did.

He stopped the mower and emptied the over-flowing catcher into the wheelbarrow.

The really frightening thought was that this guy might be a bastard. He could make life hell for a young boy. It could lead to all sorts of complications. What would happen then? Whose side would his mother take? How could any man live up to the memory of his real father anyway? He was a war hero. No way was he going to start calling some stranger "Dad" and pretending to mean it, even if his mother asked him to. No way!

The catcher re-attached, the mower resumed its slowly reciprocating motion across the lawn with Trevor, deep in thought, strolling behind.

Had his mother deserted him? After all, he was the one who got her off to bed at nights and cleaned up the mess when she had had too much to drink which had been most nights in Martinup. He was the one who had taken care of the shopping after school because she was too depressed to go out. He was the one who often did the cooking because she wasn't up to it. He was the one who calmed her down when there were strange noises in the night. Had she forgotten about all that? Was he about to be cast off like a worn-out shoe?

The lawn was finished but having had a little more time to reflect, Trevor had a few more thoughts on the subject of his mother's love life as he pushed the mower back up the slope towards the house. He'd been thinking like a spoilt child. It was time to be a bit more mature. Time to act like a grown-up. After all, he'd be fourteen soon.

His mother was a very attractive "single" woman. She had been alone for a long time. It was only fair she should meet someone who made her happy. Why not? Good luck to her. She deserved it.

'I only hope he's not a "bastard",' he muttered as he shoved the mower into the shed at the back.

'We'll find that out tomorrow.'

He scampered off inside to catch "Bonanza".

Testing Times

He was waiting for her in the morning at the usual place. Roger was always reliable. Jane easily spotted his enthusiastic wave above the crowds of students surging into the underpass leading to the campus for the last week of lectures.

'You're looking pleased with yourself Roger! What's up?' asked Jane as they exchanged a quick kiss of greeting before entering the underpass with the rest.

'I phoned my folks this morning to tell them about you.'

'And?'

'Well my mum's over the moon. She's looking forward to meeting you when we go down and she's really grateful you've helped me so much with the studies. She reckoned Suzie was a bad influence.

'What was your dad saying?'

'Oh, he thought it was great. He plays tennis with your old man and he reckoned going out with a policeman's daughter was just what I needed to keep me on the straight and narrow. HA!'

Roger was insinuating something. Jane wasn't sure what, so she aimed a slap at the back of her boyfriend's head just to be on the safe side. He ducked and giggled.

Jane turned to a more serious subject.

'Exams start next week. Are you ready for them?'

Roger took a deep breath, bit his bottom lip and clutched the library books firmly to his chest. A black thought that had been at the back of his mind for most of the year suddenly re-surfaced. He swiftly blocked it out then turned to her and nodded.

'Yep. Ready as I'll ever be. Thanks to you.'

'Oh no Roger, you're the one who's done the work.'

She suddenly stopped and turned to face him.

'Where will you be staying after the exams?'

'Well, college I suppose,' he answered, the truth being that he hadn't thought of it. He hadn't thought of anything much except study.

'Expensive option,' she said then continued with an offer Roger could hardly refuse.

'How about this then? My cousin owns a flat near the beach at Cottesloe. She's on holiday at the moment in Malaysia and she's just written to me to say I'd be welcome to stay there while was away. She's not due back until after Christmas and she doesn't like the idea of the place being empty. Fancy a beach house at Cottesloe while we wait for the exam results?'

Roger's face said it all.

Suzie looked up startled at the sudden loud knock on her door.

'Who is it?'

'Phone call for you downstairs.'

'Thanks,' she shouted back jumping to her feet, knocking over her chair and sending piles of paper onto the floor. She charged down the hall and swung herself down the banister almost colliding with the anonymous messenger who was making a more sedate descent of the stairs.

'Sorry!' she shouted over her shoulder. She clattered on down the steps in a flurry of multi-coloured Indian fabric and a jangle of silver jewellery arriving breathless at the dangling mouth-piece. Pausing for a moment to regain her composure, her hands cupped the phone and her voice took on a sense of urgency.

'Hello? Oh it's you.' Suzie's face lit up. It was the call she was hoping for.

She pulled the wild mane of hair away from her eyes and turned to the wall, the volume of her speech dropping proportionately with the intensity of her conversation.

'Is it on? Are we going? ...that's brilliant...I can't wait...yes I know it will be hard, especially at first but...yes of course I can...and I love you too...see you tomorrow....Bye.'

She delicately replaced the receiver, turned, leaned back against the wall and heaved a sigh of relief.

Minutes later, back in her room, she frantically started filling cardboard boxes with papers, books and journals. Then she started on her wardrobe. By lunchtime it was done. Stacked cardboard boxes, bags of rubbish, bundles of clothes and a small suitcase littered the floor. She was ready. She rolled a cigarette and gazed out the open window wishing the day would end quickly. Should she call her mother? No, she was far too busy with her new boyfriend to be concerned with her daughter's dreams and schemes. Her mother would find out soon enough and by then it would be too late to do anything about it anyway.

The class was silent. The angelic form of Miss Henderson began gliding down the aisles handing out the maths exam papers. Brian watched in awe as usual and hung on every word of her introduction.

'I know you've all had some exams this week so you know the rules. Keep the paper face down until I tell you to turn over. You have ten minutes reading time. Reading time is strictly for reading. You are not allowed to write anything at all during reading time…'

A paper dropped on Brian's desk and he caught an exquisite whiff of perfume as she passed.

'…You have an hour and a half, plenty of time to complete everything and of course if you do finish early, make sure you go back and check your work. Turn your papers over now.'

Brain flipped the paper over. He'd been waiting for this for a long time. Since the incident on the railway line, he had kept a very low profile and took his schoolwork seriously. Inspired by his mother, two hours each week-night was his regular homework time with several additional hours over the weekend. Under the tutelage of the divine Miss Henderson, mathematics was no longer the arcane language of disconnected symbols and disjointed facts Mr MacDuff professed. The lowly mark he got earlier in the year still rankled. Now it was time for revenge!

His greedy eyes eagerly scanned the first page.

'Find the area of this shape in square metres…draw on a number line the truth sets for the following inequations…Find the sizes of the angles marked…' '*Uh huh, okay so far,*' he thought. He turned over. '…draw Venn diagrams…solve these equations…simplify these algebraic expressions. If a man earns $25 a day and works a four-day week… With ruler and compass…A rectangular water tank…'

Brian looked up. There was nothing in the paper that looked threatening in the least. Most of the others seemed to still be reading the first page. He ached to get going. At last Miss Henderson spoke up.

'You can start now. Good luck everyone.'

Brian's pen had already hit the page and he was well into question one before Miss Henderson had scored off the time on the board.

'You have ten minutes left,' called the senior examination supervisor from the table on the stage at the far end of Winthrop Hall.

Roger glanced at his watch. He had been going flat out for two hours and forty-five minutes. Maybe he'd just been lucky but the set questions were remarkably similar to those in the 1965 Anthropology paper. It had been Jane's suggestion of course to check out what had been set in past years and it had paid off. She had also accurately predicted what to expect of his other exams.

As he worked his way through the Anthropology questions, his style of writing surprised him. His penmanship resembled the peculiar form of speech that his teacher, Professor Bernstein used in his lectures.

Not only that, appropriate academic references automatically occurred to him to support his arguments and explanations making his answers look similar to the convoluted jargon of an anthropology journal. He seemed to be speaking the language of his lecturers. But was it good enough?

He was on the last page of his answer book when the cry came from the front of the great hall.

'Time's up! Pens down please.'

The attendants started to move down the aisles of the great auditorium collecting papers while the head examiner continued to shout instructions.

'If you've used more than one answer book, make sure that you've filled in your name, number and subject on the front cover of each and ask a supervisor for a staple. No talking until all the papers are collected please.'

When Roger's papers had been uplifted, he sat back in his chair and gazed at the surroundings.

In the south wall, the great organ towered over high above the stage, its pipes embracing the spectacular rose window which glowed with every colour of the rainbow from a thousand parts like a huge multifaceted gemstone.

Above his head, great pendulous gilded chandeliers hung rigidly on lengths of cable and chain from the vaulted wooden ceiling. Along the wood-panelled walls, the coat of arms of St Andrews, Oxford Cambridge, Stamford and other great universities around the world and the portraits of past Chancellors and Vice Chancellors looked down sternly on yet another annual examination.

Roger wondered pensively if this would be the first and last time he sat in this hall. He needed at least three B's and a C for Law. The black thought came to him. If he bombed out completely, his father would not subsidise another attempt. He would be forced to leave and get whatever job he could.

Being out of full time education and physically fit, he would then be a prime candidate for conscription. The war in Vietnam was going badly for the Australians, more manpower was needed and Roger was the right age for army service. In twelve months, he could be serving in the steaming jungles of Vietnam. A shudder ran down his spine at the prospect. Time alone would tell. There was nothing he could do about it now, except wait as patiently as he could for the results. He had done his best. It was all over.

Father O'Neil seemed to have a skip in his step as he approached the church that Sunday morning. He was early for the first time ever, his enthusiasm the result of one simple fact: This would be his final mass in Martinup. He paused for a moment before the concrete steps and looked up. The magnificent bell-tower that soared into the bright blue sky above his head was *his* doing. What an achievement! He had raised the money for that much, and much more besides. Single-handedly he had transformed a mediocre building into a modern glorious edifice worthy of a city. Indeed, it was more like a small cathedral than a humble parish church and now at last his efforts were to be rewarded.

He bounded up the steps and started putting on his vestments, usually a tedious business, whistling as he did so. The sudden appearance of parishioners passing the open sacristy door giving him funny looks forced him to abort the rehearsal of his valedictory address to the mirror. He smiled and waved and thereafter kept his thoughts to himself. They would find out soon enough. '*Yes, yes, YES! Oh, to be away from Martinup!*'

Preceded by the lonely red and white figure of the altar boy Peter Haddow bearing a candle, Father O'Neill resplendent in his green and gold vestments, swept down the aisle looking neither right nor left.

Mass seemed to go slowly for the priest, his heart and mind were somewhere else. At last it was time for his sermon and at the end of it... He mounted the pulpit with determination in his eye. This was going to be a moment to be savoured.

His chosen topic for the final homily was how the Catholic Church adjusted and adapted to Change. His first word was the stimulus for John MacArthur to drift into his usual deep sleep. He was not alone. Over by the confessional, Big Arnie MacAulay started dreaming about his new harvester, Constable Finnegan was beginning a nightmare about paperwork, Luigi de Luca was in a vineyard and up the front, Mrs Jaworski was probably somewhere in Poland as Father O'Neill's sonorous, mellifluent tones rolled over their heads and bounced off the cream-coloured plastered walls and high wooden vaulted ceiling.

'...and above all...the nature of the Cath-o-lic Church...the universal church...for that is what the very word cath-o-lic means...above all...'

Towards the end of his sermon, Father O'Neill felt quite pleased with himself. The words had just appeared in his head, formed an orderly queue and fallen out of his mouth. He prided himself on his oratory skills, albeit somewhat wasted here in Martinup and being somewhat short-sighted, he failed to notice that every week a certain proportion of his congregation was sound asleep during his words of wit and wisdom.

Father O'Neill completed his oration with the sign of the cross, the signal for the spouses of John MacArthur, Donald Finnegan and Luigi de Luca to elbow their menfolk into wakefulness. Naturally, being partner-less, Big Arnie MacAulay and Mrs Jaworski slumbered on as usual until roused by the rumble of the congregation rising to its feet for the recitation of the Creed. On this occasion, the pair of them slept through an interesting announcement.

'As you know I have been in this parish for twelve years...' TWELVE BORING YEARS! screamed the little devil inside his head. Father O'Neill tried to ignore the secret voice and continued his *ad lib* statement to the rows of silent faces rapidly losing their glazed looks…' and in that time I have made many friends here…' *HA!*…but as I have just been saying in my sermon, nothing is permanent, nothing is fixed, we all must flow with the tide.'

He paused for effect.

'It is time for me to move on. I am leaving Martinup.' *"FOREVER! HOORAY!"*

'Goodbye and God Bless you.'

The silence following this totally unexpected news was profound, even by church standards. Not even a cough broke the stillness and the footsteps of the priest down the carpeted pulpit staircase were the only sounds that broke the solemn hush.

Although Father O'Neill secretly held the town and its people in disdain, his parishioners felt differently about him, although they rarely showed it. In fact, they quite liked the bombastic, flamboyant Irish priest. Sure, they all knew he had a bit of a drink problem. They could smell it on him when he swept past on his grand entrances to mass and those who invited him to the wedding celebrations of their children knew that Father O'Neill would be responsible for a good percentage of the refreshment budget. It was rumoured that he had a bit of a fondness for the women, but if true, that side of his nature was never in evidence. Not once had he disgraced himself in public although he obviously had ample opportunities to do so.

But perhaps the chief reason why his parishioners with long memories liked him was simply because he was infinitely better than his predecessor, the unfriendly, humourless and totally incomprehensible, Father Mantini, who had held power in Martinup for twenty years before succumbing to a heart attack. Before the news of his departure had properly sunk in and the first whispered comments made, Father O'Neill had reached the altar and begun to recite the Creed. The rumble of the crowd struggling to stand caused Big Arnie MacAulay to abandon his machinery and Mrs Jaworski to leave the green fields of Krakow.

At the end of Mass, as Father O'Neill trailed behind Peter Haddow, the priest noticed something odd about the congregation. Instead of the glazed eyes and tired looks that usually greeted him on his processional exit, people were smiling at him. Bemused, and a little annoyed, he gave a half-smile of acknowledgement back to each one as he caught their eyes. So they were pleased to see the back of him, were they?

Ungrateful sods!

But it was not true. He scarcely had time to disrobe and take up his usual position in the blinding morning sunlight on the front steps of the church when he was mobbed. Everyone wanted to shake his hand, congratulate him on his efforts and question him on his next appointment. The overpowering attention he received from all sides meant his thanks and answers to a fairly obvious question were brief and rather vague. 'I'm off to Melbourne,' was the only explanation he had time to give. Mrs Jaworski strode through the crowds and out the front gate unaware that anything unusual was afoot, Big Arnie MacAulay enquired what all the fuss was about and John MacArthur confided in whispers to his wife that the priest had *'obviously been busted at last…sent down for fiddling the books…sure to be in a Melbourne slum in a fortnight's time…'*

When the crowds had finally dispersed, the priest breathed a sigh of relief, tidied the sacristy and stood at the back of the church gazing around at his handiwork one last time before turning off the lights. The final moments had come as quite a shock and he could not deny unexpected mixed feelings in his heart as the heavy glass door closed with a click behind him.

But then he changed his mind.

'Oh, sod that!' he snorted to himself as he rubbed his hands with glee. He danced down the steps and hurried across the road for a strong cup of coffee and a well-earned cigarette.

The following morning, Brian drummed his fingers impatiently on the desk. It was results time in mathematics. He already knew from Miss Marceaux that his French mark had been a creditable seventy percent while Mr Newton had surprised him with a mark of no less than eighty-two percent, his highest mark he'd ever achieved for anything. English and Social Studies were in the high sixties and woodwork and metalwork were…well woodwork and metalwork. Examinations in the manual subjects were a complete waste of time. You were awarded a pass if you survived the year without cutting off your own or someone else's extremity or successfully managed to use the lathe without getting your school tie caught in the chuck. But now the divine Miss Henderson was, dare he admit it, beginning to annoy him.

'Come on, get on with it,' he muttered under his breath. Like many new teachers who have successfully produced their very first exam paper, the divine Miss Henderson had fallen into the trap of making sweeping generalisations of the performance of the class as a whole saying how pleased she was at the overall improvement of most of them. Meanwhile Brian, along with everyone else wanted only to know what they got.

When the vital paper at last dropped on the desk in front of him, Brian thought he heard an intimate whisper of 'Congratulations Brian! Well done,' as she breezed past, but he wasn't sure. Normally he would have returned any look or comment with the gaze of a lost puppy but now his total concentration was focussed on the mark scrawled in red ink and circled at the top of his paper. Surely that could not be right.

He drew the paper across the desk and whispered the mark to himself over and over again with varying degrees of emphasis to reinforce the reality of it.

'Nine-ty seven percent...nine-ty seven percent... ninety-seven PERCENT...NINETY-SEVEN PERCENT!'

Flicking through the pages he could see it was true. Full marks for most sections in red circles...ten, ten, twenty, fifteen, five... And there was the one mistake. Wrong angle. How stupid! Then the thought occurred to him, *'Shit! I could have got a hundred percent but for one silly error! Unbelievable!'*

As the divine Miss Henderson began to go through the paper, Brian could not resist trying to find out the mark of Brian Clelland, the class genius who had consistently done well in maths even through the dark days of "fart-breath" MacDuff. Straining in his seat, he just caught sight of it. Eighty-seven percent. Yes!

The siren went and the class emptied. The divine Miss Henderson called Brian over to her desk. This was the first time she had ever asked to speak to him personally. He immediately thought the worst and his knees trembled. Was there something terribly wrong? Did she think he'd cheated? Was there some dreadful mix-up in the marks? Had he been looking at the right paper?

She looked up at him from tidying the papers on her desk and a broad smile crossed her face.

'Brian, that was a wonderful result. I know the marks you were getting earlier in the year. Other people have improved too which is pleasing as far as I'm concerned, but your achievement is pretty good don't you agree? Certainly, I shall be saying so in your report.'

The colour came back to Brian's face but he could find no words. Of course, there were a thousand things he'd love to say to the divine Miss Henderson, but they were all totally inappropriate, so his mouth just opened and closed for a moment like a goldfish. Then with a mumbled 'Thank you, miss,' he made a discreet if somewhat hasty exit, tripping over the carpet as he went out the door.

The flat at Cottesloe would never win an award for architecture. Set on the fourth floor of a tower consisting of smooth rectilinear blocks of white-painted concrete rising five storeys high and above the date palms and orange roof tiles of the surrounding suburb, it hardly blended in with its environment or presented itself as an aesthetic land mark. What it did have is what Real Estate agents die for: Location.

From the balcony accessed by sliding glass doors, the sparkling waters of the Indian Ocean stretched as far as the eye could see. The balcony was the first place Jane led Roger to as soon as they entered the flat for the first time. From below, the heady scents of honeysuckle and bougainvillea and from the sea, the salt and seaweed laden air lifted up on a light westerly breeze. Roger surprised her by producing a bottle of champagne from his rucksack and as the cork flew towards the sea and glasses clinked, they toasted being together and at last free of study.

The days and weeks that followed were the happiest time of their lives. Everyday chores like shopping and cooking and the flat were adventures. Ordinary trips on the bus into Perth or Fremantle became treasured memories and they took the photographs to prove it. Neither of them had much money, but they didn't need a lot. They had each other. On the beach they laughed and joked and played in the surf. They made love in every room in the flat, on the balcony at the first light of dawn and after midnight on the beach with the crashing rollers of the ocean beside them and the lights of the Southern Cross in the darkness above for company.

'You're still worried about what's going to happen if you fail completely, aren't you?' she asked as they walked hand in hand along the beach. Jane had got her marks the previous day. A creditable if not unexpected set of four Bs. They had celebrated in style the night before and Jane was right. Roger's uncharacteristic silences that morning could not just be attributed to his hangover, bad though it was. His results were due out the following day and try as he might, he just could not disguise his concerns.

'Yep.'

'You know what I think? I don't think you have bombed out completely. I don't think that's possible. So, what is possible? Say you get something less than three B's and a C. Okay, not good enough for Law, but that's not the end of the world! There's still an Arts degree in it for you.'

Roger nodded. That would have implications. He knew his father would not finance anything but a Law degree. Or Accountancy. He shuddered at the thought. But she was right. He could earn money during his vacations on the mines up north...and end up...an anthropologist?

Jane seemed to read his thoughts. She continued,

'No, I don't think that's going to happen at all. I think what's going to happen is...'

She stopped and turned to him.

'...your marks will be good enough to get into Law. We'll both study together and then when we qualify, I'm going to marry you.'

Roger looked on stunned.

'You're not supposed to say that?'

'What do you mean?'

'I'm supposed to ask you to marry me.'

'Well, go on then.'

Roger roared with laughter at her impish remark. What was she going to be like in a courtroom?

'Okay. I'll ask you, but only on one condition.'

'Which is?'

'That we set up in practice together.'

'Done.'

'Will you marry me?'

'Only if you qualify as a Lawyer. Come on! Are you going for a swim or what?'

She broke away and made a dash for the surf with Roger in hot pursuit. He caught her as the first low roller crashed into her legs and they rolled together in the shallow surf. Roger sat up beside her, the water draining of his bare legs.

'MacArthur and Finnegan,' he said suddenly.

Jane emphatically shook her head.

'Uh huh! Finnegan and MacArthur.'

'Oh, and why is that?'

'Three reasons Roger. First, "Ladies first" remember? Second, "F" comes before "M" and third, I'm a year older than you, that makes me the senior partner.'

'But MacArthur and Finnegan sounds better.'

Jane abandoned reasonable argument.

'Bullshit Roger!' She laughed as she shoved his head under the next advancing wave.

The hands on the clock at the top of the Winthrop Hall tower moved towards three o'clock, the scheduled time for release of results in the Faculty of Arts. Although not yet a hundred years old, the sprawling sandstone edifice dominated the campus, a curious mixture of neo-Gothic long arched windows and neo Classical Doric columns. A Mediterranean tiled roof added to the confusion of styles.

As they emerged from the cool darkness of the underpass, Roger and Jane could see through the glaring heat that they were not the first in the queue for results. Across the expanse of lawn in front of the building, a crowd had already gathered in the glass-fronted alcoves where the sheets of names and marks were to be posted.

Roger felt weak at the knees at the sight but Jane urged him on, trotting across the grass ahead of him. The first sheets were going up behind the glass and the crowd had suddenly changed from an orderly gathering of nervous retrospective individuals into a disorganised rugby scrum. Whoops of delight came from unseen students at the front of the throng while others said nothing and tried to slip away unnoticed. Success or failure was easily discernible on the faces of those fighting their way back through the pack.

'Stay here, Roger,' said Jane and edged her way into the scrum.

She waited anxiously at the back of the crowd while newcomers jostled past her. Roger had disappeared from view. Arts, being the biggest faculty on the campus obviously attracted the biggest crowd when results were released. Jane remembered her first year. The marks were all arranged alphabetically on a series of lists and of course when she finally reached the front line, she was at the wrong list. Trying to move sideways in the ruck was practically impossible and she nearly fainted in the heat and the crush. In fact, it was her friend who found her marks and together they were able to wade out of the chaos.

Jane strained to catch sight of Roger but there was still no sign of him. What if she was wrong? What if he had failed completely? The implications of that were just too terrible to contemplate. Conscription.

Vietnam. She slammed the door on that and bit her lip, a tear beginning to well up in her eye. Angrily she wiped it away and strained again to see him through the mass of bodies.

Suddenly, he was there beside her. 'A and three Bs!' He could not remove the grin from his face and the mood was highly contagious.

'WHAAAT!'

She threw her arms around him and squeezed so hard it nearly took the breath away from him. He lifted her high over the crowd around and around and around they turned, the sandstone buildings and tiled roofs becoming continuous blurs of orange and yellow until at last they collapsed together on the soft grass in a giggling heap.

She stared at him with that impish grin that always melted his heart.

'So, what was the A for then?'

'Anthropology.'

'Fantastic Roger, you're into LAW!'

He didn't need reminding. They kissed and rolled over in the grass until Roger broke clear and sat up looking serious.

'MacArthur and Finnegan. Definitely sounds better.'

An Unlikely Hero

'It's Brian's report card John,' said Mary MacArthur handing the document to her husband who had almost finished his tea. He put down the knife and fork and wiped his mouth on a handkerchief.

John MacArthur studied the brown card intensely for a moment then flipped it over with a flourish to check the name on the front before returning to the marks and comments of Brian's teachers.

'This can't be right. Have I got someone else's report card here? I didn't think you liked maths, Brian! What's this? Ninety-seven percent? That's only…ah…three off a hundred!'

His astonishment and incompetent arithmetic was of course a not-so-elaborate sham. Mary had phoned with the news and he was to pick up a surprise for the boy on his way home. John MacArthur was in fact delighted that his youngest son had done so well in his first year at high school. As he could recall, his own best ever mark at secondary level was seventy-five percent and that was for woodwork. Now he had to accept a mathematical genius in the family. He read aloud some of the teacher's comments,

'Good results all year, Brian is a pleasure to teach. P. Newton.'

'Brian has shown a mature consistent attitude to the study of this language. M. Marceaux.'

But his eye was drawn back again to mathematics that extraordinary mark.

'Outstanding achievement. Well done Brian! P. Henderson.' he read out.

Brian was starting to become embarrassed and his face was beginning to show it.

Mary sensed it and stepped in.

'I think Brian deserves something for all the hard work he's done, don't you dear?'

John MacArthur smiled and nodded and reached in his pocket for a slim brown packet which he passed over the table to Brian.

'You've worked hard boy. Congratulations!' Brain thanked his parents abandoned his custard pudding to unwrap the surprise gift.

'Speaking of work, Brian,' said his father, Kenny McIntyre is dropping off a load of mallee roots on Sunday. You'll give me a hand to shift them, won't you?'

Brian groaned at the mention of the name of his nemesis but naturally agreed. The unwrapped parcel revealed a brand-new fountain pen, the first he'd ever owned.

'I've got ink for it,' said his father. 'I'll get it for you after tea.'

His mother had an idea.

'Why don't you write a letter to Trevor? Margaret sent a card with their address…'

She left the table to rummage in the cabinet by the wall.

'Here it is,' she said, dropping the postcard in front of Brian who was still busy examining his new pen.

His mother's idea was a good one. He'd get straight into it after tea. There were one or two stories that would amuse his old mate. But his father as usual, had played his cards close to his chest. He had another surprise for his son.

'Oh, by the way Brian,' said John MacArthur casually, 'when I was talking to Kenny McIntyre about the mallee roots, he told me he's bought a plane. It's just a little two-seater Cessna mind you. He wants to start a crop-dusting business next year. Anyway, when he heard about your marks, he offered to give you a trip over Martinup someday next week. Do you fancy that?'

Brian's eyes assumed the size of saucers and his head nearly fell off with the enthusiasm of his acceptance of the unexpected offer.

His mother's face however showed a little concern. This was news to her.

John MacArthur laughed. 'Don't worry Mary. Kenny's had his licence for years. I'm just annoyed he didn't invite me.',

203

Father O'Neill paid the driver and retrieved his luggage from the back of the taxi. This was all new to him but he'd get used to it. He was at Perth Airport and about to catch a plane for the first time in his life. It had been an ocean liner that had brought him to Australia and air travel was still a luxury alternative to the railway. But the church was paying and obedience was one of his vows so he stooped down, grabbed his bags and crossed the road, a buzz of excitement in his stomach. It was happening. It was really happening.

Ceiling fans inside the main terminal made a vain attempt to circulate the air, but the temperature inside the building hardly seemed lower than the searing heat outside. Father O'Neill bent down to deposit his bags on the shiny linoleum floor before tugging at his dog collar to relieve his discomfort. Not long now before he could get rid of the damn thing forever.

He squinted into the distance, his myopia a distinct drawback in situations like this where signs had to be read. He stepped backwards to improve his view and in doing so collided with a young couple coming through the entrance causing them to drop their luggage.

As Michelle bent down to receive her handbag the priest, apologising profusely, had already recognised her partner.

'I know you,' he said helping Paul with his suitcase. You're from Martinup aren't you? And you,' he said to Michelle as she rose to her feet. 'You're the young couple that...you know, that train thing,' he said shaking their hands enthusiastically.

'That's right Father,' sighed Paul trying not to show that he and Michelle were thoroughly fed up hearing about "that train thing".

'And you're the catholic priest in Martinup aren't you? asked Michelle.

'Not anymore, but that's a long story. Tell me, do you know where to catch the plane to Melbourne?'

'Just follow us Father. We're on the same flight as you, said Michelle striding ahead with Paul.

'Are you going to Melbourne too?' enquired the priest struggling to keep up.

'No Father,' Michelle said over her shoulder. 'We're going to Sydney but we stop in Melbourne on the way.' Although Perth Airport had the status "International" due to the arrival and departure of thrice-weekly flights to Singapore and places beyond together with weekly flights to South Africa, was still a minor airport by world standards and internal flights were the mainstream business. That morning Michelle, Paul and Father O'Neill were booked on a scheduled Anset Airlines flight for Sydney, stopping at Adelaide and Melbourne.

Having helped the priest through the checking in ritual and all now armed with boarding cards and only essential hand luggage, Michelle suggested they go through to the departure lounge to await the boarding announcement. Father O'Neill's eyes lit up the sight of the bar and he insisted on buying the young couple a drink.

'The Catholic Church is not short of a bob or two,' he assured them with a *wink* patting his wallet on his way to the bar.

'That was a lovely weekend with your parents Paul,' said Michelle from the comfort of her arm chair.

'It was, wasn't it?' he answered, smiling at the thought of him having to translate his parents' thick Scottish brogue for her. They thought she was wonderful but he just enjoyed being the linguistically competent one for once.

Father O'Neill was back at the table with the drinks, a glass of white wine for Michelle a beer for Paul and a double whisky for himself.

'Cheers everyone!' said the priest. 'Here's to a good flight!' With that, he gulped down half the contents of his glass as Michelle and Paul exchanged quick glances. Within minutes, he'd completely drained his tumbler and was making to go back to the bar, but Paul, rising to his feet, said it was his round.

'I'll get it Father. Double whisky was it?'

Father O'Neill nodded. 'Johnny Walker Black please Paul.'

Michelle leaned across the table to engage the priest in conversation. 'So, Father, will you be a priest in a suburb of Melbourne?'

Father O'Neill's tongue was already beginning to loosen with the effects of the drink, so he was quite happy to be more forthcoming about his future than he was with the good folk of Martinup. Besides, it was a long time since he'd been able to chat to such a gorgeous young girl.

'Well, still be a priest, but not a parish priest, so I won't have to wear this anymore.' He jabbed a finger at his dog-collar.

'No, I'm to be the bursar of St Xavier's, it's a seminary in Melbourne. Very nice place I believe.'

'Bursar?'

'He's in charge of the money. You know, allocating budgets, raising funds, that sort of thing.'

Paul had just got the drinks on a tray turned away from the bar when a girl pushed past him almost upsetting the tray. He recognised her immediately.

'Susan? What are you doing here?'

Suzie looked back at him from the bar with a strange expression on her face. What was he doing here? Was he following her or something?

'Oh, hullo Paul,' she said trying to sound nonchalant. She circumvented any more questions by introducing the dark-skinned man standing behind him.

'Paul, this is Ananda…Ananda Viswanath.'

Paul turned, struggling to put his tongue around the name, juggle the drinks tray and shake hands at the same time. Suzie added,

'He's my yoga teacher.'

From her position at the far side of the bar, Michelle watched Paul in conversation with a familiar-looking female while Father O'Neill droned on about what a wonderful little town Martinup was and how difficult it had been for him to leave.

'What's she doing here?' she hissed in Paul's ear when he finally made it back to the table with the drinks.

Paul laughed and shook his head as he sat down beside her.

'She's on our flight.'

'Oh no!'

'But only as far as Adelaide. You'll never guess what she's up to. She's going to set up a yoga school in the Adelaide Hills with her teacher. That's him over there now with her.' He nodded in the direction of the bar.

Michelle looked over her shoulder then turned back.

'So, she's got rid of her boyfriend, Brian MacArthur's brother, what's his name? Roger?'

'Yep.'

'But she's finished her honours degree?'

'Chucked it in apparently,' said Paul taking a sip of his beer.

Michelle shook her head in disbelief. Father O'Neill stood up, burped quietly and asked if anyone else wanted a drink.

St Xavier's College, an old rambling brick building on the banks of the Yarra River was Australia's training school for the priesthood. High walls surrounding it together with a thick canopy of gum trees ensured that the fifty or so theology students therein had ample peace and quiet for study and prayer.

But all was not well with the College. A sharp-eyed observer would notice the brickwork required attention, the paint was peeling, the garden was overgrown and the gutters were in need of repair. But these were only symptoms of an unseen malaise. St Xavier's College was in a financial crisis. There was no money to keep the place going and the Roman Catholic Church could not afford to lose its only seminary in Australia. Frantic discussions had gone on at the highest level but there seemed no way out. St Xavier's would have to close and the Cardinal would then have some awkward explaining to do in Rome. Word came through of a priest in Western Australia who had performed an economic miracle in the tiny parish of Martinup.

Father O'Neill closed his window on the top floor of the college that looked out over the walled garden and the swift-flowing river beyond.

'Ah, this is the life,' he muttered to himself as he settled into the luxurious comfort of his leather chair behind his mahogany desk. He loosened his tie. What a joy it was to wear something normal after all these years. No more sweltering in the heat in a uniform of basic black. The only indication now of his priestly status was a tiny gold cross on his lapel. It was the concession he'd won in taking up the post. He was still a priest, he just didn't look like one.

He picked up the financial pages of the Melbourne Age and scanned down the figures. The phone rang. The priest's conversation was short and swift.

'Hello...oh Harry...yep...yep...Kalgoorlie mines? ...38? ...yep sell...thanks Harry...OK...bye.'

Father O'Neill rubbed his hands with glee. This was only his second day as Bursar and he'd hit the ground running. He got up from the desk and studied one of the charts that he'd drawn through his years in Martinup which now lined the walls of his new office. Drawn in different coloured pencils they looked like seismograph charts, horizontal shaking lines that here and there suddenly peaked as if an Earth tremor had occurred. His concentration was lost by a knock on the door.

'Come in!'

Father O'Neill knew the face of the tall stranger but he wasn't expecting visitors and couldn't immediately place the name. His visitor spoke first.

'Ah there you are Father! Great to see you again! You remember me? Father William Harding?'

The Jesuit held out his hand in greeting and Father O'Neill warmly invited him in. Their last time of meeting had not been so pleasant, both being locked in the sacristy for several hours.

'I was just passing through and heard you'd got the job, so I thought I'd look you up. So, this is your new office? And these are the charts you were telling me about?' asked Father Harding as he wandered over to the wall.

A machine on a table in the corner suddenly sprang to life. It made a chattering noise and slowly began to spew out paper.

'Telex machine,' Father O'Neill explained. 'I've just had it installed. Excuse me a moment won't you?' He hurried across to the machine and cocked his head to read the incoming information on the extruding sheet.

The Jesuit sat down by the desk until the telex message was complete. Father O'Neill carried the paper back to his side of the desk and himself into the leather chair still absorbed with the contents of the message. He looked up suddenly.

'Oh, sorry Father. Would you like tea or coffee perhaps?' Father O'Neill's finger hovered over a buzzer on his desk.

'No, no, Father O'Neill, I can't stay too long. I just wanted to know exactly what you are doing, because I had to explain to my superiors and I must have done it reasonably well because you wouldn't be here I suppose, but basically you make money buying and selling shares. Is that right?'

The priest nodded. The Jesuit continued,

'Surely, that's very risky. You can lose money too. But you say you have a method using these charts to make sure you don't lose. Correct?'

'Precisely,' said Father O'Neill. 'Come and have a look at this.' He walked over to the wall inviting Father Harding to join him.

'First,' said Father O'Neill, 'you need a good stockbroker. My cousin Harry deals on the Perth Stock Exchange. He got me interested in this in the first place and he keeps me up to date in the market. He does what I tell him to do. Fast. I read everything I can in the paper. There are all sorts of companies, but I only deal in mining. Now the value of mining shares pretty much depends on the price of the metal being mined. The gold price goes up, the price of the company that mines gold goes up. Okay?'

Father Harding was beginning to catch on and made a contribution,

'So, if you know when the gold price is going up, you buy gold mining company shares...' Father O'Neill nodded while the Jesuit continued, 'you sell them... The priest finished the sentence for him '...when the price is going to go down.'

'But how do you know when the gold price is going to go up or down?'

Father O'Neill smiled. 'Look at this chart of the price of gold over the last twenty years.' He pointed to a line showing irregular peaks and troughs. 'Now if I take this chart over the same twenty years of the silver price and put it next to gold, do you see it's the same pattern...but not quite. The peaks in the silver price occur two months before the peaks in the gold price. In other words, *silver is predicting what gold will do two months later!*'

Father Harding struggled to see the similarity between the two graphs but went along with the priest,

'So, when you see the silver price going up, you buy gold stocks and when you see the price of silver going down... The Jesuit's voice tailed away in admiration. Father O'Neill was clearly a gifted man, even just being able to see the patterns in the graphs, but he had even more to offer.

'Mind you,' said the priest, 'it's not always perfect, so I also work with aluminium and copper. There's a similar relationship between them too. Look...' he pointed to two other charts which showed similar jagged lines which again proved incomprehensible to the Jesuit.

'Here, aluminium predicts copper, but again not always. I'm right seventy-five percent of the time but by working with reliable companies that mine those four metals, I can pretty well cancel out any losses. I generally stick to the same twenty or so companies. The rest of it…well, put it down to the luck of the Irish!'

'But you lost money one month back in Martinup didn't you?'

Father O'Neill pointed to the telephone on his desk.

'That was the problem in Martinup. The phone line would go down when you least expected it. I was trying to tell Harry to sell but the line went dead. By the time I got through it was too late. No problems like that here.'

'But why should there be a connection between these metals?'

The priest shrugged his shoulders.

'It's beyond me I'm afraid.'

'Why hasn't someone else spotted this?'

Maybe someone already has. Who knows? This is a tricky business. Nothing I deal with is an absolute certainty. Asbestos is a bit dodgy but uranium and nickel can be interesting. I haven't found out how to predict them yet, but if you want a hot tip, Harry says Poseidon is a good bet.'

'Poseidon?'

'Poseidon, nickel prospecting company,' confirmed Father O'Neill. 'I've just picked up a few thousand shares myself this morning. Good value at five cents a share Harry reckons.'

The phone rang.

Father O'Neill answered. The Jesuit got up slowly and mouthed to the priest he had to go. Father O'Neill waved him goodbye with his free hand.

As Harding gently closed the door, he could hear the priest shouting down the phone, 'Sell, Harry, sell. SELL!'

'*Poseidon, Poseidon,*' he muttered over and over to himself as he walked thoughtfully down the stairs.

Paul had a bit of a hangover. It was a bright summer's morning and he was sitting on a deck chair under the shade of a parasol on the back lawn of the palatial home of his future parents-in-law. Henri and Kristel had picked them up from the airport in a very expensive-looking foreign car. Henri was a tall man with a military bearing and looked every bit the retired diplomat with his grey slicked down hair and pencil-thin moustache. His wife was obviously Asian, but taller than Paul had expected and he saw immediately where Michelle got her stunning looks.

Paul had been received like a long-lost son and the presentation of the ring to her parents by Michelle was the signal to open the vintage champagne from the cellar. Seriously impressed that a modern home in Australia should possess such a thing, Paul said so to Henri as he was being shown the collection of fine wines by his host. The old man laughed and told him it had caused all sorts of construction problems. In the end he had to resort to a firm specialising in swimming pools to build it as no other contractor would take on the work.

Over a meal of the finest French cuisine, the wine flowed, the conversations never ceased and laughter echoed around the vast open living area.

They had wanted to marry the following Easter in Martinup. Paul's parents had agreed but would Henri and

Kristel be prepared to make the long journey to a tiny rural town?

Henri's English was good, but when Michelle put the plan to him, his enthusiasm was more naturally expressed in his tongue which Paul had no trouble understanding,

'Enchanté! Bien sur, ma cherie!'

It was the after-dinner cognacs that did it for Paul. He groaned at the thought as he sat in the sun reading the "*Sydney Morning Herald*". An article about the Vietnam War caught his attention. He sat up suddenly. It couldn't be…surely not…

A shout came from the house. It was Michelle, obviously excited about something. Paul gently put the paper aside as she arrived beside him, breathless.

'We've got the house!'

'Really! That's wonderful!'

They embraced and kissed and Michelle continued.

'I've just had a call from the Estate Agents in Martinup. Our offer has been accepted! All the papers are ready! All we have to do is sign them when we get back. Isn't that wonderful?'

Paul took her hands and laughed.

'I've just thought of something. I'd better start digging straight away when we get back to Martinup.'

'Why is that?'

'Well, Henri will be expecting a wine cellar when they come over for the wedding!'

They laughed and sat down together in the sun and talked of the plans they had for their new home, of the kitchen, the bedroom and the garden.

Then Paul suddenly remembered what he'd just been reading in the newspaper. He picked it up carefully.

'Look at this Michelle. No wait, I'll read it out.'

'The soldiers were on a routine patrol when they came under heavy enemy fire. Corporal George

Jackson (21) of Kalgoorlie Western Australia...'

Michelle interrupted, 'That's Jacko!'

Paul nodded, 'I think so. He must have signed up after he left Martinup. Anyway, I'll read on.'

'...radioed for helicopter support from Da Nang. Despite gunshot wounds to his legs, he provided covering fire enabling the rest of the platoon to be evacuated safely. His body was later recovered and returned to Western Australia He will be buried with full military honours in Kalgoorlie...'

'Jacko,' said Michelle softly.

Paul nodded with a lump in his throat.

'Jacko.'

In a small one-bedroom flat in Kalgoorlie, Tracey Jackson, a bride of just ten months cut out an article headed:

"LOCAL HERO RETURNS" from the *West Australian* newspaper and carefully stuck it into her album.

Jacko had done the right thing and married her in a short civil ceremony soon after she told him she was pregnant. Then he was gone. She only saw him thrice during his training program and then only briefly before he was sent to Vietnam. Apparently over a thousand people had turned out for the funeral. But that didn't matter much to her. Hero or not, he was dead.

She walked over to the window and picked up the only decent picture she had of him. The wedding photos were crap. He smiled at her through the glass pane, looking handsome in his uniform. A tear welled in her eye.

The sound of a baby crying caused her to put the photograph down and wipe her face.

'Just coming Michael, Mummy's just coming!'

Roger's van was still going strong after a year of abuse at his hands. Jane had always loved it and that was how she first noticed Roger. They were now only a dozen or so miles out of Martinup and the light was fading fast. Jane had dozed off but awakened when the van slowed and stopped by the roadside.

'Who are they Roger? she asked referring to the figures walking towards them.

'Don't worry Jane. They're old friends of mine and I bet they want a lift into Martinup. You don't mind, do you?'

'Of course not. Your friends are my friends too.'

Roger wound down the window as the familiar figure approached.

'Hello Peter! I suppose you want a lift. Whose funeral is it this time?' A female voice suddenly called out from the advancing crowd.

'IS THAT YOU RUDJAH? HAVE YOU GUT A FARM FOR ME YET?'

'It's a letter from Trevor. He can't have got yours yet surely? I only posted it the other day,' said Mary MacArthur handing the envelope to Brian.

'They must have crossed in the post, mum. Thanks. By the way, where's Roger?'

'He's still fast asleep in the van. He's exhausted after all that studying the poor thing.'

'Yeah, of course.'

Brian dashed away to his room, threw himself down on the bed and tore open the envelope. He retrieved the letter and threw the rest into the bin beside his bed. Trevor's handwriting was not the best in the world but he managed to read the first page:

'...Auntie Jean died... Granny died leaving them the house... the house is huge...I go to a private school... uniforms...really good...nothing like Martinup...'

Brian's eye suddenly stopped at a really interesting bit on the second page. He read it softly aloud to himself.

"My mum's got a BOYFRIEND! She went back to nursing and she met a doctor called Tom. When she told me about him, I went, oh shit! Maybe this bloke's a complete bastard! Maybe

he's going to make my life hell you know what I mean? Like if he said 'do this' and I said 'piss off, whose side is my mum going to be on?' And then I thought wait a minute! My mum's got a lot of money now. Maybe this bloke's just after her cash?

Turns out he's BRILLIANT! He doesn't want me to call him "dad" because I wouldn't anyway. He rides a motorbike and lets me ride on the back. He even bought me a crash helmet. He knows LOADS about aircraft. He's going to buy a camping van so that me and my mum and him can go to Surfer's Paradise next year. I reckon my mum will marry him eventually which is fine by me. Then he would be my step dad, but he's just like a big brother. Which is great. Before I forget, looks like we've sold the house in Martinup. Someone called Newton's bought it. Funny if that turned out to be "lofty" Newton the science teacher eh? How did you get on in science by the way? I got 75% but I did better in maths. I got 79%. Hope that doesn't make you jealous! Only kidding!

One last thing. The package with this letter marked SECRET FOR THE EYES OF BRIAN MACARTHUR ONLY is because Tom is…

Write soon,

Your mate
Trevor."

Brian screwed up his eyes at the last sentence. Trevor had started to write something then scratched it out. Tom is what? And what was this about a package marked "secret?" He turned the letter over then got up and looked on his bed. Had he dropped it or had Trevor forgotten to put it in the envelope? The envelope! Of course! He dived over to the bin and retrieved the screwed-up paper. Sure enough, inside was a slim packet marked in the way that Trevor had described.

With care, Brian opened it. The first thing he found was a slip of paper containing Trevor's last sentence with an explanation together with the suggestion that the note be safely destroyed after its contents had been noted.

"Tom is a member of an amateur rocket club. I now am a member too. We build decent rockets, not fireworks. I hope you

find the enclosed plans interesting. I got them from the club. See you in space one day. Or Sydney.

Trevor."

Intrigued, Brian unfolded the other document and gently breathed a sigh of astonishment. Printed on the thin paper was a complete set of plans and detailed instructions on how to build a three stages rocket that could reach a height of sixty thousand feet using ordinary household chemicals.

Brian was immersed in the details of the mercury-based system for the second stage when a shout came from his father outside which caused him to hastily hide the controversial document.

'BRIAN! ARE YOU IN THERE BOY? MALLEE ROOTS HAVE ARRIVED AND I NEED A HAND TO SHIFT THEM!'

Brian held on to his seat belt as the wheels of the Cessna lifted clear of Kenny McIntyre's improvised runway. The pilot could not be heard over the roar of the engine but Brian pretended to hear him. He gave the farmer a thumbs up whenever Kenny shouted something at him. They were still climbing through patchy cloud, the translucent circular blur of the propeller scything through the mist. Brian looked out at the smoky stream over the wing rising and falling with the turbulence and remembered Trevor trying to explain to him about air pressure. But this was for real! He was flying!

The plane levelled out and the sky cleared. Brian suddenly recognised the terrain below. They were half way between Kenny's farm and Martinup, following the road that snaked ahead of them towards the town. On both sides of the black bitumen track the golden squares of ripening wheat fields stretched in a giant patchwork to the horizon, broken here and there by the brown and dusty-green bush.

Kenny indicated something of interest below and he banked the light aircraft to the left. It was Martinup already. Brian could clearly see the white bell tower of the Catholic Church as they passed over it. He cast his eye over the rectangular network of roads to the other side of town. There was the hospital and yes, there was the school and coming up below them was his house. Definitely. He knew it from the light brown circle set in the bush nearby which was obviously the race-course and the distinctive bright green rectangle that had to be Roger's van. He thought he saw a figure waving from the back lawn, but he wasn't sure.

They circled the town again then Kenny increased the altitude. When the Cessna finally levelled out, Brian looked down to see that Martinup had virtually disappeared, swallowed up in an endless sea of farmland, mallee scrub and bush that stretched as far as the eye could see in every direction.

He realised for the first time that his world was a very, very small one indeed.

But it would not always be so. Oh no.

'*One day*,' he said to himself, '*One day...*'

THE END

Epilogue

Shortly after his meeting with Father O'Neill, Father Harding, for the first time in his life took a gamble. He had some savings so he bought two thousand shares in Poseidon, with Father O'Neill's help of course, securing them at five cents each.

The months passed and nothing happened. Father Harding quite forgot about the shares. Then the news broke. The price of nickel had gone through the roof, an event that few, except perhaps Father O'Neill would have predicted.

The price of Poseidon rocketed. The Jesuit was persuaded not to sell by Father O'Neill when the price reached ten dollars. Again, he was dissuaded when the price reached twenty dollars. Father Harding was nearly beside himself when the share price of Poseidon hit sixty dollars, but Father O'Neill was adamant.

'Trust me,' he said and reluctantly the Jesuit agreed to hang on.

'Sell,' said Father O'Neill when Poseidon hit ninety dollars a share. The Jesuit did. The price continued to climb, but just by four before plummeting back to where it had started. The bubble had burst in spectacular fashion.

Father Harding left the priesthood and became a skiing instructor.

A delighted Father O'Neill received a phone-call from the Vatican with an offer he couldn't possibly refuse.